# VOTE
## *of*
# NO
# CONFIDENCE

*A Novel*

# VOTE
### *of* NO
# CONFIDENCE

*A Novel*

## Carla Stalling Huntington

SUNSTONE
PRESS

SANTA FE

Sunstone books may be purchased for educational, business, or sales promotional use.
For information please write: Special Markets Department, Sunstone Press,
P.O. Box 2321, Santa Fe, New Mexico 87504-2321.

Book and Cover design ›Vicki Ahl
Body typeface › Book Antiqua
Printed on acid-free paper
∞

Library of Congress Cataloging-in-Publication Data

Huntington, Carla Stalling, 1961-
  Vote of no confidence : a novel / by Carla Stalling Huntington.
     p. cm.
  ISBN 978-0-86534-865-3 (softcover : alk. paper)
  1. College presidents--Fiction. 2. Universities and colleges--Fiction. I. Title.
  PS3608.U59497V68 2012
  813'.6--dc23

                    2012001498

**WWW.SUNSTONEPRESS.COM**
SUNSTONE PRESS / POST OFFICE BOX 2321 / SANTA FE, NM 87504-2321 /USA
(505) 988-4418 / ORDERS ONLY (800) 243-5644 / FAX (505) 988-1025

For Art's Joy

*It is often tragic to see how blatantly a person*
*bungles his own life and*
*the lives of others*
*yet remains*
*totally incapable of seeing*
*how much the whole*
*tragedy originates in themselves.*
**—Carl Jung**


*Your only obligation*
*in any lifetime is*
*to be true to yourself.*
**—Richard Bach**

# Oh, for Tenured Sake!

*Spring 2003, Southwest Arkansas*

A
s she drove, farms, tractors, rolled up bales of hay, and flat land laughed at her through her 2003 Volkswagon window, which she'd bought new, trading her BMW for it. Hell, she was even scared to stop for gas or food once she got past Peculiar, especially after crossing the bridge over "Coon's Creek" and passing the gigantic white Praying Hands Monument along US Highway 171. You could see it from miles away. She checked her printed Google map, steering with her knee, to confirm she'd taken the correct turn for the university.

When the campus came into view, it was dotted with a few old buildings from the 50s. Mostly brick, with concrete, cream-colored cubic columns accenting the corners. Plain white lettering tacked onto the brick identified the buildings "Administration," "Athletics," "School of Business," "Public Safety." The roads were named Scholars Avenue, University Parkway, and Faculty Row, so on the campus map they seemed impressive. But as she drove along them her car shook from the bumps and potholes. 'There's *no way* I'm moving here,' she promised herself. She was looking for a quiet place to work while she healed from the divorce from Tyler, from being redundant after Shane's greed, and Sebastian's ungrateful—well, look don't even go there. In whatever southern state that university turned out to be while she finished her dissertation, she needed a return of dignity coming from being able to pay bills, stop her rising debt, and eat decent food. But how desperate was she? Surely not *this* desperate.

Driving along Old Highway 29 Boulevard to the Palm Garden Inn only convinced her how wise this promise was. Her jaw dropped from the shock. The street was littered with billboard signage and low-end retail. Dollar General, Walmart Super Center, and all manner of fast food joints lined both sides of the road. People drove their vehicles, mostly Chevy and Ford trucks, like they were going to a funeral in the 45 mph zone. She passed the one story mall with JC Penney and Sears as anchor stores. She shook her head.

Olivia sighed. "God, 'bet they ain't got a decent ballet place nowhere."

At six a.m. the next morning, wearing a black wool crepe business skirt suit, altered by her tailor back in Palo Alto for better fit, and black leather three-inch stacked heel Cole Haan pumps, she checked out of the hotel.

Outside, annoyed with the whole thing she told the sky, "Even though this place is like some nineteen sixties hold over — oh well, I'm here. I may as well go on with the interview," got in her car and drove to the university.

Dr. Patrick Berry, the Associate Dean of the Business School, met with her at the end of the day, after the interviews with other faculty, and the indigestion of a Norm's breakfast and an inhaled Olive Garden lunch. It was his twenty-sixth year at the university, and he was looking forward to *finally* making the business school reputable, expanding the faculty to include people that weren't homegrown unproductive morons who only cared about "working out at the college" for retirement benefits.

When he came to work at the university he had no idea that he would get stuck there but he made the most of it. Now he had the opportunity to get himself positioned so that when he retired he could have great accomplishments on his CV. In his mind he savored the image of collecting his retirement while he worked as President. His wife would have to take back her criticism and disdain for his decision to move to Roadims in the first place. It would be sweet. He puckered his thin red lips a little.

By hiring Olivia, he knew he would be able to improve his CV in a different way too: that he had contributed to the diversity of the institution, that he hired someone with a doctorate that was unique. As he showed her around the building, he pointed out classrooms equipped with modern ergonomic seating and technology.

"We recently invested in new classroom furniture to facilitate group discussion," he bragged.

"Great," she said but thought it was weird. Olivia reflected on her graduate classrooms that were all small conference room-types, where she sat with students around a table. But for undergraduate work, all the classrooms were auditorium size. She didn't know anything about teaching at that level except the lecture format, which clearly would not be conducive to a group setting.

Before leaving the building he toured her around faculty offices. They were generous, about seven-by-eight feet, most with windows to outside views, and privacy on the inside.

Now he was escorting her to meet the university President.

As Patrick walked her across campus, her mind was somewhere else, remembering the drive from Palo Alto to Kansas City, hurting whenever she probed the scab over the sore spot of the life she was kicked out of. Now she wondered if Tyler was right. He always said she was making a big mistake by going into academia. But that was only because he wanted her to keep making the money so he could leech off her. He was such a wimpy ass but only the most recent example of how she people pleased. It was killing her. At 38, in the most *Hope for the Flowers* way, she determined to jump off of ladder-climbing ambition, and let life take her. Looking around, she thought now perhaps she'd over done it.

It was Eileen who pointed this out to her in no uncertain terms.

"What are you doing?? Don't you know that Roadims is backwards and full of Republicans?," her advisor nearly yelled when Olivia first told her about the job. Olivia knew that Eileen wanted her to be a pearl in her string of protégés she wore like a gift from a lover. Being Olivia's advisor was going to make Eileen look bad if she took a job in a business school.

"Yes, that may be true but I need a job," Olivia tried to be respectful but firm.

"Understood, but you are going into a *business* department, not a *dance* department," there was disgust in her voice. "You'll have to re-tool, and I'm afraid you won't get to continue the research you're doing." She wished Olivia would just do what she told her to do. But she never had, and never will.

Eileen took a deep breath, reaffirmed this was why people shouldn't be admitted to doctoral programs after they've turned twenty-eight.

"True, that's because none of the *dance* departments will even look at me, I can't get an interview for even the little one year, thirty-two thousand dollar fefore taxes appointments, since they're too locked in their thinking to *understand* my research. Here I'll also be able to make enough money to live on, continue my research with a tenure track job in the *business school*," she said softly.

Eileen didn't work in a dance department any more either, after the sheer unfrofessionalism she experienced with the sexual harassment. She was penalized for not being lesbian, had to hide her marriage, waited until she was damn near getting ready to give birth before the pregnancy announced itself. Relief came when she was able to move back to the sociology department where people were at least sane.

"Okay Olivia, but I am strongly advising you against this."

This was why Olivia waited until after she moved to Kansas City to call her.

"Olivia, we're here," Patrick's voice brought her back to the present.

"Okay, great!" she tried to sound as if she heard everything he'd been saying along the stroll across campus.

"I'm going to introduce you to the President, a man who has controlled this institution for nearly twenty-five years. *Before that* he was the Dean of our business school, and *before that*," he paused to give emphasis to just how long the President had been there, "he was a faculty member."

"Oh wow."

"President Fontecillo's from Chile, his wife from Hong Kong," Patrick added.

"Really?" she expressed genuine curiosity.

"Yes, so you're not alone, though you *will* be the first African American to be hired by the business school since the institution's inception back in the fifties. If I recall, we have about three hundred full time faculty, four are minorities. I think there's some Democrats around but we like to remain anonymous."

Why do they assume Black Person equals A Democrat? It was really annoying. Olivia was Republican—until just before Clinton. Olivia raised her eyebrows, rolled her lips as if to spread her lipstick, and thought it would be best if she didn't say anything.

Patrick continued, "The college just received university status, and now we're trying to hire more PhDs, since we're offering graduate programs and degrees. Of course, people who started here with a two-year degree objective will be allowed to finish within a certain timeframe and are not turned away. However, we're not accepting any more students into the Associate's program," he said matter-of-factly, smirking, and giggling a little. "I'm glad we're rid of them." He slipped his left hand in his pants pocket.

"Oh, okay." Olivia had no clue about how to respond, like he was making jokes she didn't get.

"We're also able to give faculty money for travel to conferences and travel abroad with our international program," he smiled. This was a coup he personally won in a recent battle with Luis so he could recruit faculty. Luis didn't understand the world had changed, that the university was going to stagnate if policies only stroked his ego.

"That's good, since I have relationships with folks in France and Germany. I did my doctoral fieldwork in Stuttgart, and I've presented papers in Ireland and The Netherlands." She tried not to sound like she was selling herself too much or to give away that her feet were killing her. She measured each step she took over the rocky path, hoping pain wasn't showing on her face.

"Good. Well, make sure you mention this to the President, and after you sign your contract, I'll connect you with the faculty in the international program across campus; the business school needs a champion so that would be good for you."

"Yes, that would be great!" She actually felt some excitement beginning to stir, and that felt weird to her. What had it been, eons since she felt that? "What about publications for tenure?"

"Well, you just need to stay current in your field, publish where you'd like, research what you want, just stay current." He nodded at her, easy, reassuring, like a relaxing massage so that her shoulders immediately dropped an inch. At that she was convinced. It didn't matter that Roadims was way south of reality.

"That's so great," she said. There was a rapport she felt with him, he seemed nice, genuine.

They arrived at The Administration Building. Patrick opened the door for her, directing her to the left. The building had olive-green plastic upholstered couches and chairs from the sixties in the foyer, with stark concrete block walls that were painted dull enamel-shine yellow. Amid dim florescent lighting with flickering bulbs needing replacement, old-fashioned blinds with kinks in them covered the windows that you cranked open outward. Linoleum government grade flooring of some kind of un-descript shade of light green with black specks spanned out in front of them. It was a three-story building with the President's Office on the main entrance level, the second floor. Stenciled on the windows and the doors of the presidential suite of offices were "Office of the President" the black lettering dared. What, did they think build it once and that's it? Who was in charge here? Patrick opened the door and she went through. She liked the way he treated her as a woman without being asinine.

President Fontecillo's suite was large and spacious, complete with the outer reception area, along with the conference room, a more secluded personal office, and a full bathroom and kitchenette. The conference room was furnished with a teak colored wooden desk and matching conference table. A large clock with the university logo on its face hung on the wall, in the center, behind it. The retro chairs around the table could have been purchased from Goodwill. A couch with some floral pattern on a light blue background was also taking up space in the room, with an oval coffee table perched between it and two more retro looking chairs. It would have been a great decorative look if had been planned, and they'd ordered the furniture from Restoration Hardware or the accessories from Martha Stewart. But they didn't.

Olivia noted that it could have been nice, but the windows were covered by drapes that had a few broken hooks, and cheap brown unpadded industrial carpet covered the floors. This was a picture of pure aesthetic poverty parading as frugality in a public institution of higher learning and frankly Olivia found it embarrassing and shameful, like when your girlfriend been hit so hard in the face and she make excuses to you rather than go.

The President emerged from his inner office, meeting Patrick and Olivia at the end of the short hall that spilled out into the main area.

"Hello, Dr. Fontecillo. This is Olivia Clarke, a candidate for our Assistant Professor of Marketing and Management position. Ms. Clarke, this is Dr. Fontecillo."

Dr. Fontecillo and Olivia shook hands, and both recited, "It's a pleasure to meet you," in unison and laughed nervously.

"Won't you sit?" he gestured them to the couch, then he took one of the sitting chairs, crossing his legs. He cocked his head a little to the right, with black rimmed bifocals pushed up close to his face. Brown creamy taught skin, thin dyed black hair with a part on the left side, he was tall and slender. He wore a light wool, pin-striped navy blue double breasted business suit, with a white collared starched shirt, long red tie, black leather shoes that laced up, socks neatly hidden.

"Welcome to Western State. I trust you have had a good visit?"

His Spanish accent was charming, and she was amazed that this university had a Latin American man as President. Her father, Raul, would've loved to have seen this. Olivia sensed an immediate connection so that she would work hard to live up to Dr. Fonticello's expectations. At the same time she felt that he would take care of her.

"Yes, it has been quite nice."

"Good, well tell me about your research."

She talked about the classical performing arts, and that her dissertation was covering the economics of professional ballet companies in the United States, Canada and Germany.

"That's very interesting, as we have here the Western State International Piano Competition. My wife is the founder and director of that organization. Perhaps you can assist her in her efforts."

"Yes, absolutely."

"Ms. Clarke will finish her dissertation very soon, and I have shown her the plethora of arts organizations here, especially over in Springfield, that will need her help. She will have a natural fit for the service aspect of her position." Patrick sounded like he was trying to convince Luis that her out of field doctorate wasn't a problem.

What the hell was Patrick thinking? Olivia wouldn't fit in in Springfield, any more than he himself would fit in at a Juneteenth celebration. Olivia's work was much more classical.

Patrick and Luis had both been at the university for a long time.

Patrick was ambitious and wanted to walk in Luis' footsteps. But, Luis here lately, was being prodded by the Board to retire. He looked weary, sitting there in the chair.

Dr. Fontecillo nodded his head, without contradicting Patrick, and then placed his palms together and rested his chin on the tips of his fingers, elbows perched on the arms of the chair. His diamond and gold cuff links sparkled next to the end of the jacket sleeve, as his matching wide wedding band reflected light.

His eyes gazed away from them for a moment, so he could compose himself. Then he said in a more solemn tone, looking her in the eye with his brows furrowed, "Are you familiar with this area of the country, Ms. Clarke?"

"No, not really, I've been in Kansas City, well, Lee's Summit actually, the last six months, working on my research and writing. I am a native Los Angelean, and lived in southern California most of my life," she summarized quickly, adjusting her seating so that her leg wasn't falling asleep.

Olivia sensed that there was some unspoken conversation between Patrick and the President, she looked from one of them to the other trying to read what it was. Patrick just looked at his notebook and after a moment he picked up the notebook and started doodling. He was a lefty.

Though she was great at putting on a poker face, it didn't hold as Olivia's furrowed brow revealed her wondering about what Fonticello was referring to. This place was not the place for a single black woman from the city but she had pretty much figured that out. Fontecillo leaned back and crossed his arms.

She didn't say anything for a moment, and they all sat there listening to the clock tick.

"Oh, um, yes, I understand," she finally managed. "Fortunately I have friends in Kansas City and of course I can always take a plane to Los Angeles," she reasoned, reading his face to make sure she reassured him and trying to deny that racism would affect her.

"Good, naturally you can imagine the cost of living is very low, so you will be able to buy a nice home here. My wife Michelle and I have been here for over twenty-five years," he explained, uncrossing his arms and leaning forward, adjusting his glasses.

"Sounds like you have a nice life."

"Yes, it is a lot different from Chile or Hong Kong," he forced a chuckle.

In reality Fonticello got waylayed here, when he was only passing through. At the time he was thinking he'd stay for a short while and move on to a real institution of higher education. But the opportunities started coming his way at the college because while the Board would pay him more with each contract renewal, they would never pay market rate for a new president. Fonticello found himself getting promoted but not getting commensurate experience, becoming more of a figurehead as time went on, skills not being necessary, but pay and perks increasing. And Michelle, well, she'd nursed her piano competition along, and as a result, the Fontecillo's rubbed elbows with the mucky-mucks of Roadims. There came a point then when, if he did want to leave, he couldn't. After a time he didn't want to leave, because he was too old and bitter.

"I can only imagine."

"Well, Dr. Fontecillo, we don't want to take a lot of your time, and we have an appointment in human resources next," Patrick interrupted. He looked up and closed his notebook, twisted his pen, put it in his inside shirt pocket.

"Fine, well it was a pleasure meeting you Ms. Clarke and we look forward to having you here." He extended his hand as they stood.

She reached out and shook it, "Thank you, Dr. Fontecillo," she replied, holding his gaze.

As they turned to walk out of the office, Patrick and the President exchanged a few words. "Make sure you tell her what she's facing here," the President told him.

Strange. Why didn't he tell her himself?

"Yep, sure will," Patrick lied. "Thanks, see you later." He opened the door for her, and Olivia again felt an unresolved something between them.

"Dr. Fontecillo is an interesting man and this is an even more interesting community," Patrick started as soon as they were out of earshot. "They don't take change well."

"Yes, I can see that." Olivia wasn't sure what she saw, but it sounded good.

"Next stop is human resources. Not my favorite people but it's part of the deal. When you finish with them one of the secretaries will bring you over to our building. We can talk about next steps, okay?"

"Sounds good."

By then they reached the door with the stenciled words "Human Resources Office" on the glass, just down the hall from the President's Office. He held opened the door and, standing in the doorway said to the assistant, "This is Ms. Clarke, she has an appointment to discuss the benefits we offer tenure-track faculty," he said.

"Thank you Patrick, yes, we are expecting her. And we will make sure she gets back to you on time," the assistant smiled at him, answering his question before he asked it.

"Great!" Feeling confident he'd sold Olivia on the place, he left her to the assistant's care. He succeeded in getting her to a certain emotional point with him, and now dropped his façade a bit, nodding and saluting her with his left hand, forefinger and middle finger outstretched to his temple as he closed the door behind him.

Olivia liked Patrick. He seemed nice, down to earth, very mannerly but warm and friendly. She figured he would be easy to work with.

After spending an hour listening to the human resources assistant, Olivia was ready to leave for the drive back to Kansas City. It had been a long day. With all the choices of health care and self-funded retirement explained *ad nauseum*, the assistant walked her back to Patrick's office. They walked in silence, and Olivia was grateful. Sleeping in the hotel had been impossible last night, and being in the spotlight constantly for the last eight hours was grueling. She was surprised that she didn't have to do a community lecture. All of her other campus interviews required it. She was glad though for the reprieve, because she didn't have to keep up with the overhead transparencies or talk to these people about the nonprofit classical performing arts which she was sure they'd be bored with, except maybe a few of them like President Fontecillo. He was a curious sort. She wondered how he'd survived here for so long, serving at the pleasure of the Board of Governors.

"Well here we are," the human resources specialist said when they'd arrived at Patrick's office. Olivia thought her name was Jan, Olivia didn't notice they were even in the building.

"Thank you so much for your help, Jan," Olivia smiled, trying to express her gratitude.

"You are welcome, good luck to you," Jan had what was now the familiar thick southern drawl. Patrick didn't have a drawl and of course neither did the President but the locals did.

Patrick stood there confidently in the doorway, tall, lean, with salt and pepper hair. Now she allowed herself to look at him. He was a very attractive man. Olive skin, under a five o'clock shadow, his wire-rimmed glasses giving him that intellectual look. He dressed just like Olivia's idea of a professor, with dark blue khaki pants and a green dress shirt, both had seen the washer a few too many times, with a Looney Toon's tie.

"Nice tie, Patrick."

"Thanks, it's one I got from my boys for Christmas a few years ago." Not waiting for Olivia to ask, he added, "One is a freshman and the other is a junior. High school," he laughed.

"Ah. Yes, I understand, we have those fond memories of our children, when they were, well, cute!"

"Right, exactly."

His brown corduroy jacket was worn at the elbows, and was too big so it draped off his shoulders. And his loafers, brown and black leather, were so broken in Olivia wondered how they stayed on his feet when he walked. She imagined his wife probably held him on a pretty short leash. A glimmer of desire flashed through her, she was totally unfamiliar with it. No matter. He was definitely off limits as were all the men she'd ever worked with. It was a Ru-elle.

"So what did you think? I know this isn't the Ivy League but, do you think you could be happy here?" He asked, smirking a little. Olivia was beautiful, brown, intelligent. Five feet four, a sleek ballet dancer too, oh my god. He imagined her in *Pointe* shoes and a pair of tights and leotard. Maybe he could get her to do a performance. He didn't want to think about what his wife was going to say when she found out he'd hired her.

"About??"

"The benefits aren't that great but they are pretty good. It used to be that we had a more defined benefit for retirement, but the Board changed that after a battle Dr. Fontecillo lost to them to give new faculty a portable plan with TIAA Cref. If you'd like to enroll in the State of Arkansas's plan, you'll be eligible after the end of your sixth year, and that will be a retirement system based on years of service and age." He thought maybe he should tell her about the local ballet school, but decided no.

"However, the good thing is that you can take your TIAA Cref plan with you should you decide to leave; you can't do that with the state sponsored plan." Olivia listened with complete ignorance to his sales pitch. She had no idea about retirement plans or anything like that because where she came from those plans were always self-funded.

"Okay, that's good to know," she managed to croak.

"This is an interesting area, and I have to tell you it has limitations, faculty are dated, the town is slow to change, and I've been here for twenty-five years myself, started here when it was a junior college. You can drive easily to Little Rock if you need to get a dose of culture, my wife and I do that often. I'm from Washington and she's from Oregon so we're used to driving for what we need."

"Why do you stay here then?" she asked, trying not to get too personal but trying to understand.

He diverted his eyes and said, "Come sit down in my office," noticing they had been standing in the outer office where his secretary Amy sat working at her computer.

The Dean's outer office furniture consisted of old metal filing cabinets and desks, and metal blinds covered the windows. The carpet was worn and unpadded. There was an adjoining conference room that had been left undecorated, with a cheap oval cream-colored table that filled up the room and eight chairs made of pre-fab plastic with seats that were too low for the table.

He led Olivia into his office, where the surroundings were no different, only he had an antique wooden desk, credenza, and bookshelves. It wasn't what she thought a Dean's Office was supposed to look like. The ones back in her graduate school were plush, with expensive furniture and carpets. She expected the Dean's Office to be nearly as well furnished as the President's.

As if sensing her distaste for the décor, he said "We're getting new furniture this summer. Please have a seat."

"That's a relief," she said before she could keep the words from spewing out.

"Yeah, don't be shy about your feelings," Patrick made light of her *faux pas.* "There's a lot that needs to change around here."

Laughing at herself and Patrick's levity, she sat nearly eye level with a ceramic vase on the desk scolding her with the words 'Ashes of Disobedient Faculty.' That's deep, needs people to obey, she thought. Along his credenza and on top of the bookcases were framed photographs of two boys, a wedding photo of him and who Olivia assumed was his wife, and ceramic pieces. His wife was definitely older than he. Olivia figured at the very least he had a mommy complex.

"Wow, do you make pottery?"

"Yes, I do. Several of us here in the community are artists as well as business professionals." We have to do something to stay sane around here, he thought. The place will drive you crazy without some creative energy flow. Besides, it was a way to get people to like him. He thought about The Watsons, The Pierces, and the rest of the donors at the Hudson Art Gallery, the movers and shakers in the area. They were valuable connections.

"Very nice." She meant it.

"So, this area is very Republican, very conservative. But you can do what you want to do, as long as you do what you are supposed to do, that is teach and take care of the students. We'll support your travel to France and send you to conferences where you're giving papers. Many of the faculty go home at noon, this has been known as the barbeque school — teach in the morning, barbeque in the afternoons. That's changing a little as we're on a push to hire more PhD-types and move the university into growth. It's the only way to get this place onto a level playing field with our competitors. I've been able to get a lot out of being here, and next year when you arrive, I will be the Dean. The current dean, Jim Brown, doesn't have a PhD and no intention of getting one, is stepping down as he recognizes that the winds of change are upon us. He's been the Dean for the last fifteen years and wants to return to teaching. Do you have any questions?"

She had no new questions, but she noticed he didn't answer her about why he stayed for so long. And she wondered how someone who had been Dean for so long could just want to return to teaching.

"No, I don't have any more questions. Thanks for a nice day, Patrick. I really enjoyed meeting you and your colleagues. This looks like a nice friendly place to work."

"Good, we're enthused as well. We'll meet — the faculty search committee — in a couple days, and be in touch. Should make a hiring decision before the end of April," he said confidently, nodding, and moving his hands in circles away from his body as he spoke.

"Okay, thank you" she stood when he did, they shook hands. Then she walked out of his office, through the outer office past Amy, saying goodbye as she went. Down the stairs out the door to her car. She started the car and began driving away, down the main drag. She remembered that Grady Harryman, the department head for marketing and management, had driven her around yesterday, showing her the sights. Now *he* had a drawl being that he was from the Mississippi Gulf Coast. Like he said, "They're some real nice places to live, but you couldn't say Roadims was purdy." Real estate was reasonable though, much better than in California. Well, she deliberated to herself, it *was* a new university, it did have international opportunities and the cost of living there was good. She could continue her research, they would support her finishing her dissertation. They covered her moving expenses as well. She broke her original promise to herself; she should consider this job. It was the middle of April and classes began in August. Who should she talk to about getting a house, she wondered?

"Hello?" she answered the phone hanging on the kitchen wall of the tiny little three-room midcentury house she'd rented in Lee's Summit.

"Hello Olivia? This is Patrick Berry from Western State."

"Oh, hi, how are you!" she breathed, moving around in circles, then looking at the calendar laying on the counter. It was May third. She'd stopped holding her breath a few days ago, figuring they'd decided not to hire her.

"Very well, and we're extremely pleased to offer you a position as Assistant Professor of Marketing and Management in the School of Business Administration." He hoped she hadn't accepted another job somewhere else, or decided in anyway against Western.

"Thank you very much Patrick! That's wonderful."

"So you accept the position? It's tenure-track, you'll mainly teach marketing, and you'll need to take some postdoctoral work at the University of Arkansas as a condition of your tenure. But we will cover all the costs for that. And once you finish your diss, you will receive an annual increase of three thousand dollars. Your starting salary is sixty thousand. All of this will be spelled out in the contract we'll mail you."

Screw Eileen and the hell with Tyler she thought. Shoot, this is more money than a tenured full professor of dance will *ever* make.

"Absolutely I accept! Thank you very much, and I look forward to the opportunity."

"Good, and when you get here, we will get you involved in our international program. By the way, there will be a Blackboard training this summer; perhaps you can come down and take the course."

"What's 'Blackboard'?"

"That's the online platform we use to deliver online content and also to enhance the traditional course design. Many faculty resist this but it is a fact of the future of academia."

"Okay, well yes, I'll see what I can arrange, I'm sure I can make it," She didn't want to spend her summer doing that. She would figure out how to get out of it, or something. The job was great but she needed to stay in Kansas City as long as possible. Already her friends were telling her it was a mistake, saying things like "Don't you know the Klan lives in Smithville, that's only a few minutes south of Roadims." She didn't care. She could get tenure, build a career, have a quiet lifestyle. Bring her son Sebastian down to the house she'd buy, and when her family wanted to come visit they'd finally approve. The short newspaper article about the 44-year old black man shot seventeen times came creeping into her memory. Before it took a hold, she turned it off, and tried concentrating on what Patrick was saying.

Patrick continued, "Fine, you'll get an email letting you know when the course is, and in the mean time you will receive the contract from the Vice President of Academic Affairs, who you met, Larry Martin. Sign one copy and return it, keep a copy for your records. And you can talk with Prudential Realtors about finding a house. They're online. Keep your receipts for moving and we will reimburse you. Let me know if you have questions."

He fired off this information, she wanted to ask him questions while she racked her brain to keep up but didn't want to look stupid. Pro who? What moving company? What's my email address? When will the contract arrive? It was like her brain was in slow motion but his words were hitting her in warp speed.

"Thanks, I will," she'd get her questions answered later.

"Okay, have a nice weekend, Olivia, bye-bye."

"You too, bye." She hung up, and looked at the ceiling, 'Roadims, Arkansas? Okay, whatever,' she talked to the space, shaking her head in disbelief, shrugged and threw her palms up at shoulder height in surrender.

They were walking towards each other on Ward Parkway, near the Hall's Department Store on the Plaza over in Kansas City. It was a fine spring day, with the sun producing a nice 74 degree crispness through a slight breeze.

"Hey Xena!"

"Hey 'Livia, how you doing girl?"

"Fine, fine, I got the job down in Roadims."

"Great, that's GREAT! You know those tenure track jobs are hard to come by. At least at my institution we've been cutting back. An when we do hire, it's someone they been coveting for a while."

Olivia didn't understand what Xena was talking about. "Is that right?"

"Um-hum," Xena touched her hair. Her sunglasses sat on the end of her short nose, and her dark brown and drapey paisley smock contrasted with her fair and smooth completion.

"Let's go in Hall's?" Olivia started towards the door.

"Oh absolutely, they're having their winter sale, and girl you know I could use some boots."

"Right, and not the kind where you gonna fall over and break your hip." Olivia waited for a moment, till Xena had gone in. "So what about you? You okay?"

"Yeah girl, I'm fine, but I just got a call from the Kansas City Ballet's artistic director pleading for some more money from the hospital. I told him I'd have to get back with him. Oh, 'Liv look at that! That's so cute!"

Xena pointed to a purple, black and pink skirt suit.

"Sure is, that would be a great suit to have. You know they got good quality stuff here."

Olivia was as close to heaven as she could be. Being on The Plaza was fantastic. Shopping in Hall's was reason enough to move to Kansas City. It gave new meaning to upscale, and the way the store was laid out it was just fabulous. The clothes weren't jammed in too close, and the racks carefully placed. And the home décor area was to die for by itself. You could buy lawn furniture and dining accessories that made you feel like you were on Martha's Vineyard. The whole place reminded her of when they'd go downtown to shop in Philly.

"Yeah they do, but you pay for it. I'd love to get this but," she slid the suits down the rack, "they don't have my size. What are you, a four petite right? There's one," pulling a suit from the rack.

Holding it up to herself, "Sure is sharp," Olivia admired herself. "They may have it in your size in the women's department."

"That's a thought, let's walk over there and see."

Olivia knew Xena wasn't going to buy anything but she went along with it anyway, placing the suit back on the sparsely populated dress rack. They were going to shop till they dropped.

Walking past the chocolate counter on the way to the plus sizes, Xena slowed down, and held her chin. Her purse dangled off her shoulder and bumped into her hip. You could the wheels of desire turn. All she did was look at Olivia, and the two went up to the glass display cases and ordered caramel and almond milk chocolate candies.

Reaching into her white paper bag, Xena said as she held a candy between her fingers, "Well at least when you move to Roadims you can get off the ballet's board. I'm stepping down as president as soon as my term is over in December. Besides, one of these days, I'm going to start looking for a job closer to New York. Daddy's getting old, and my family — well you know."

"I understand completely," Olivia gave Xena a reassuring touch on the shoulder. "But you'll have to come visit before you go."

"Oh, definitely. We should do the holidays together, at least Thanksgiving, since I do go home for Christmas."

"Let's make it a date! And tell your kids to come on down. Y'all can stay with me."

"Yeah, let's do that." Xena took a tiny bite from her chocolate.

Olivia frowned at her. "What are you doing?"

"Gotta make it last," Xena smiled and took another shaving from the candy.

"Come on, let's go look at the shoes," Olivia laughed.

"Oh girl you know that's right."

They meandered through the store, just being girlfriends. For Olivia, *that* was chocolate.


By August Olivia moved to Roadims, Arkansas driving again past Peculiar, a little less afraid.

*Spring 2008, Newhall Springs, Arkansas*

Standing at the mailbox she read the envelope's return address embossed with 'Vice President of Academic Affairs, Western State University'. She turned the letter over quickly, hands shaking, pushed her right index finger under the left corner of the flap, and ripped it across, not caring if she got a paper cut.

*Western State May 18, 2008*

*Dear Dr. Clarke:*

*On behalf of the Interim President Dr. Renee Gruber of Western State University and the Board of Governors and the Governor of the State of Arkansas, I am pleased to inform you that you have been granted tenure. It is with distinction that you should carry this honorable achievement with you; much will be required of you as you shape and lead the organization in the future with your colleagues.*

*Congratulations on his remarkable accomplishment. Please contact me should you have questions or concerns. Under separate cover you will receive notification of your promotion, granted along with tenure status.*

*Sincerely,*

*Dan Fogerty, PhD, Interim VP of Academic Affairs*

Her heart stopped while she acknowledged that breaking a promise to herself by accepting this job nearly six years ago had been a good thing.

"Hello Olivia," one of the neighbors waved.

"Hi Lee, how's it going? Congrats on your lawn," she said, trying to sound genuine. She faced the little sign they'd stabbed into and left in his lawn like a campaign endorsement of "Landscaping for Mayor" shouting to all the inferior neighbors that he'd won the city's best landscape award. Her lawn meanwhile was only green half the year, uneven, since she wouldn't take her entire pay for two summers and devote it sod. Damn lawn was covered mostly with acorns dropped from the trees, full of holes from moles and digging squirrels. Olivia tried — but gave up quickly — to clean up the acorns but there must have been fifteen years worth of them under the grass.

At one point she half believed her son would help her with the yard. Being stupid and tricked again, Sebastian didn't do anything after he talked her into letting him move in. Every time she looked at the yard she got mad and remembered having to put him out. Naturally he never helped after that, never even asked her if she needed something. She should have told him to stay in California. Her stomach turned when she thought about it, so she pushed the memories back into their box.

"Yes, thanks. It was a lot of work," Lee bragged, oblivious to Olivia's shoulda-woulda-couldas. Lee was in early 70s, gray haired, pot bellied, glasses, what she'd come to know as the usual non-descript Roadims look. He was really involved in his church, but he'd only proselytized Olivia once. She would often see his church's bus sitting in his driveway.

"Well you deserve it, I know it's a lot of work, especially with these Arkansas rocks trying to pass as soil and all them trees and dad-gum squirrels. I can barely keep up my yard." She knew that was an understatement. That yard was running *her* worse than a dog walking his master. She needed a man who cared about the lawn to help, but she could only hire guys who didn't, who'd come over every two weeks and "cut the grass" as they called it.

"True, but you got a huge piece of God's earth and you got all them trees. You still out at the college?" He leaned on his short shovel.

She cringed whenever anyone said 'out at the college'. It made her feel like she was at some low level diploma mill or something.

"Yes, I am, I just got tenure," she didn't correct him.

"Good for you, I don't miss working, I'm retired from Pitt State you know."

"Yes, I remember, but, I gotta go in now, looks like the storm's 'bout to hit," she wiggled out of the conversation. He was the kind of old guy who would talk your ear off and she didn't feel like listening to it today.

"Yeah, it's gonna hit soon, take care, let me know if you need anything living by yourself in that big ol' house."

'Right Lee, you don't need to rub in the fact that I'm alone,' she thought. 'I really do hate it but...'

"Thanks, I will," she turned and walked down the long driveway to the door off the third garage, and went in. Earlier she prepared the house for the storm, brought in the lawn furniture, the decorative flags, and anything that could be lost to the winds. Getting the mail was the last step, and she intended to spend the evening at home hunkered down, having already bought groceries in anticipation of not getting out.

Inside the house, still both numb and in shock from achieving tenure and promotion, since somewhere deep, deep down inside she really didn't think she would be able to measure up, she paced the kitchen's hardwood floors around the center island. She wondered if Harmony would be home right now. For a split second she thought she'd call her mother. "Now that is still stupid. Think about it. You know she's only gonna act like tenure ain't nothing," she said looking out the kitchen window. It was a little after four o'clock Saturday. Maybe Jonathan? She walked quickly from the kitchen, through the living room, down the long hall of the rambling empty house to the middle bedroom converted into her office, picked up her Motorola cordless phone. Thumbing quickly through the calls list, she found Harmony's number and pressed 'talk.' With the phone to her ear, she stood in the doorway, admiring the décor and the paint, hoping she wouldn't get any storm damage. The lawn was good enough, she told herself, and the outside of the house had a great paint job, doors and trim in red and the house white. Then she took the phone down from her ear, pressed the 'off' button, and scrolled again, finding Harmony's cell number.

"Heeeyyyy Liv sweetie!" Harmony answered.

"Heeyyy! Whatcha doin'?"

Harmony said, "right now, Justin is going for a tennis lesson, and he'll be spending the night with his friend. I'm dropping him off as we speak. Oh god, he's getting ready for his bar mitzvah next fall and it's costing me SO much money, I'm going in debt! Like four thousand dollars!"

"Yes, I can imagine, I'm still going to try to make it if I can. I haven't been to Philadelphia in years. Where's Brock?"

"He's out in Springfield for a unexpected visit with Elizabeth. Her mother has gone crazy again."

"Oh, sorry to hear that," Olivia soothed.

"No, I'm okay, really."

Olivia could tell she was trying to convince herself. After a moment, Olivia asked, "Hey, how about, do you have time for dinner tonight?"

"Would love to have dinner. Where you wanna go? Is Jonathan here?"

"No, unfortunately he's not. But how about the noodle place on Old Highway Twenty-nine?"

"Fine I haven't been there this week. Hmm, let's see. It's about four-thirty now; will seven, will that work?"

"Sure, do you think the storm will cause problems?" Olivia asked.

"What storm?" Harmony sort of chided, Liv was always worried about the weather. It was going to rain, no big deal.

"Never mind, I'll see you then at seven, okay?"

"Great, bye, see you soon!"


Olivia pulled her '97 Mercedes E320 into the parking lot, trying to park as close to the door as possible. The rain was coming down in torrents, the wind blowing at least 30 miles an hour. It was a good thing she traded her VW for this car, it was better against the weather here. She parked, got out and ran to the restaurant, grateful for the opportunity to be with people even if they were near strangers.

"Hello, one for dinner?" the hostess asked, smiling, nodding her head, eyebrows raised. She was dressed in traditional Thailand costume, and spoke with her native Asian accent. Olivia closed her umbrella, shaking the water off her hands, and placed it in the umbrella holder. She made a mental note to get one of those for the house.

"No, Harmony's meeting me tonight," Olivia soaked up the smile from the hostess, and smiled back.

"Oh, okay, your usual table then?"

"Yes please." Olivia loved being known, it gave her the illusion of not being alone. They walked past the wall-inset fish tank full of blue and orange koi and big screen television perpetually tuned to tennis matches, to a white table-clothed table with four leather chairs next to the window. *The Buddha*, sat at the back of the restaurant, made of sculpted marble, at least six feet tall and four feet wide. She felt relieved that it guarded her peacefully. She sat down, and waited for Harmony. It was just seven p.m. her watch said. Harmony was always late; she operated on colored people's time. Olivia laughed. Yes, CPT applied to other cultures besides black folk's.

"Ginger tea?" the waitress asked loudly, as if she was speaking to someone hard of hearing.

"Yes, thanks I would love that," and she disappeared and returned with a cup, steaming with hot tea. Olivia sipped, it was so good, warming, reassuring.

"Hey Liv!" Harmony said, walking up to the table. Harmony had a wonderful broad smile, it was inviting and nurturing. Olivia loved her long, thick, wavy mostly gray hair. It reminded her of her own. Harmony's pale skin, and tiny body frame, about five-feet tall was obscured by her expansive mind, and talking to her was always an adventure.

She wore purple rectangle-framed glasses on the end of her nose, and her dangle jade earrings caught the light. Long flowing black skirt with a purple wool turtleneck sweater, little beads of knap standing at attention, peeking out from the red silk wrap. These made her look Arabian or Egyptian. Her shoes were a black plastic two-inch heeled boot, and her purse beige mesh macramé. Olivia loved her eccentricity and how Harmony was true to her vegetarianism and stance against consumerism. No meat and no leather, no matter what.

"Hey!" Olivia said getting up to hug her. Harmony dropped her soaked umbrella on the floor next to the table just before embracing.

"Been here long?"

"No, not at all, just long enough to get my tea."

"Great." They settled down at the table, not studying the menu. The waitress came up and smiled at Harmony, and asked if they wanted their usual: Harmony, her Buddha's Delight with fried tofu, and Olivia her Tom Yum noodle soup. Without writing anything down, the waitress smiled and retreated again.

"Harmony, I got tenure!" Olivia blurted out.

"Oh my, wonderful. When did you hear?" Harmony leaned into the table, resting her arm on it.

"I got the letter today."

"Awesome, that means next year you can get us out of rubber-stamping the administration's decisions without fear of retaliation from the old Dictator Fonticello," she said, nodding to the waitress who had just brought her tea. Harmony's brow furrowed, and she shook her head as she spoke. "Of course, I've been here for seventeen years and so far, no Faculty Senate President has been able to. But we have confidence in you." She smiled at Olivia over her glasses.

Olivia felt a knot in her stomach. She'd only agreed to run for the office two academic years ago because it would look good on her CV, imagining the great opportunity to work with Fonticello. And serving as president-elect last year was no picnic. But she said to Harmony, "Thanks, we'll see. I'm looking forward to working with the new guy, Dr. Williams."

"Kevin is really hopeful you'll get some changes through," she continued.

"Oh really? I like Kevin. He's brilliant" Olivia concurred.

"Yep, and he's not afraid of the administration either," she laughed.

"I know, he was telling me that over dinner last night, and how he deliberately taunts them," Olivia confided with a toothy smile.

The waitress brought the steaming food on a tray she held on one palm. Olivia breathed in the aroma from her soup, and then started slurping her noodles, trying to avoid splattering juice on her blouse. 'I should have worn something else' she thought, but she'd long ago determined not to stoop to the Roadims dress code. Whenever she went anywhere, she put on something that looked nice. Plus the fact that she ran in to students and other folks from the university and her community involvements all the time. At restaurants, grocery stores, the mall. There was no place for anonymity in this town.

Today she had on her favorite rose colored long-sleeved cotton silk knit, and a long, Jones New York jean skirt, no back split, with Bandolino stacked three-inch heel, zippered inseam knee length leather boots same color as her top. These reminded her of the trip she took to Dallas to go shopping. One time Harmony told her that she never bought clothes, but somehow they showed up. Olivia couldn't imagine anything like that. Tonight, she also wore an oversized cotton multicolored wrap that Harmony gave her, and a dark green Liz Claiborne brimmed hat. Her salt and pepper hair spilled out under the hat onto her shoulders, and made a frame for her face. The humidity frizzed her hair, so wearing a hat made it more manageable.

"Dinner? With Kevin? Well now, how was that? He's very attractive, only a couple years from tenure," Harmony teased with a little song in her voice, taking a bite of her veggies.

"Yeah, I know, like I said before he's too young — fifteen years younger than me."

Olivia knew there was this new push for older women with younger men, but it wasn't for her, what were they called, Barracuda's or something? Sebastian was only five years younger than Kevin. Besides that, younger men leave when their biological clock starts counting on heirs, and they finally believe what Olivia told them in the first place, that she truly wasn't having more children, no matter how much in love she was. That was the last thing Olivia wanted at this point in life. Plus, he was a white boy from the wrong side of Mobile, not that there was anything wrong with that.

They laughed. "Oh, your only problem is there ain't no pickins in Roadims," she said. "I mean, I met Brock in my *department*, and he, like other faculty in Anthropology and all over campus, was married but I *stole* him."

"Yeah, you two been living together twelve years, y'all oughta get married."

"Nah, I don't think so," she pulled her hair off her neck and rearranged it, looked at the floor. Harmony thought about Brock and the whole marriage thing, and she was not interested. Sure he wanted to get married and he asked her all the time. But two divorces under her belt was two too many. Maybe, just maybe, if Brock needed to be on her health insurance when he was old, and after retiring from Western State she would marry him. She loved him but there was no way she was marrying him under any other circumstances. His temper, his bipolar disorder. No way.

"So you think Luis was a Dictator? Do you think he was forced out by the Board last year?" After a moment of silence about campus coupling, Olivia returned to the topic.

"Absolutely, and retaliated against anybody who crossed him. I think the Board was fed up with him," she said. "Hey, how's your house coming along?" They both loved the way they meandered mentally.

"Just fine, I'm pretty much done now, the dance studio is finished, and the colors are so artsy-fartsy, purple and yellow with the wood flooring and fifteen-foot ceilings. I love it! The basement is done too, finally. I had the carpet put in a couple weeks ago, and had it painted a nice earth-tone green. The house is absolutely fabulous, transformed from the *wreck* it was when I bought it. You saw the lawn, the back yard and stuff, right?"

"Oh, yes, it's very tranquil. Just like your own personal park," she said, smiling and playing with her cold fried tofu. She loved Olivia deeply and even though she had only known her for five years, it seemed like a lifetime.

"Thanks. Oh, and the decks are done too. One of them spans the whole north side and entire back of the house," Olivia reported, a proud homeowner. They chatted on over dinner for hours, as usual. "Have you met Williams?" Olivia asked.

"Yes, I've met him. He's okay, I mean, he does have a doctorate in Anthropology!"

"I don't know, Harmony, I'm not sure about him, how he was hired, how he acts in public—

"I'm giving him the benefit of the doubt. You haven't worked with Luis but believe me anything is better than what we had," she pleaded with her face, rolling her eyes at the thought of Luis.

After that the conversation ebbed, and they both said, "Well, it's getting late," and they sighed and prepared to leave. The check had long been paid, and so they gathered their things, put on their rain gear and walked out into the cool air.

"See you soon, sweetie," Harmony sung, and the two friends embraced, kissed each other on the cheek.

"Okay, absolutely. Let me know when you drop Justin off at the airport to start his summer in Philly with his Dad, and we'll make some plans!" Olivia promised.

"Will do, bye," Harmony grinned and walked quickly to her car to avoid getting too wet.

On the twenty-five-minute drive home to Newhall Springs, Olivia dodged the fallen trees and branches left by the storm and hoped everything was okay at the house. She was so engaged with Harmony that she'd missed the tornado warning alarm.

Loneliness, her all too familiar companion, took its seat in her ribcage, now accompanied by Fear jumping around in her stomach. She needed to pull herself together so she could hide these feelings from Jonathan when they talked later that night.

Then she started rehearsing in her mind next Tuesday's meeting with Williams.

"When I get home," she told the air, "I'll email an agenda to his secretary."

*The things we think*
*are the things that feed our souls.*
*If we think on pure and lovely things,*
*we shall grow pure and lovely like them.*
*And the converse is equally true.*
— Hannah Whitall Smith

# Down with the Dictator

*Fall 2007*

President Fonticello normally strutted onto the stage prouder than George Jefferson ever could before all three hundred faculty-members assembled and waiting expectantly for his opening message for the academic year.

Of course they looked *more* forward to the after-the-speech-hidden-meanings-in-his-words meetings; the small informal gatherings where faculty assured each other that what he'd said was pure bullshit. Many of these faculty had listened to the President drone on and on for hours over the years, made bets beforehand as to the content and length of his speech "this year." They played "Bingo" to the letter and number of possible topics to be covered in the speech the night before. It was the defining rhythm for the year's dance between the faculty and the administration, choreographed by the egotistical whims of state political leaders who pulled Fontecillo's puppet strings.

Faculty entered the auditorium after having milled around in the foyer for the continental breakfast, wanting some kind of compensation for the agony of sitting through the stupid speech, and the thanklessness of their lots in life as professors here. They got there at eight-fifteen in the morning for a nine o'clock meeting to eat the campus-food-service catered fair of tough and bland tasting cantaloupe and honey dew, pineapple that was mostly pine and not much apple, and little stale muffins that nearly choked you to death, getting stuck in your esophagus when you swallowed if you didn't have something to wash them down with. That was the purpose of the weak, lukewarm coffee because it surely wasn't the taste people liked. Most of the juice-from-concentrate was gone by eight-twenty.

Inside the auditorium, flags hung all around the semi-circle shaped space, each representing the international-themed semesters the university held over the years. They ranged from Argentina to New Zealand, virtually no country left uncelebrated. Lights were dimmed, and the lectern sat like an abandoned yet repossessed parked car waiting patiently for a buyer under the lights on the center of the raised wooden platform. The emblem on the lectern "Western State" shone proudly, in green and gold with the lion's head logo. President Fonticello considered himself above technology; so there was no screen, no handouts, only a microphone to ensure no distractions from his godliness or his sacred word. At eight-fifty-nine, the Vice President for Academic Affairs, Dr. McAllister, walked onto the platform stopped next to the lectern and stood still, smiling at the assembly for a few counts until people noticed he was standing there ready to begin the performance.

"Good morning and welcome to the 2007 2008 academic year. I trust you had a restful summer and are anxious to get back to teaching." He was enthusiastic, this being only his third year at the university.

"I would like to thank our Food Service Department for the wonderful refreshments we enjoyed," he started applauding, gesturing so the faculty would follow suit.

"Welcome, members of the press," he added. Dr. McAllister was a droopy fellow without any facial affect whatsoever. His blue gray suit and white unpressed shirt were too big, and the style of his clunky black shoes didn't match. He wore several gold rings that looked like wedding bands in no particular order on his fingers. But they were arranged above his knuckles on some fingers, below the knuckle on others. And he wore copper bracelets on both wrists. Pale skin, with dull brown hair that he compulsively swept to the left side of his head, he looked out at the world through his small brown eyes and large brown plastic-rimmed trifocal glasses. He was like a scared little mouse trapped on a sheet of sticky paper.

"While you were gone, we tracked enrollment and retention. We have, as you know, been taking part in the Program for Excellence in Higher Education, and many of you have served on committees and subcommittees to support this effort. This year, in April, the Higher Learning Commission will visit our campus in conjunction with renewing our accreditation."

It was clear that Dr. McAllister thought the faculty at Western were a sorry lot of lazy bums. They wanted him to do all their work for them, came to meetings with little or nothing prepared. A few faculty could be counted on but for the most part, not. After the accreditation site visit, Dr. McAllister would announce his new position as president at North Dakota, starting next academic year.

He continued, smoothed his hair to the left using his right hand, stooped over towards the mike in perpetual bad posture.

"As you also know, our enrollment trended downward over the last several years due to our area's demographics." He paused, looking out over the assembly, waiting for the words to settle. Faculty fidgeted in their seats, Olivia rolled her eyes, thinking not this crap again.

"Dr. Fonticello therefore, has been working with our partner universities in China and Russia; his goal is to bring some ten thousand of those students here. He will speak with you about this in a few minutes. In addition, the State of Arkansas faces considerable financial constraint. As such, an agreement between the universities across the state has been signed, allowing disbursement of funding to each of the universities based on need. This means we will receive a one-time allocation of nineteen million dollar in addition to our annual flat appropriation. That money will be used to build a new health sciences building, and more information on that will be forth coming."

There were murmurs of disagreement from the faculty.

Olivia overheard Eric say "Yeah, we need a new health sciences building like we need a hole in our heads," and the faculty within earshot chuckling in agreement with him.

"And finally, as you saw if you attended last night's welcome dinner, we have a number of new faculty that have joined us this year. I will read their names by school and department; please hold your applause until all the names have been read. And when I call your name, please stand."

Dr. McAllister read the names in his most reserved academic voice, bringing renewed hope to pomp and circumstance. Fifteen eager looking faculty stood up, all of them being appointed with tenure-track status.

"Wait till they been here a while, they won't be so bright eyed and bushy tailed," Alex whispered. He was sitting next to Olivia.

She hit him on the leg, "Stop Alex, now, don't make me start laughing like you did at the graduation ceremony last year," loving that Alex spoke like she did sometimes.

"Oh Miss Oliv-ya, you know I wouldn't dare do a thing like'at," he smiled, and looked down, his face turning red from being a little embarrassed at teasing a black woman.

After the applause, Dr. McAllister continued, "Now, I would like to introduce the President of Western State, Dr. Luis Fonticello." Again he began the applause and the faculty joined in.

The doors next to the platform opened and the President emerged, smiling, standing in the spotlight, like a beloved political leader of a small third world country. He wore his signature suit and exuded charm. His hair was extremely black, impeccably cut, and parted on the left. His black wire-rimmed oval glasses sat in their usual place pressed to his face. His olive brown skin and white teeth shone. He stood in front of the doors, faculty applauding, flash bulbs winking all over the room, and before turning to walk to the three steps up to the platform, he held out his left palm face up, towards the front row.

His wife, Michelle, stood up and turned to the assembly and bowed humbly, with her palms facing each other at her chest, tips of her fingers just under her chin. Faculty applauded louder. Olivia didn't though; she remembered working with Michelle a couple of years ago on the piano competition. Boy was she ever the unrelenting knit-pick. She had to have her finger in every little detail. Olivia was stunned at how she pushed even the largest donor to do more and be more. Most faculty had no idea that she was so difficult to work with, tolerating her because she was the President's wife. She wore white pants, and a red jacket, with a black blouse and accentuating black, red and white silk Gucci neck scarf. Her dyed-black hair was held in ponytail by a barrette decorated with pearls, the hair just touching the nape of her neck. You could see the foundation she'd applied to her face, and the red lipstick and thick mascara, her make-up just another sign of her perfectionism.

After a moment of acknowledgement from the crowd, Michelle returned to her seat. Her face was tired from the perpetually plastered smile she wore, and she was weary from traveling with him to Russia and China. She hadn't wanted to go because she had her own work to do, but she had to be dutiful and supportive of him. If she stayed behind, people would talk and Roadims was a most unforgiving Peyton Place. She watched without showing any emotion as he ascended.

"Welcome to the 2007 to 2008 academic year," President Fonticello's accented voice bellowed with confidence, "and I trust you had a wonderful summer, writing, traveling, teaching, or spending time with your family and friends."

The audience responded with soft smiles and whispers of acknowledgement.

"Please sit."

Then after everyone was seated and quiet, he continued. "Summer is the ultimate reason for choosing this career because we all know we're not in it for the money or the glamour." He chuckled and so did the faculty.

"But, I must tell you, that my summer did not go as I planned. There were many, many changes at the state level, with budgetary problems and the transition of funds from ACHEIP, the Arkansas Cooperative for Higher Education Investment Pool. It was in hindsight definitely an overly ambitious investment agreement. As you know, we were to receive approximately thirty million dollars from that agreement composed mainly of surplus state revenue. But as with many agreements forged between university presidents and Republican politicians when the economy is good, the money's been, well, let's say, 'held up' due to a projected deficit." He waited for the laughter to subside.

"Yeah, well I read that agreement and it was the university presidents' all over the state that sold their souls to the devil," Olivia whispered to Alex.

"Really? You'll have to tell me about that."

"Basically, the presidents agreed that they would take the one-time allocation from the investment pool earnings. To get the money, they had to agree that they would accept the 2003 budget allocation levels from the state — no increases — and agree to hold future increases in tuition to equal the rate of inflation."

"Oh, so they have to find ways to fund raise now? That's not going to go over well in this part of the state," Alex acknowledged.

They turned their attention back to Fonticello.

"And last year, here on our campus we faced challenges in finding closure to gaps in revenues and expenditures. However, for more than twenty-five years, we faced those kinds of issues, successfully solving problems, and we never reduced staff or forewent salary increases. Sometimes, yes, meager increases, yes." He paused, the faculty softly buzzing agreement.

Olivia thought "meager" was an overstatement. One or two percent adjustments boiled down for her to about twenty-five dollars a month after taxes. She leaned over to Alex "What can we do with twenty-five dollars a month?"

Alex looked at her "Well Miss Oliv'ya, you could buy yu-self anotha hat," and again the two laughed, trying to keep it down. She liked Alex because he didn't hide the fact that he never knew black folks like Olivia.

"We were instrumental in forging relationships with our international affiliates. Our newest agreement was just signed by colleagues in China, I have a copy on my desk. And of course we have been working closely with Russia. I expect an agreement from them very soon. These are areas of the world in which education will prosper and this university can play a role in that." He paused, waiting for applause from the faculty. While he was getting it he took a sip of water from the glass on the table next to the lectern, like he was posing for a Kodak. Next, he wiped his forehead with his breast pocket handkerchief and carefully replaced it in his pocket.

"The Board of Governors asked me to take a number of actions at the regularly scheduled monthly meeting last week. However, I was not willing to comply with their requests." The room grew completely silent. He let this information sink in for several beats. "As you know, the Board of Governors for this university is comprised of individuals appointed by the Governor of Arkansas, and it is to be bi-partisan representation. This arrangement always makes for interesting dialog." He forced a smile. Still nothing but silence in the room, and faculty were on the edges of their seats.

"Effective today, this morning, I submitted my resignation as President of this university to Chairman Doolittle. He accepted it. And so, let me say that I enjoyed working with each of you over the years, and I only envision your continued success. Thank you for the support you have shown me and Michelle and the loyalty with which you served Western State over the years. For new faculty, I wish there was more time to meet and work together but I am sure your experience with the Western Family will be warm and fulfilling."

He stopped to look over the faculty, contemplating what he should say next, but decided he was finished.

"Dr. McAllister, won't you come and instruct the faculty in what they are to do today?" And with that, he backed away from the lectern, walked down the steps to the front row, waited while his wife Michelle stood up.

The faculty began clapping wildly and standing for an ovation. More flash bulbs. The President and his wife interlaced their arms, and together, they bowed to the audience. Then, they turned around and without looking back, walked out of the two double doors from which he'd emerged.

Olivia was dumbfounded. "Alex, what was that?"

Alex shook his head slowly, "That, Miss Oliv'ya was Fontecillo's ego, right Patrick?" Patrick was sitting in the row behind them, but didn't say anything, only smiled, raised his eyebrows, and took a long deep closed-mouth breath.

Dr. McAllister returned hurriedly to the lectern, and trying to calm the crowd yelled into the microphone, "Please, please meet with your individual schools and departments, and more information will be forthcoming on how we will handle the Presidential Search. We are officially dismissed. Have a good semester!"

It was certainly a good thing he had another position to go to next year. Dr. McAllister would never do what Fontecillo just did. He wouldn't ever have to because he was a different kind of leader.

"The Dean will hold the School of Business Administration faculty meeting in Cornell Auditorium at nine-thirty," the voice mail from Patrick's secretary reported. Olivia walked back from the all faculty meeting to her office, dazed. She looked at her watch. It was 9:20. She didn't have time to do anything but go to the ladies' room and walk to the auditorium downstairs. She put away her purse, stepped outside her office and closed and locked her door. Patrick was standing in the hall.

"So, this is going to be your opportunity to change things here, Olivia, as the Faculty Senate President-Elect with a new university President coming," he beamed.

"Really? I'm sorry to see him go; I was really looking forward to working with Luis, learning how he functioned," and hoping to get pointers about being successful at administration Olivia continued in her own head. Never would she say that much about what she wanted to Patrick.

Olivia felt sad he'd resigned. And the way it sounded to her was like he was forced to leave. True, it was time for him to retire, after all, over thirty years had passed. But wouldn't it have been better to give him another year and have him go with honor?

"Believe me, you didn't want to work with him. Now, for sure, you're in the most advantageous position. Luis was too hard and too controlling for too long. The administration needs to be decentralized so that Deans have more power over their budgets, faculty have more say, and the focus of the university is on growth," Patrick rattled these things off very quickly, and Olivia listened to him as if he was speaking another language. She nodded her head, and smiled.

"Well I'm sure you will help me with these issues next year; this year, Mike Frasier over in Environmental Science is Faculty Senate President. I think the first meeting of the senate is next Monday. But, let me catch up with you after your meeting, I've got to get to the ladies' room before you start."

"All right, no problem, I've got the presentation I'm going to make all set up so you'll see what we're doing in the School of Business this year." He walked away, down the hall of offices where faculty were gossiping, toward his office, and then eventually down the stairs to the classroom auditorium.

Patrick's power point presentation was already on the screen when she walked into the auditorium, and the twenty-eight Business School faculty were sprinkled all over the room in *cliques* like they all suspected each other carrying latent H1N1. No one sat in the front row as 'Dean's Disease' was also catching. She sat in the middle row, in the center, as if she was going to the movies, by herself, as usual. Olivia thought most of the faculty were, well, Patrick had his hands full of whining children really. She caught snippets of conversations, "It's about time he left, you know he was just so old" and "Maybe now we will get a good president that can help us grow."

Patrick interrupted.

"Well as you saw, Luis is no longer President!" he said, arms held up over his head, he looked like a teenager with his first iPhone with unlimited texting screaming "Yay!!".

"Yeah, and whose gonna to take his place?" It was Abe, who always shouted from the peanut gallery.

"Dr. Renee Gruber is going to serve as Interim President while a national search is held. I received an email right after the meeting this morning informing the deans," he reported as he hid behind the lectern.

Oh great, Olivia thought. Renee's a piece of work.

"Was he fired? Why did he leave like that? He only had one more year on this contract, right? Will we still have to pay him? I could use that money." Eric asked.

"I don't know, you know as much as I do, and yes, he had another year on contract. However, at this point right now, we need to talk about this academic year, and what we're doing in the Business School." Patrick changed the subject and hid his irritation.

The faculty grew silent, and Patrick began showing charts and graphs of statistics on enrollment, projected growth in the School of Business students, and how students want more distance level classes.

"We are no longer teaching under an old model. Students don't want to hear you wax eloquent. No more sage on the stage. They want to get lectures on their iPods. Each of you needs to make sure you can deliver your courses this way." But Patrick knew the faculty could care less. The only way they were going to do this was if they somehow got paid to do it. He knew there was money available for faculty who wanted to modify a course for Blackboard, but he'd be damned if he'd say it to them. He wanted them to do something because it was the right thing to do, because they wanted to work in a real business school, not some trumped up one in a masquerade.

He started talking about student course evaluations, and showed some statistics on this. "By and large, the Business School is right in the average of the range, and that's great. However, I want you to set goals to get your evaluations in the upper third range," he pointed his electronic red dot to the place on the graph. Then he turned to the accreditation renewal process for undergraduate business schools, which included a visit from representatives of ACBSP in 2011; then he talked about the new MBA program that just came online and students will be enrolling for 2008 2009; He moved then to shoot them with the next level of accreditation he was seeking from AACSB, but this was for schools of business offering master's degrees.

"How could we do all this?" Claire asked no one in particular.

"As part of this accreditation, you will need to make sure you have publications within those on *Cabell's* list of journals. This will also be necessary in order to get promoted from now on. You need two publications every five years. And by the way, we have several open lines for new faculty. I hope to get Dr. Gruber to approve a recruitment this month." Patrick thought that he could create a healthy competition and fear among the faculty to get them to do what he wanted them to.

He clicked his remote mouse and a slide popped up with a bell-graph of the ages of the Business School faculty, showing that one half of them will retire over the next few years, leaving a shortage of faculty.

"As you can see," Patrick used his remote red-dot pointer, "I'm in the group approaching retirement. Believe me, in August 2020, I'm going to be gone, and you'll be facing a new Dean. Whatever that'll look like, in order to teach graduate courses, those of you not in the retirement stage, you have to be academically and professional qualified, and only a handful of you, those hired within the last five years, are," he threatened. "When we recruit new faculty we are going to hire PhDs only so if you don't have your doctorate yet, and you aren't retiring soon, you may want to get going on that. Or, you can see about going to work at one of the local community colleges," he chuckled. "By the way, we won't be paying for you to finish your doctorates anymore."

Patrick read the faculty's faces with seriousness in his. He knew exactly which of them didn't have doctorates, exactly which of them would fight, and which ones would bury their heads in the sand. Get them off the bottom line if they're not of the caliber I want, he thought. He hoped he'd provoked them.

"Do you have any questions?" he clicked his mouse again, and the next slide said 'Have a good year!'

"Yes, Patrick, are we going to get raises for becoming "academically and professionally" qualified if we aren't retiring?" Chris asked.

"That's not something we have determined yet, however, we do want to move to a merit-based system rather than the blanket system we have now. We want to encourage and reward, rather than to keep the status quo of no matter what you don't do, you get the same percentage adjustment as everyone else." Patrick liked Chris; he was willing to work. Hopefully, he would go ahead with his doctorate. Chris was guaranteed coverage of the expenses for it when he was hired four years ago when Olivia came in, but so far he hadn't done anything about it.

"What's this new accreditation you were talking about?" Claire threw out. She was the newest hire, on an annual contract without the possibility for tenure. Patrick hired her to take advantage of her skill and experience in this area. But so far he was disappointed in her performance. She was never on time, never followed through, and embarrassed him at meetings she managed to fall into late. She was too busy with her real estate business, gazing at herself in the mirror, and flirting with the married male faculty. She'd tried to seduce him many times; and while her breasts were huge, and she was in his opinion, somewhat sexy, she wasn't worth it.

"Good question, and that's one of the reasons you are instrumental to the school. Claire as you know comes to us with extensive experience in the double-A accreditation process. Why don't you tell them about it?" Maybe putting her on the public spot would get her to perform, he thought.

"It's the accreditation that business schools get if they want to remain competitive in graduate programs. We can't have a graduate program of any distinction without that level of prestige. Students will go somewhere else because the degree from an AACSB institution says positive things about their education. And faculty in business who we will recruit will only want to teach at such accredited schools." Claire sounded very competent.

"Any other questions?"

"Yeah, uh, Patrick, if we're gonna teach more distance learning courses, do we have to have ten office hours each week? Is our course load gonna get reduced?" Eric was only concerned about not being on campus if he didn't have to be.

"Those are faculty governance issues; you should talk to Olivia; she's the Faculty Senate President-Elect. There are mechanisms to change those kinds of rules through amendments to the *Faculty Handbook*. So start with the senate on that," he directed.

Olivia was glad she sat in the middle, forward of everyone but she could feel them looking at her. 'Right Patrick, deflect the question to me, put me on the spot,' Olivia thought. They already resented her because she carried Patrick's initiatives without question when no one else would. Now though she had no idea what the hell he was talking about, it sounded like garbled mumbo jumbo paraded as academic-ese, but she didn't say anything, only nodded her head.

After a moment people stopped asking questions, and he told the faculty to meet with their department heads, turning off his power point, and waving them away like disloyal servants from the first School of Business faculty meeting for the 2007 semester.

Back in her office after the meeting, Olivia wanted to sit down and start looking for a card to send to Dr. Gruber. But before she could, Nancy Shepperd, the new department head for marketing, popped her head into her door. Patrick appointed her last May after Grady Harryman retired. There were many a time when Grady said "I don't need this job, anybody who *wonts* it can have it, I was doin' the Dean a favor when I took it, and I can retire any time," sounding and grinning wide just like Andy Griffith. Nobody believed he would retire but he did.

"We're goin' to Johnny Carino's for the department meetin' in about thirty minutes," Nancy said in her Arkansas drawl. She stood at the door, smiling, with her bleached blond hair that didn't budge in any Arkansas wind, bangle bracelets on both arms, costume jewelry on her neck and fingers to match her outfit, made of polyester, her eyebrows drawn on giving her a look of surprise all the time.

"Okay, sounds good. We takin' your car?"

"Sure can," Nancy agreed. She loved her new Cherokee.

"Meet in front of the Dean's office as usual?"

"Yup, good deal," Nancy chimed, tapped the door twice with her acrylic French tip fingernails and walked away.

Alone in her office, Olivia's hip ached, it had only been three weeks ago that the left hip had been completely replaced. She wanted to ignore that she was still recovering from that, but the pain drew her down. Olivia sat at her Ikea L-shaped desk, remembering that when she arrived in 2003 she'd decorated her office so that it would look like a den, and none of this government issue stuff. She'd hung Rodin art work on the walls, and decorative clocks and a calendar. She had a thing for beautiful clocks. In the mirror sitting at eyelevel she studied herself, and ran her left hand over the short hair. 'Yuck, that looks awful,' she said shaking her head. Long hair was better, but for the surgery she cut it short to make it so she had less hair to fuss over. She turned on the floor lamp to give the room a soft appearance. She was lucky to get one of the offices with windows facing southwest and a decent view of the grassy areas, just beyond a parking lot. She resumed searching for her blank Crane note cards so she could address one to Dr. Gruber. She pulled one of the cream-colored cards out of the box, and a light blue envelop out of the ribbon tie and thought for a moment. Then she wrote:

*Friday, August 17, 2007*
*Dear Dr. Gruber,*

*Congratulations on being appointed Interim President. Please know you are in my thoughts and I wish you all the best.*
*Sincerely,*
*Olivia Clark, PhD, Assistant Professor, Marketing*

Instead of sending it through the campus mail, she addressed and stamped it, placed it in her purse to put in the regular mail on her way to Johnny Carino's.

At lunch, all six of the marketing department faculty speculated, and wondered what happened with Dr. Fontecillo.

"We don't know anything — us department heads — more than you do. I DO know last year, there was some scuttle-butt about Luis and spending for his personal pleasure. I got that from Renee one day when we were out shoppin' at Macy's. And I know the folks over on the Honors Committee were P.O.ed when they couldn't just get their budget increased like usual. You know with Luis it was ask for forgiveness and not permission." Nancy was no refrigerator: she couldn't keep nothin', so if you wanted word spread she was the go to.

Today she was more than glad to spill the details however irrelevant for the group, this being her first 'first of the year department meeting'. They all listened.

Olivia remembered once when Grady took them out, how everybody ordered water to drink at first.

But Grady said "I'mo have me some water too but I'll take some Bourbon in mine."

Olivia laughed a little at the memory. Or the time he said, "Well, I b'lieve I need to go'on over and tawlk to the folk in Administration about this here change to the course. Seems they're a might bit upset about this'un." He was something, Olivia wishing he wasn't gone too.

Jim Brown said, "You know, I don't like to interfere, and as the only other Dean of this business school until this year, I have to be careful."

They listened very attentively to Jim, who was totally gray with a great big potbelly that stretched the buttonholes of his plaid shirts, always wore black polyester pants and man-made materials black loafers, and huge gold wired-rimmed glasses.

"But it would be my guess that the Board followed the Chairman's lead to get him out. Now. *He's* wanted him gone ever since the International Mission was set, and the establishment of 'university' status," Jim said, gesturing quote marks when he said university, rolling his eyes. "And you know, Darnell is in bed with the Governor. Now that's my two cents," he stopped talking, crossing his arms.

Nancy took control back, "Yeah, Renee did say that the Board was pushing for budget reductions but tol' me she presented the budget to the Board and they weren't real happy with it. She said Luis wouldn't take no for an answer to his plans for expanding to China. But don't quote me on that, but that's what I heard."

The waitress appeared with everyone's order lined up on her arm.

They ate in silence for a while and then Nancy added, "Well we won't have too many department meetings this year, but we will do what Patrick asked for accreditation, and we have to comply with McAllister's needs for the Higher Learning Commission in April. I'm gonna be a-askin' y'all to pitch in, and you know we *got* to get them faculty evaluations set up. You know how Patrick is," Nancy gave a fake smile bearing all her teeth like Charlie Brown's Snoopy and drummed her nails on the table.

After a moment, Olivia and everyone around the table stopped listening. It was a familiar tune sung every fall, and everyone volunteered to dance to it with the same pathetic tenured apathy in the name of retirement. Eventually, they finished eating, and went back to the university, one of two Friday afternoons they would do such a thing for the entire year; only because students were waiting to get enrolled in classes starting on Monday.

Later, Olivia heard Patrick's footfall coming towards her office. The halls were empty, all students and now faculty gone too. It was about 4:45; she just logged off her computer. He knocked twice on the door, didn't wait for an invitation. He took her keys, which she left in the door purposely, out of the lock and handed them to her, and closed the door.

As he sat down in the chair next to the door he said, "So, they finally got rid of Luis, and now we can move forward." He had a big smirk on his face. He scootched the chair out from the door, tilted it back so that it teetered on its two back legs.

"He ruled this place too long, he should have retired at the end of the last contract two years ago," he said, lacing his fingers in his lap, resting his head on the wall.

"Hmm, you really think so? I don't know, but like I said, at least they could have given him till the end of the year to retire, rather than humiliating him like this. That was mean. I'm... He deserves—"

"Yeah, I think they're planning a reception for him or something later in the year. But believe me he's doing fine. He gets to keep getting paid and keep his benefits without doing anything," Patrick argued.

Olivia figured he was jealous.

"What's going to happen to the Piano competition and Michelle?" She smoothed her hair, took a glance in the mirror.

"That could stay intact as it's a stand-alone organization, but the Board's been trying to get rid of it for years." Patrick put his hands on his head, keeping the fingers laced, looking out the window behind Olivia.

"Yeah, Michelle is a hard driver I know that. What's up with Renee? Did she fund your positions?"

"She said she had to ask Darnell first and get his approval, since McAllister can't make the final decision. But you know I've known Darnell for at least ten years and whenever he sees me at any of the fundraisers he never even speaks to me."

"Wow, that must hurt, why does he do that?" Olivia checked to make sure her jacket was closed so that her breasts weren't revealed. She didn't want to find herself in any kind of sexual harassment situation again.

"Because he's a jerk, and between him and the area's representative, all three are in cahoots, they basically run the show here. Luis was able to make changes through the years despite the strong hold because of our lobbyist in Little Rock, and because he had some clout. But with the signing of ACHEIP, that's all gone. Luis underestimated the impact that signing that would have. Sold his soul to the Devil." He dropped the chair down on all fours, picked up a rubber-band sitting on the table next to him, and started stretching it between his fingers.

"Do you think they'll let Renee stay on as President?" She took off her glasses, flicked the crusted sleep out of the corners of her eyes, and put the glasses back on.

"Absolutely not. They're going to go out to national search I'm sure. But that'll be interesting because no one's had to do it in the history of the institution," he laughed.

"You gonna apply for it?"

"Me? Oh no, I'm not ready for that yet. Maybe if the VP position becomes open, I might, but no, I don't want to deal with Darnell," he smiled and started to get up. "Well hey, have a nice weekend, and get ready for the fireworks at the senate meeting," he said, turning the knob on the door, opening it to its limit, and walking out.

"Thanks, Patrick. Let me know if you need anything from me, and have a good weekend."

"Will do, and you too. Oh, how's the bionic hip?"

"Fine, recovering fine, thank you. Probably won't be dancing for a while, maybe a year. But it's been two years since they told me I needed it replaced. Oh well. I really appreciate you and Nancy visiting me in the hospital. And thanks again for you and Jane comin' over, bringin' food, taxi-ing me to the doctor, and... You know, just thanks for everything." She smiled at him.

"Yep, great, well, let me know if you need anything; the boys will come and take care of your leaves when the time comes, as usual. Have a good weekend, and be careful," he smiled, saluted, and left.

"Okay, you too." She listened as he walked away from the door.

Olivia started to pick up her purse, after she reached for her cane. Her cell phone was ringing. "Hey Harmony, what's goin' on?" she answered with happy relief in her voice. Talking to Patrick was fraught with landmines she had to negotiate carefully.

"Hey sweetie, how are you? Can you believe Luis? Wow!" she screamed and laughed.

"No it's really amazing, isn't it?" Olivia laughed too. She sat back down in her chair.

"Still wanna have breakfast tomorrow at Panera's? I can pick you up if you need me to."

"Yeah, breakfast is great, yeah pick me up. I'm doing okay but been on my leg all day and it hurts. With classes starting next week, I should take it easy."

"You still using the cane, right?" As usual, Harmony was being parental.

"Oh, yeah, absolutely, though I should be off it soon."

"Liv, the surgery wasn't even a month ago yet, and even though you don't think so, it was major surgery. Honey, please take it easy."

"Oh, yeah-yeah-yeah, definitely, I promise."

"Okay, then, nine-thirtyish tomorrow. Brock's doing a book signing up in Kansas City today, and Justin is still in Philly with Tom, so I am free for the *entire* day. Yay!! After breakfast, we can go run errands if you need to."

"Sounds good. I can't wait to see you, my dear!" Olivia tried to convey her complete adoration for her in her voice.

"K, see you soon, love you!"

"Love you too," and they hung up.

Olivia leaned on her cane, gathered her purse, turned out the lights, and locked her office. She hobbled down the long hall to the elevator feeling so grateful for Harmony. She missed their long walks at the Nature Center trails, Harmony with her binocs looking for birds. But the doctor said she could walk and should, so maybe in a week? She thought back to the day she checked out of the hospital. Brock and Harmony were so unconditionally loving, they were the surrogate family she needed.

"You ready, Sweetie?" Harmony asked walking into the hospital room the room and going to sit in her usual seat. Brock followed, towering over her; he was at least six-five. The room still smelled like iodine despite the lavender potpourris and candles Olivia'd brought to cover it. She had a white comforter too that she'd brought from home. Between those things and the flowers people had sent, it made the room as inviting as a hospital room could be.

"Hey Olivia," his voice deep and sexy, "when you gonna stop giving these people hell and get out of here?" he laughed, leaning in to kiss her on the cheek.

"Hey yourself, man, what's crackin'?" In the wheelchair Olivia had to stretch to turn her cheek up so he didn't have to bend so far.

"Nothing, just getting ready for the semester to start, keeping out of trouble."

"Don't remind me, it's like only three weeks away!"

"So did the doctor come in yet?" Harmony interrupted the banter between the two.

"Yes, he did and I'm all set to go. I have my crutches and my Vicodin!" she held up the bottle and they all laughed.

"Well, Brock'll carry you from the wheelchair to the car if needed," Harmony said, gesturing to Brock who nodded his head in agreement.

"Let's go then, I've had enough of this place." Brock started pushing her wheelchair and Harmony grabbed her bags.

Back at Olivia's house, Brock played big brother and helped her out of the car, while Harmony was like a close sister as she took her key and opened the door. Inside, Harmony made sure the handicapped toilet seat and all the gadgets were in place. "What else can we do for you, honey?" she said, bubbly as usual.

"Besides getting rid of that good old geriatric feeling? I can't think of anything."

"Well, let us help you with lunch and make sure you can maneuver around," Brock said.

"For a change, I'm not gonna object," Olivia smiled, "Let me sit here in this hard ass chair, and y'all just make yourselves at home," she breathed heavily, suddenly very tired. "Doctor said this is the best type a chair to sit in." She slowly lowered herself into the wooden straight back chair, having arms of the chair curved supported by wooden slats, with a rounded bottom with grooves for your butt cheeks and thighs. It reminded her of an old school-teacher's desk chair. Before the surgery she picked it up from a yard sale and refinished it in black. She put it between the leather recliner and the high-back over sized sofa, and the baby-grand rested behind it so she could see the TV. Olivia's furniture sat on white carpet opposite the stone floor-to-ceiling fireplace under the vaulted ceiling in the living room, with a double door leading to the deck. Her walls were painted soft yellows. She wanted the living room to be where people felt embraced but Olivia was particular about the need for color, and made sure they were matching and contrasting.

She closed her eyes and waited for the pain to subside, absorbing the spirit in the room. Harmony and Brock sat down on the couch, and Brock turned on the TV. It was his favorite, a *Law and Order* marathon, and handed out the Subway sandwiches they'd stopped for on the way, using the coffee table for a sideboard. After they ate, they sat for a while. Then there was a loud knock on one of the patio doors in the dining room.

"I'll go," Brock volunteered.

"Hello, is Olivia here?" a woman's voice asked, as Brock opened the door.

"Yes, whom may I say—

"Hey Kathy, what's going on?" Olivia interrupted, she could see them through the living room glass doors.

"Brock, she's okay you can let her in, she's my neighbor from around the corner."

Kathy barged in with a hot baking dish, followed by Thomas with a great big roasting pan. They set them on the kitchen island.

"We just were grilling some food and thought we'd bring you some," Kathy shouted to Olivia in the other room. She was stout built like Shrek's girlfriend, standing on pure muscle calves, with flaming red hair. She didn't know the meaning of the word 'whisper'.

"We got grilled lemon chicken, macaroni and cheese—homemade of course, and we figure you can make your own salad," she yelled from the kitchen.

"Hello Olivia," Thomas came into the living room and squatted by her chair. "How are you?"

"Fine Thomas, thank you. I heard from Kathy you just got out of the hospital yourself, with a heart attack?"

"Yeah, but I have them all the time."

Olivia knew Kathy kind of pushed Thomas around since he'd lost his job. Whenever she saw him he seemed sad. Kathy said they had to cut their country club membership, and were spending into their savings. She said he never imagined he would be discriminated against in the job market but being nearly sixty, he didn't get considered. Not having a formal college education was also a liability. Kathy went back to work in a collection agency, her salary covered mainly his portion of the premiums she got for company paid health benefits. Thomas was a tall man, attractive even though he was overweight, and gray-haired.

Kathy came by Olivia's often, and over a cup of coffee she complained about his drinking and the financial mess. With Kathy, who was not an academic, Olivia talked about girl stuff, went looking for plants, and she helped Olivia with making decisions on her house. Over the years they'd grown quite close. In a pinch Olivia could count on her.

"Hey you guys, what are you doin'? Aw, Kathy, that's so sweet, you didn't have to do that. I'm gonna weigh a ton before this hip heals so I still won't be able to walk." They all laughed.

"Well, we ain't stayin' just brought over some food so you won't starve. I'll call you tomorrow, maybe stop by on Sunday and have a cup of coffee with ya. You call if you need anything, hear? Come on Thomas, we gotta go," and in the next second they were out the door.

"'Bye Olivia," Thomas yelled, waving as they walked around the deck to the driveway.

"Wow, that's a lot of food," Brock laughed.

"Yeah, that's them," Olivia replied.

"Well, honey," Harmony motioned to Brock, "we should get ready to go, don't you think? Let's let 'Liv rest?"

"Good idea," Brock said. He rubbed Harmony between her shoulder blades.

"All right, thanks for everything. I really appreciate it."

"No worries, we're family, so it's all good," Brock said, he and Harmony collected their things. Each of them came over to her chair and hugged her and she kissed them both.

"Bye, see you soon," they walked out of the living room through the kitchen and out the garage door.

That was just a few weeks ago, but at least she could manage the pain with only taking ibuprofen now. Olivia finally got to her car, got in, and looked forward to seeing Harmony for breakfast.

On Monday afternoon, Olivia hobbled into the 'Royale Commons' meeting room on the third floor of the Student Center. She scanned for Harmony and met her eyes. Next she searched for Kevin. He saw her walk in, and she saw him sitting there looking at his papers, purposely not at her, but nodding softly. Twenty-five faculty sat around old fold-up tables joined forming a U, name cards sitting like little tents in front of them letting them know who they were. The Executive Committee sat at tables strung together that formed a bridge over the two ends of the U. The EC included a recording secretary, a Parliamentarian, and a member at large. Mike sat in the middle and Olivia sat on his right. The Administrators sat opposite the EC at the U's curve. It was like two unequipped and ill-prepared armies getting ready for a battle in a war that had no strategy. Dr. Gruber sat in the middle, flanked by Dr. McAllister on her right, and Mr. Johnson on her left.

"The first meeting of the 2007 2008 academic year of the Western State Faculty Senate will come to order," Mike stated.

The room quieted.

"We meet here every first Monday of the month during the academic year at three p.m. for those of you that don't know. First order of business: Do I hear a motion to approve the minutes from the May 2007 meeting?"

"So moved."

"A second?"

"Second."

"Motion carried. We will now hear from Renee, uh, I mean, Dr. Gruber, Interim President," he declared with a wide Bubba-like grin. Olivia scanned the framed ghosts of past board members hanging on the walls, and tried not to focus on the grimy carpet. This meeting was a total waste of time.

"Thank you Dr. Frasier," Dr. Gruber smiled and looked around the table at the faculty. After a moment, she continued, "We have been directed by the Board to establish a search committee and hire a new president by the first of the year," she said, her voice so soft it was barely audible. Her body slumped in the chair, the fat rolling down her elbows onto the table and cascading off her hips down the sides of the chairs, and down her legs spilling over her shoes. She had thinning stringy ear-length brown greasy hair, huge glasses and red lipstick contrasting against her lily-white skin.

"I do not intend to apply," she informed the faculty before they could ask. "In the meantime, we're going to try to finally, at last, get a fall break institutionalized so that you'll be able to have a breather before Thanksgiving."

The Senators applauded, and she sucked up what she thought was approval like it was the last of a chocolate shake. The truth was that nobody—none of the faculty—liked or respected Renee. She was nothing but a fake, constantly shifted her responsibilities onto other people because she was doing a job she wasn't qualified for. Yes, maybe she could have been an average HR director but she'd been promoted the same way that Luis had and now she was plain incompetent.

"I know this is something you have wanted for years," she said after the applause. "We're also beginning the construction on the much needed new Student Center, but our Interim Vice President of Business Affairs, Gil Johnson, will talk with you about that. Thank you Mike," She sat back in her chair, her fat jiggling when she moved.

Renee Gruber in fact probably thought she deserved to be the President. After all it was she who prepared the budgets, saw to it that the financial statements were presentable, and the audits were done appropriately. It was she who went to the meetings in Little Rock and negotiated the legislation, and worked with the international partners to get staff at Western to forge agreements. If you asked her, she would swear she did everything to hold the institution together, as well as advance it, but they took the credit. Unfortunately, everyone knew her staff did all her work for her. Luis took advantage of her insecurities, and the Board members talked down to her. At least for the moment she could get the faculty to credit her, especially if she gave them something they wanted.

"Thank you Dr. Gruber. Now we will hear from Mr. Johnson," he said.

The meeting progressed this way. After Mr. Johnson, Dr. McAllister spoke, and repeated the same thing he'd said at the faculty meeting Friday.

After each administrator gave their report, and none of the faculty of the senate standing committees had anything to report, Mike said, "Thank you for attending. We're doin' a new thing so Administrators are dismissed after their reports. This is so we can talk freely among us without bein' scared of getting' in trouble like when Luis was here," Mike's face was beet red, his skin looked like weathered cowhide. In his Hawaiian shirt, khaki shorts and flip-flops he flaunted the fact that he believed being Faculty Senate President had no real meaning and certainly no power.

"But if you'd wont to we can meet at Gusano's Pizza and have a beer later!" The three administrators managed a chuckle and got up, and paraded out of the room bumbling like the three stooges. Mike would never have dared such a bold slap in the Administration's face if Luis was there. He was so embarrassing.

"I met with Darnell, over the weekend at his house and he's leadin' the search committee for the new president," Mike began. "A national search will be carried out, placin' ads in *The Chronicle*, and other academic administrative position announcement—"

"Since we haven't done this before, don't you, or rather doesn't the Board and Chairman Doolittle think it would be better to use a recruiting firm for this?" Kevin asked.

"No, the Chairman said the search needs conducted by a in-house committee," Mike retorted, the corners of his mouth downturned, his wiry blond hair sticking out around his face.

"And what Darnell wants he gits." In the next breath he dared, "Any other new business to take up?"

The room was silent.

"A motion to adjourn?" Mike announced more than asked.

"So moved," someone replied.

"Fine, see you next time," he said, and faculty silently and slowly filed out, leaving their name tents on the table.

*October 2007*

Jonathan did an online search of Olivia Clarke, and came across websites containing information about her. "Wow, that's pretty impressive," he said out loud. "So far, I don't see any red flags." He made sure he checked her out thoroughly; the last woman he'd met online nearly took him to the cleaners. And it was years before he tried to meet someone again. But Olivia seemed different. Jonathan sat in his upstairs bedroom at his glass desk with the massive Apple monitor surfing the Internet as usual. "Oh, I should print out my boarding passes," he talked to himself. Swinging around in his chair to face the mirrored closed door, "Uh, maybe I should shave?" He rubbed his cheeks.

Standing up in front of the mirror now he thought maybe he shouldn't go. "I mean, the only thing that's gonna happen is she's gonna take one look at me and say, 'yeah, thanks… so uh, I have to go.' Nobody's gonna want me once they get to know me. Besides I'm too geeky and weird."

Jonathan looked down at himself, wearing worn out shorts and sneakers, with a frumpy looking, moth eaten polo shirt. "I shoulda got a haircut," running his fingers through his hair. "I can still get one, it's still early," the clock on his computer read 6:37. He'd been out of bed now for three hours. "I can get dinner while I'm out," Jonathan reasoned.

A couple of hours later, Jonathan closed the garage door, and went up the stairs to the kitchen, carrying his left over pizza. "This'll be great for breakfast—Oh, God-damnit!!" He yelled and slammed the box into the sink. "I forgot to get a haircut. Damn, damn, damn! Oh well, I guess she'll just have to see me this way. Unless… maybe I can get a haircut in one of the airports? We'll see."

After playing *World of Warcraft* for a few hours, Jonathan packed his suitcase with enough clothes and medicines for two days, and set it by the door so he would remember to take it. He put his boarding pass on top. Then he set three alarm clocks in his bedroom so he would be sure to wake up in time to make tomorrow's 6:30 a.m. flight.

"Hey Jonathan, how are you?" Olivia answered but tried to be cool.

"I'm good, how are you?"

"Great, I'm nearing Little Rock, and should be there in about a half hour."

"No worries, I'm just landing now so that should work fine."

"Good flight I take it?"

"Yep, perfect. I thought I might get a little nauseous having to connect from San Diego but it was okay.

"Glad to hear that. Hey, I thought we could go to the Clinton Library, and have dinner maybe?"

"Works for me. I'm kind of a picky eater so don't feel bad if I don't eat much, but I've always wanted to go the Clinton Library. Actually, I have a goal of going to all of them, and so far I've been to Regan's and Truman's. Oh, and uh, that one up in Ohio, I forget now."

"Okay, well good. So I'll see you soon. Wanna just meet at the Clinton then? Or, I could pick you up from your hotel…"

"No, no, that's okay. Let's just meet and go from there." Jonathan didn't want her to get the idea that he was going to have sex with her on the first date.

"All right, I'll see you soon then." Olivia snapped her phone shut.

Olivia felt irritated. 'Wow, all the gall. Like I'm gonna have sex with you and I've just met you? What a tremendous ego.' She shook her head and figured it was something to do anyway, better than sitting in Roadims all weekend — alone.

Jonathan got out of his rental car and walked over to the entrance to the Clinton Library. He had deliberately not looked at Olivia's picture so he relied on her to introduce herself to him.

"Are you Jonathan?" Olivia stood up as he approached the area.

"Olivia? Hi, yeah, I'm Jonathan," extending his hand.

She ignored his hand, "How about a hug, I mean, I know this is the first time I've seen you but we've talked a lot," opening her arms to hug him.

He stepped awkwardly into the embrace, careful not to touch her. "Shall we go in?"

"Have you had lunch yet?"

"No, I haven't, and now that you mention it, that may be a better idea."

"Great, 'cause I'm starving. How 'bout we go over to Sonny William's? It's not too far from here, and I can drive us."

"Okay, sure, but I have my Tom-Tom so I can drive too."

"All right, if you feel more comfortable driving that's fine with me," Olivia acquiesced.

An hour later they arrived at the restaurant. "Sorry about the delay, but I forgot to update the software before I left San Diego, so it didn't know there was a Sonny's here."

"No worries, let's get in and get a table. It's three o'clock now, so we probably won't have a lot of time for the library. We can go out for a walk around the mall after that?"

"Yup, that works for me. I love to shop—look really. Window shop." Jonathan felt so nervous and stupid.

"Me too. I been looking for a meat thermometer lately so maybe we can look around William Sonoma's," Olivia glanced at him.

Jonathan barely ate anything, afraid that his stomach, his acid reflux, or both would get out of hand. The last thing he wanted to do was spend the afternoon in the bathroom with Olivia waiting for him to finish. Olivia, on the other hand, ate without reserve, a rib eye cooked medium, garlic mashed potatoes, and veggies, with a salad before hand, followed by peach cobbler a la mode. It was something Jonathan was unaccustomed to as women he'd dated before ordered all kinds of expensive food and only nibbled.

"Here, let me get that," Jonathan took the leather folder from the waiter, placed it down on the table-clothed table and reached in his back pocket for his wallet.

"Thanks," Olivia said.

At least she's not presumptuous. "No problem," Jonathan chuckled, knowing he had at least two-hundred-thousand dollars in his checking account, not to mention a sixty-thousand-dollar credit limit on his credit card. Of course he would never tell her that.

"Did I tell you I'm having a house built?" He waited for her reaction.

"Really, that's great. Where?"

"In East County."

"Oh, fantastic, so tell me all about it. You bought land and then got the plans done? When're you moving?"

"Well, I think it'll be by the end of the year," Jonathan was careful not to say it was a townhouse in a development where he didn't have any say over anything. He wasn't expecting her to know anything about building houses. "You ready?"

Olivia noticed he went out first, not holding the door for her, and this was a pattern of his. Nor did he open the car door, or do any gentlemanly things. She was irritated by it but of course it wasn't something she would say anything about. They looked through the Clinton Library without any real enthusiasm and then wandered over to its store.

"Here, Jonathan, take a picture of me next to Bill Clinton," Olivia stood by the cardboard rendition of the former President.

"You favor the Democrats?" He snapped the photo and handed her back her flip phone.

"I do nowadays. You?"

"Absolutely but I don't understand how we got here with George. Baffles me. I really wanted to move to Canada or France or somewhere."

"Me too! I remember I was in Germany when he was re-elected and I was totally disgusted."

"Hey, look at this," Jonathan picked up a cookbook. "I think I'll get this for my Mom."

Olivia smiled, "Does your Mom like to cook?"

"She likes to but she sucks at it," he laughed, walking to the checkout counter. "You like to cook?"

"Sure, it's great when you don't have to, and people aren't waiting for you to make dinner."

Jonathan didn't understand what she was talking about because he didn't have children and had never been married before. Actually, he'd never lived with a woman either. So he didn't say anything. He did decide right then though that he was going to hang on to her. When his mom and dad found out he'd met a woman like her, they'd finally stop thinking he was a loser. Well, except for the fact that she was black.

"Jonathan, it's getting late and I need to head back to Roadims. I've got a long drive ahead of me."

"No worries, let me walk you over to your car."

They walked the short distance from the library store to her car. He resisted the urge to show his excitement about her having a Mercedes, and said, "You know, I have a Land Rover."

"Yes, you told me. Midnight blue, right? 2006?"

"You remembered? Yes, that was one of the things I bought with my most recent liquidity event."

Olivia didn't say anything.

"Thanks for such a nice day," he extended his hand.

"No, thank you," Olivia ignored his and gave him a hug.

"Oh, okay," Jonathan again embraced like he'd never hugged anyone in his life.

Olivia turned to get into her car.

"Text me when you get home," Jonathan backed away from her car door, waving.

"Right, I will."

Driving away from him, Olivia didn't know what to think. She sensed he was lying about stuff and felt insecure. Maybe it was only because they didn't know each other? Either way she hated that he didn't treat her like a woman and he was so arrogant.

"Um, I don't think so Jonathan, but thanks anyway."

She determined that she would write him a goodbye email in reply to the next one she got from him, when ever that was.

*Thanksgiving Day*

Xena arrived for Thanksgiving Dinner with her hands full of platters of food.

"Hey Xena," Sebastian let her in. "Come on in, we're in the kitchen."

"Sebastian, how you doing? This is my daughter Faye and my grandson Stuart. You guys, this is Sebastian."

"Xena girl, you made it!" Olivia came up and took one of the platters from her. "You look great! The food's almost ready," motioning them into the dining room.

"That's great, we been snacking all day, and it sure smells good in here."

"Sebastian, introduce your friends," Olivia inclined her head towards Sebastian's two friends.

"This is Nuck-Nuck, and this is Nicole." The two waved at Xena. "And this Faye and Stuart."

"And this is Didier, he's an international student from France." Olivia added. "You all make yourselves at home. You can put your coats in the closet there next to the door."

Olivia disappeared into the kitchen, putting the platter on the island countertop. Xena followed her, while the others settled down into the living room and turned on the game.

"Make a fire, Sebastian," Olivia shouted around the corner.

"Okay, in a minute." Sebastian ignored his mother.

"So how you doing?" Xena pulled her jacket off and hung it on a dining room chair.

"Fine, fine, no complaints. Getting ready to go to DC pretty soon to see Jonathan and meet his friends," Olivia tried to sound enthusiastic.

"What, you guys gonna meet there?"

"Yeah, we're going to see Avenue Q, but you know he wouldn't buy my plane ticket? I thought that was real chicken of him, 'specially with him bragging all the time about how much money he got."

"That is strange. Usually a man will cover that."

"You know, I wonder if his selfishness will be a problem. I'm tempted to end the relationship with him, but of course I'm not doing that before the holidays are over."

Olivia opened the oven, pulled the bird out.

"Good idea, you know I always said that when Robert finally died, I'd had enough. Men are just they always, always gotta try to keep you off balance." Xena took her scarf off and hung it over her coat.

"Cold out huh? Yeah you right, I know you right. Robert's been gone now what, four years?"

"Yup, seems like a day. I miss him, but I don't, you know? And if you don't feel comfortable with Jonathan, then, you young, you got plenty of time and there's sure more fish in the sea."

"We got lamb and duck too, sweet potatoes, macaroni and cheese."

"I brought some greens, and cheesecake."

"Oh Lord, we going to heaven now," Olivia knew Xena was a good cook.

"How's Sebastian?"

"Same, just the same. I'm wondering what it's gonna take for him to change." Olivia lowered her voice and looked over Xena's shoulder to make sure she wouldn't be overheard. "He just won't stop. You see how he look. Hair all over his head, looking like a homeless person. On my last nerve all the time. Won't go to school, lies about it, says he's in but he ain't going to class. Getting tazered by the Sherriff. Girl, it's a mess. And you know this a small town. It's really embarrassing."

"I know how that goes, but you know at least he's here, and you know you have to let him do his thing, don't do no good to interfere and coddle them too much. 'Specially boys. Black boys."

Xena and Olivia looked into each other with a knowing that could not be articulated, a love that just transferred.

"Here, let me set the table," Xena grabbed the stack of plates from the end of the counter. "We still going to the movies later on?" Sebastian shouted from the living room.

"As far as I know," and Olivia kept her Thanksgiving tradition going, enjoying what little family she had.

It was a reprieve from thinking or being lonely or afraid. For just a few hours, she was grateful to God for a house full of black people she could communicate clearly with, who except for Sebastian, only wanted to be around her because they loved her and her company. It was the kind of thing she had wanted her whole life but it eluded her. Sebastian never complied, or when he was compliant quickly became defiant the moment it occurred to him that he was going along with the program. And as much as she loved Joy and Brock, Kathy and Thomas, and was invited to all sorts of events with Patrick, Luis, and Nancy, time with them, well it just wasn't the same. They would always slip up with some kind of ingrained point of privilege. Being around black people with a common language and history, and experience, that was what Olivia longed for. It was not something she even considered when she left Los Angeles. It didn't occur, wasn't even able to imagine that she would need. Now, through all the changes and striving for what she didn't know anymore, she felt like she was a drift. These people were anchors she needed to steady her ship. Maybe another white guy was a mistake.

"You wanna use these glasses, 'Livia," Xena asked, pointing. "Your table is beautiful. I love the amber table cloth and red plate changers that match your bronze stoneware."

"He's gonna tackle you! Watch out! Oh man, did you see that?" Sebastian yelled at the TV.

Faye and Stuart played "Go Fish" on the floor.

Their shoes were scattered everywhere, and the chip bowl needed to be refilled.

"Sebastian, you guys need some more snacks?" Olivia shouted and waited for an answer.

"I guess they didn't hear me. Yeah, those are fine," Olivia standing at the sink looking out the window, glanced over her shoulder, spoke through muffled tears.

Xena nodded her head in understanding, without looking away from the table. "Let's make this a tradition, getting together at Thanksgiving." She put a crystal tumbler at each place setting.

"That's a good idea, I'd like that."

"Me too. I need it too 'Livia." Xena started folding the napkins and then treaded them through the napkin holders. "I do."

After a moment or two, having put all the food on the table, "Ready to call them to dinner?"

"Yeah, I think we got everything now 'Livia," Xena walked around the table. "We got it."

"Food's ready you guys." As Faye, Stuart, Sebastian, and Didier walked into the dining room, Olivia pointed them to their seats.

"This looks great," Didier said with his French accent.

"Well I hope you all enjoy."

They began eating and Olivia felt safe and loved.

Olivia met Kevin for her morning walk, in spite of the cold. Her circuit when she didn't walk with Harmony but with Kevin was around the Big Raven Statue. As she got out of her car in the otherwise empty parking lot Kevin bellowed, "Dr. O-livia!"

"Hey my man, what's crackin'?" Olivia asked, walking up to hug him. He was so tall, at least as tall as Brock, and much more substantial. His beard was closely and impeccably trimmed, shading part of his rosy cheeks, encircling his red lips. He wore a black beanie on his head.

"Like the hat, looks like you come straight outta Li'l Rock," she laughed.

"Girl, it's cold out here, I ain't playin'," he was laughing. "How you doin', how were your holidays?"

"I'm good, good. Holidays were fine. Stayed around here for Thanksgiving. Brock and Harmony came over and helped me move some furniture. Had Christmas dinner with them too, her Mom and Dad were down from Chicago. That was funny since they don't celebrate Christmas. Where's your dog?"

"Yeah, that is funny, no didn't bring the pooch, I'll walk him later. So you had dinner with Harmony's family, huh? I don't know Harmony well, but I see Brock at the gym all the time. He's quite a character."

"Um hum, he is definitely funny. And Harmony is an absolute joy. But yeah, we had dinner at the Thai Restaurant, it was fun. Brock was in rare form, his satire in high gear. Then I went to Cali for a few, right around New Year's, and came home on the third. Figure I give myself ample time to get ready for the new semester."

"I know that's right, shoo."

Their pace was now steady, walking around the path, over the river's bridge, ice and snow on the grass and trees.

"How 'bout you?"

"Oh my holidays were fine, went and spent time with my Mother and Grandmother, you know, no big deal. It's hard since my Dad's been gone. But they were fine. And just like you, I came back so I could get ready for the semester, and to prepare for the crap we gonna hear from the administration."

"I know I understand about losing your Dad, it's never easy no matter how old you are." Kevin didn't say anything, just turned his head, cleared his throat, and adjusted his beanie.

"Can you believe the way Williams was brought on board? I mean really, the last guy standing and they didn't even do a background check on him, sources tell me. So I did my own, and the guy is a total fuck up, never been a president nowhere, and got a bad track record from every place he ever been."

"Wow, really? I know the hiring process wasn't on the up and up, well, it wasn't at the level it should have been, you know, with the search committee being all internal, and with all but Williams withdrawing from consideration."

"Yeah, weird. Really weird, but you know it's what the Board wanted."

"Hmm. They have that much power? It seems like they ain't done nothin' for years and now they fire Luis, and then hire this guy this way? Odd, don't you think?"

"Very. But he starts in February. February — nobody starts a job as university president in fuckin' February!" his voice rising.

"That's right, it's supposed to be July, right?"

"Right, and at first he was gonna start in March, but the folks at his current place said, 'no no, you go now,' that's how bad they wanted him gone," Kevin speculated with conviction. "It don't' take a rocket scientist to figure that shit."

"Well, maybe it'll work out so we can make the university a real university, with the faculty leading and get out of the habit of just going along to get along."

"That would be nice," he agreed. They walked along the path and were so engrossed in talking they were already back to the parking lot.

"All right Kevin, thanks for the fine walk, as usual!."

"No, thank *you*, and I'm glad to see you're recovering," he smiled.

"Thanks, and the doc says I'm a exemplary case," she smiled a little. "Let's do it again in a couple days?"

"Absolutely, I love these walks. So yeah, gimme a call tomorrow or Sunday, and we'll set it up. I don't have any plans to be outta town for a while now."

"Okay."

They hugged, and got in their cars, he letting her back out first, and drove away.

Ten minutes later she was at home, a little after eleven. Standing in one of her bedroom closets, sweaty clothes in a pile around her feet, trying to figure out what to wear, the phone rang. She padded quickly as she could on the white carpet the fifteen feet across the dark purple painted room around the bedposts at the foot of the bed to the nightstand, read the phone. 'Brock Liebermann,' the caller ID said.

"Helllooo Harmony, whatcha doin?"

"Olivia. Brock's dead," she said the words so softly.

"What? Are you kidding?"

"No, I'm not kidding," she whispered.

"Okay, honey, I'll be right there."

*Look well into thy self,*
*there is a source of strength*
*which will always spring up*
*if thou wilt always look there*
*—Marcus Aurelius*

# A Replaced Reality

*Early January 2008, Spring Semester*

Harmony and Brock's corner house was surrounded by emergency vehicles. A station wagon with the words "Jackson County Coroner" written on the sides and back sat out front. Olivia parked in the driveway facing the side street. She walked past the overgrown bushes and pushed a branch aside to open the storm door; the inner door was already open, even though it was twenty degrees outside.

"Harmony?" Olivia called to her softly. She sat at the little antique table just opposite the kitchen, her back to the front door. She didn't turn around when Olivia walked in.

"Liv, thank goodness," she got up after Olivia touched her. They hugged. "You were the first person I called, and I just can't believe it Brock's dead. He's dead," she was smiling in that way people do when they can't feel the pain.

"Oh, honey, what happened, where is he?" Olivia rubbed her arm gently.

"He's in our bed, he's dead. The coroner is in there with him." She pointed to the front bedroom.

"Oh, Harmony, I'm so sorry, my God," Olivia hugged her close.

"We have to find out what the cause of death was because under Jewish tradition he has to be buried within a specific period of time, and I don't know, we weren't married, so his brother has to handle all the details." Harmony voice was muffled, talking into Olivia's collarbone.

"Where does his brother live?"

"Jeff lives in Chicago, and so does his mother. His daughter is only seventeen; she'll be eighteen in a couple of months so she can't do all this stuff," she kept going with her stream of consciousness.

"So you talked with, Jeff? It's Jeff, right? His brother, already?" Olivia let Harmony go.

"Yes, I called him right after I called you. Oh Olivia, what am I going to do without him? I don't believe this," she held her face in her hands, still smiling.

"It's really not fair, I know. Have you called Justin?"

"No, thank God he's living with Tom this year, so this won't be so hard on him. But what a mess just before the bar mitzvah. Oh Liv, what am I going to do?"

Olivia held her close again, "Honey, it's gonna be all right," tears rolled down Olivia's face.

People from the synagogue began to arrive, then people from the Anthropology department, and soon the little house was full. The synagogue folks started taking charge where Harmony couldn't, making phone calls, doing laundry, cleaning the kitchen, and making arrangements.

Harmony sat there, and each time someone new came into the house, she explained, "Brock came home from the gym this morning complaining of a headache. He lay down on the bed next to me and I was just holding him in my arms rubbing his head. He said, 'my head hurts my head hurts, I want to go to the emergency room,' and I told him okay, let's go, I'll take you, but before I could untangle myself from him, right in the next instant he stopped talking. I called him 'Brock? Brock?' and he didn't answer. Next I felt for his pulse and it wasn't there. He told me the other day he wasn't feeling well and I should have listened more closely." Harmony trailed off, guilt gripping her. Simultaneously, people assured her it wasn't her fault.

After a moment of listening but full of denial of their assurances, Harmony repeated, "I don't know, we have to wait to see what the cause of death is, but he's dead. He was only fifty-four."

Olivia hated death and funerals. She relived her father's death when anybody in her life passed away. She hated that she involuntarily mourned all over again every single time.

Olivia ran to him when he came in.

"Hi Daddy!" she chimed. He reached down and hugged her close, now she was too big to hold in his lap or pick up and carry. She hugged him back, searching for his familiar scent of stale tobacco and liquor. He loved the way she looked at him, unlike any look he'd ever received from his best mistresses or wives. He stared at her and drank in her unconditional love and adoration for him.

"Hi sweetheart. Daddy has a question to ask you." Olivia looked at him and noticed his lips and teeth, blackened and stained from years of smoking, against the creamy Cuban skin that showed no signs of hard living. He'd been gone to the store for what seemed like hours. She looked at the clock and it was just about 4:30. There was silence in the apartment—her two sisters were in the bedroom and her mother was in the kitchen but no pots were rattling. The television was on but there was no sound.

"Yes Daddy?" She didn't want him to beat her for saying 'yeah' so she was careful to say 'yes'.

"Olivia, were you stealing?" he whispered in her ear.

Feeling the tickle of his breath, Olivia giggled, "No Daddy, I wasn't."

He let her go as he kissed her cheek, and she backed away from him.

"Daddy has some business to take care of." He walked over to the living room closet, opened the door and reached up and pulled the string and turned on the light. He reached up again to the top shelf. He grabbed his gun, stepped back, turned off the light, and closed the door. He checked the chamber. Satisfied, he lifted his brown leather jacket and placed the gun in the small of his back, between his belted wool maroon pants, and tucked in, white shirt. He straightened himself, smoothed his precision cut black wavy hair. Olivia studied every one of his moves.

"Tell your Mama I'll be back," he directed Olivia as he winked at her, then walked out the front door.

Olivia ran behind him, "'Bye Daddy," she yelled. She was scared because he'd left with his gun but didn't want to show him or anyone she was afraid. Instead, she watched till his brown booted foot left the bottom step. She closed the door and turned the lock. As she was sitting down to continue watching television, her mother came out of the kitchen.

"Was that your father?" Her mother wanted to know what Olivia knew.

"Yes, but he left again," Olivia wouldn't betray him.

Her mother stood there in the undefined space between what was marked off as the living room and dining room. After a moment she went to the large corner window in the dining room and looked out onto the street, left then right. Then straight up the street as the apartment building was situated at a perpendicular intersection, giving it two streets for a view. Then Olivia watched her mother as she walked over to the front door, checked the locks and turned off the porch light.

The clock ticked past 5:30 and the television blared in the background. Olivia sat on the couch hiding in a book. At dinnertime, she and her two sisters sat with their mother at the formica table, fake leather chairs with metal legs sitting on the over-cooked-spinach-green colored hi-low carpet. The cheap curtains covering the corner window billowed gently with the spring breeze, not yet dark out, the last of the sun cast hazy light through the window, showing dust particles in the air.

Joanna thought about the home she left, Philly was long ago and south central Los Angeles would never be a haven. Why had she run from him only to have him here now? Sounds drifted up from the street, men signifying and selling wolf tickets, engines revving, a mother calling her children, voices echoing off the high-density residentials, muffled by palms, and bouncing on the packed ghetto dirt that used to spread lawns.

It was bedtime, baths were taken, dishes were done, Disney was watched. The phone rang, as the girls got ready for bed.

"Hello?" her mother answered after waiting two rings.

"Nothin', really how you doin' 'Nez?"

Olivia eavesdropped while her mother talked to Inez from Philly. It was their weekly call.

"Yes, he's doing okay, got a job finally."

In the silence, her mother's head nodded, her red-auburn Afro proudly sat on her head, "Yes, of course, the girls are fine. Ever since the last incident, things have been quiet."

She crossed her long, brown, skinny legs, right over left, bouncing the right leg and snapping her house shoe on her heel. Then she tucked the tip of her right foot behind her left ankle, making her leg look like a snake.

"Yeah, you right. How's everything out there?" her mother said holding the phone with her bony shoulder to her ear. "Uh huh, uh huh, umm."

Inez and her mother talked for hours most of the time, but this night her mother cut it short.

"Okay, well good talkin' with you chile, talk at you next week, and I'll call you so you don't have to worry 'bout the bill," she managed a smile, with a fake laugh. She uncrossed her legs and put her knees together, and looked down at her toes.

"'Bye, 'bye." Olivia heard the receiver go back on the cradle.

It had been a long day for Joanna. She snatched the moment of peace and quiet finally when she got off the phone with Inez, and headed to her bathroom. Standing before the mirror she got the facial cream out of the drawer. Her children were in bed asleep, her husband wasn't there, but her mind kept on re-visiting the moment when Olivia came home saying she was detained by the store security guards accusing her of shoplifting. She wanted to kick herself. Her first thought had been to tell the girls they couldn't go, but she didn't want to be too hard on them, after what they'd been through, so she let them go against her better judgment. After she'd come back from arguing with those bastards, Joanna saw red. God couldn't they see this was a twelve year old genius? No, they stereotyped everybody. She wished either Malcolm or Martin or somebody'd change this, but no, five years ago they made sure no black leader could succeed.

At the moment, Joanna noticed she was holding her breath as she put the facial on her face, looking in the mirror at the acne scars on her dark brown skin, and hoped this time, this stuff will help. She figured it'd been nearly six hours. "No news is good news," she repeated to herself, praying aloud. She shouldn't have told him what happened, she thought. He was in the shower when she left to go talk to the store security guards. When she got back she told him they had detained Olivia. She watched his anger come up, "I told you not to let the girls go out by themselves," he yelled at her, his face covered with shaving cream. She cowered back, avoiding the swing. He got dressed, she stayed in the kitchen, and he went as she figured he would. Grabbing a towel, she dried her face after rinsing the mask off, and looked in the mirror to see if she could see signs of the success. Nope, she looked the same.

She never knew when he was going to come home, being out drinking till all hours on Saturday nights, wanting her to nurse his hangovers on Sundays. But tonight, she paced the bedroom floor at the foot of the bed. Then she felt it. She went to look for the gun in the living room closet, and it wasn't there. "Oh God!" she said, her hand to her mouth because she knew and didn't want to. At the eleventh hour, the phone rang. Standing in the living room, she stared at it, two rings, three. The girls awoke and wandered out, rubbing their eyes squinting from the light. Six rings, seven, then eight.

"Hello? Yes, this is Mrs. Gonzalez? Who? The Los Angeles County Coroner's Office? Oh my God no, oh my God." The receiver fell to the floor.

Olivia sat in Harmony's den, while people milled around, and Harmony told the story of Brock's death over and over each time a new person entered the house.

*February 2008*

"I belong here," Olivia constantly tried to convince herself when she batted away the thoughts that chided her into thinking she was merely an academic imposter. Often she felt inadequate, especially when she measured herself against these people who she perceived to have been academicians all their lives.

Her mind raced back to the interview, when Bob Johnson asked her "Why do you want to come here? There are no black people here. When you all do come, you don't stay. So why don't you just go on somewhere."

Olivia's answer was so clear then, resting on waves of indignation: she could handle any situation with white folks at work. In no uncertain terms she told him she had been the only African American at the executive level in many white male dominated high-powered environments. And, by the way, "if you must know" she said as she leaned forward so he wouldn't miss her words, "I made them millionaires." This university, she told him without wavering, needed some diversity. He didn't say anything in response to Olivia's emotions, but Olivia guessed he probably voted against her candidacy for the appointment.

His office was next door to hers, and she felt badly that she hadn't made more effort to befriend him before he died, either before or right after Brock did. But her respect for Bob declined even more, as she understood now that he spent many years recycling all his mimeographed handouts and hadn't changed one iota of his materials — the Dean asked her to take his class until the end of the semester. He had the nerve to die at this inopportune, inconvenient moment. She didn't feel bad when she decided it was good that he no longer stood in front of this group of students, cheating them out of an education. My God his notes were in purple mimeograph ink, his transparencies were typed in Courier, his lesson plans had no mention of today's business needs. Good riddance, and maybe someone with a clue will be hired to replace him.

It was the same feeling she had when her father was declared dead. Dingdong the witch is dead, the witch is dead, the witch is dead, she remembered singing and dancing around when her mother came home from the coroner's office.

Standing there at the reception surrounded by champagne and gaiety, she watched Chairman Doolittle walk up behind the lectern, and step up on the stepstool. He was a short, stout man, reminiscent of Boss Hog, wearing a heavy wool plaid unlined Walmart blazer and gray polyester pants, and a tie that reached the center of his mid section. Olivia wondered how someone like him got to the place he was. He was an idiot.

"Good afternoon," he said into the microphone, which was bent down to reach him, in spite of the stool. People paid no attention, they were so engrossed in their conversations, and not to mention that there was alcohol on campus out in the open. "Good afternoon," he said again, a little louder. The third time, he yelled "Good afternoon!!"

"Good afternoon," the crowd responded.

"I'd like to welcome y'all to this reception for Dr. Arnold Williams, our new President." He started clapping as did the others. "I hope you're enjoying the refreshment. We have with us today several of our Board Members, and we welcome them. In the interest of time, we won't let them all give speeches — even though we'd like 'at. But our program today does include an invacation by Rev'rand Peters from our Grace Baptist," he motioned to the reverend, who came to the lectern as Darnell moved aside.

Oh no, not that. This was exactly the type of rhetoric that made you understand what was wrong with the place. Separation of church and state? Had anyone heard of that around here?

"Please bow your heads." The Reverend lifted his hands and closed his eyes. He was someone Olivia had seen before, it was rumored he was an alcoholic. He was about six-seven, with thick salt and pepper hair, jowls hanging. His hairy arms stuck out of his white short-sleeved pressed Oxford shirt, which was tucked into his grey wool pants. "Father, we give you honor and praise, and honor to George W. Bush, and the Governor of Arkansas, and thank you for the strength of the Western family. We ask that you continue to bless us and Dr. Williams, as he takes the lead for this institution. We ask this in the name of your precious son, Jesus, and all God's people said, Amen." The crowd collectively amen-ed and people who bowed raised their heads. Olivia did NOT bow, and as far as she was concerned George W. could go to hell.

Darnell returned to the lectern and stepped up, as the Reverend moved aside.

"Thank you Rev'rand for that fine invacation. Now, I would like to tell you a little about our search for the new President and his qualifications. The search was conducted nationwide through the normal channels of academic administration recruitment. All of you were involved in the process from developing the announcement, to reviewing candidate files, to interview and selection.

"We had some forty people apply for the position, even though it was off cycle for this kind of recruitment. Most of these jobs are filled in July. Three people were invited to campus for interviews; y'all interviewed them and had time for question and answer. Students were invited as well. I came up here from Smithville, leaving my law practice, to participate in each one of 'em. The search committee, after all this, unanimously selected this man for the position. That selection was presented to the Board, and further with their unanimous approval, and then to Governor William Lacey through Gary Follet, our representative, for his approval." Olivia wondered to herself, if the search was legit, why you trying so hard to convince everybody it was? As if you followed some procedure and all o' us know you didn't. It was insulting.

"Therefore, we are very certain that we have followed a diligent process and have the backing of all of our stakeholders. All of that notwithstanding, not insignificantly our new president comes to us from one of the finest state university institutions in North Carolina, having served as Assistant Provost and then Interim Provost at UNC. Before that he served as Chairman of the Anthropology department at Aberson University, a state institution in Virginia. His doctorate is in Anthropology from the University of Nevada, his Masters from University of Iowa and his bachelors from University of Pennsylvania. Dr. Williams has published several books and numerous articles, and taught for more than twenty-five years. He and his devoted wife, Carlotta, have three adult children. Please help me welcome Dr. Arnold Williams." The crowd returned an obligatory applause. This message was worse than a corner preacher's on a New Year's morning in the ghetto.

Darnell looked over at the President as he stood there to his right, greasy dandruffed hair covered by a black felt Fedora, crooked teeth, ruddy looking skin, tie stopping at the top of his belly. He had on a heavy wool suit, black, again a Walmart original, and a blue shirt and shiny tie. As Darnell backed away from the lectern, he took his hat off and laying it on the table next to the lectern, he began, "Thank you."

In a split second, Olivia reviewed her success over the last six years and tried to ignore the premonition she was getting, the kind that like make you shake your head and say 'WTF?' with a lilt in your voice. They were trying to make you believe something and asking you to suspend your experience with the world. She no longer had pain from leaving her old life, never thought about the divorce from Tyler or the fact that he was gay. The pace of her life was great, not having to do the corporate dance to the frenetic rhythm of capitalism. She was happy with her publications, and the fact that there was no real pressure on her made her prolific. And while she did have to deal with her family, she did so from fifteen hundred miles away, their blame less apparent every day.

After thirty-five years she was getting to where she didn't feel responsible for her father's homicide and was able to have relationships — good, healthy ones — with men. She been dating Jonathan for a while now, he was smart, gainfully employed in the right social class, straight, available emotionally, didn't abuse, and three years younger than her rather than twenty years older. He was the exact opposite of everything she knew and it was great.

But, here, now in this room, Oh God, Brock was dead. Daddy's dead. Child out of wedlock and then divorced from a gay man. If what Darnell was saying was true, then she had misjudged reality again. It was like when her father pulled down her pants, but when she turned around to look, he quickly pulled them up and pretended to be looking in on the baby in the crib.

She felt like she was about to lose all she'd gained her grip on reality was slipping.

She looked around for Harmony. It was in this very building, on the third floor in the ballroom that Harmony had come up to her, after the 2003 faculty dinner. Olivia was so excited to be working here. The then interim vice president for academic affairs, Mary Hollingsworth introduced her. "Ms. Olivia Clarke, Assistant Professor in the School of Business, ABD from the University of California, MBA from California State University, and BA in economics, from the University of California. In addition to Ms. Clarke's academic accomplishments, she has fifteen years of experience in corporate executive leadership and entrepreneurship." As she listened, Olivia thought they were talking about someone else. But most importantly, they were proud that they'd hired someone black, and Harmony was ecstatic.

She came up to Olivia and introduced herself, saying "Hi I'm Harmony Schwab, I'm glad you're here. Let's go to dinner sometime soon!" Harmony was very bubbly.

"Hello, hi, thanks. It's nice to meet you, and sure, I'd like that." Olivia didn't know a soul in Roadims, but she instantly connected with Harmony's twinkle in her eye.

"Okay, I'll give you a call tomorrow," and before the end of the week, they were out to dinner.

Between Olivia's introduction to Harmony and now, Sebastian had finally decided to get it together. He was at boot camp with the US Army, glad to have income, bonuses, somebody telling him what to do and when, three hots and a cot. She feared he would call and say he'd gotten kicked out. But at least there would be no more embarrassing newspaper articles or visits to see him while he was being held for a 96-hour observation at the psyche ward. No more avoiding questions from faculty asking if he was her son. No more unasked questions from him about who or where his father was. She felt the weight of her life, her shoulders rounded while she exhaled. It made her tired to think of it. Maybe she should break up with Jonathan, she thought. She felt insecure about her perceptions and maybe she wasn't seeing him clearly. The whirling dervishes of her mind seemed to take over. Finally she spotted Harmony standing by the door. She was thumbing through the Reception Program, standing there looking entirely bored.

Seeing Arnold Williams standing in front of the gaiety gave Olivia pause. He looked like something out of a Cracker Jack box. This can't be real, she thought.

"Thank you, I am very glad to be here with you today. Thank you Darnell for that introduction, and please everyone call me Arnie. I trust you're enjoying the champagne and the snacks. Our food service department is wonderful. I know we don't have the legal right to drink on this, a dry campus. But, my first duty as President was to authorize drinking on campus and I did it gladly. Apparently, no one else on this campus could," he laughed, and so did everyone else. Great, so he's good at getting drunk and getting other people drunk. Wonderful.

"I'm told that you have some budgetary crises that need handled, and the Board's given me the directive to solve problems related to that, and I intend to do that. I have an open door policy, and I'll be looking forward to talking with you individually. Just call my secretary and make an appointment and we'll go from there. Oh, by the way, Dr. McAllister has tendered his resignation; he accepted a position as President of North Dakota University. Fortunately, and we are extremely grateful for his generosity, he agreed to stay on with us until the HLC site visit is completed. As such, his last day with us will be April 5, 2008. We will announce the reception date to see him off properly."

"Thank you for the memorial service for Brock Lieberman. It was a wonderful and moving service, we will miss his contribution to campus life. We send our prayers to his family and loved ones. I understand we sent flowers and a donation and we often do that sympathetically and when people are in the hospital; however, with our budgetary crises, we are no longer going to be able to do that but we will send a card."

For Christ's sake! How much can it cost to send flowers to people's families? Surely someone has to see this guy's nuts? Olivia couldn't believe her ears.

"I would like to conclude my remarks with a toast to Western State, to our future." He raised his glass and the rest of the crowd did as well.

Darnell came up to the lectern and stood beside him grinning from ear to ear. He stepped up on the stool. "Thank you Arnie. Thank you all for being here. Please continue to enjoy the refreshment. We'll both be here until the champagne is gone, so feel free to come up and talk to us. We are very proud to have Arnie here with us. We think he's going to lead Western in the direction it needs to go." He stepped off his stool.

Olivia thought, 'It's refreshments you ass!' Does anyone else see this bullshit? Apparently they didn't, because the people went back to drinking and talking.

---

"Hi Patrick, hello Jane," Olivia stood by their table at the annual St. Thomas Ball.

"Hi Olivia, so nice to see you here." Jane motioned her to come sit next to her.

"Thanks, I appreciate you both including me at your table. Wow, lots of people here, huh? Everybody who's anybody is here!" Olivia surveyed the room and saw many of Roadims high profile executives she'd mainly seen at her Rotary group.

"Yes, it's 'the ball' to be invited to, so you've arrived," Patrick assured.

"The decorations are beautiful, this red and gold China theme," Olivia rubbed her hand on the back of a covered chair.

"Yes, and did you see the silent auction? We both have pieces being auctioned," Patrick pointed to the large double doors of the Sheraton's ballroom.

"Really, come show me where your art is, and I'll bid on it," Olivia twisted around and the three of them got up.

"Olivia, you look beautiful," Patrick said.

"Thanks, yeah, it's not the university professor look." Olivia wore a long taffeta skirt that was a hint of olive green with a matching silk crochet tank top that rippled over her torso like waves of pearls. "I got this the last time I was in France. The shoes I got from Kansas City." Olivia wore some Donna Karen shoes that were pointed toe sling-backs that were killing her with each step.

"It's very nice," Jane said.

"Here's our art work," they pointed to two ceramic pieces, and some weird looking textile thing with a woman's rights motif.

Olivia never liked Jane's art. It was too harsh for her tastes, but she had bought some of Patrick's stuff, and put it in her meditation room.

"I think I'll bid on this one," she moved over to Patrick's display, and made a note on the card.

Patrick didn't say anything, "Let's go back to the table, I'm sure they'll be serving dinner soon.

The three of them walked back to the Ballroom, and found their way to the table and sat down. Eating while the big band played familiar tunes such as those from Count Basie and Louis Armstrong, it was a very pleasant moment.

When the waiter arrived and put the big tray of meals down and removing their silver dome covers, Patrick noticed immediately that there was beef on the plates.

"You still vegetarian, Olivia, right?"

"Yes, I asked for a special meal."

After the waiter served all the guests, Olivia turned to Patrick, "I'll trade you my beef for your rice?"

The two scraped the food off of their plates onto each others and continued eating.

When the dessert was finished, the band played more current songs, like Earth Wind and Fire's *Shining Star*. Olivia liked the music.

"Wanna dance?" Patrick asked.

"Sure, Jane, you wanna dance too? We can make it a threesome."

"Okay Olivia, but no showing us up. There's no way we can dance a well as you," Jane joked.

Olivia already knew that but it was an opportunity to dance socially, which she never got.

They walked out to the dance floor, and the three of them danced until Olivia's feet flat out objected.

"I gotta sit, my feet, they're killing me," Olivia yelled to them, walking to the table.

Jane and Patrick waved at her and continued dancing, while Olivia watched them and the rest of the crowd from her seat. There wasn't a single other soul that was black in the room of over two-thousand people. Olivia felt that feeling starting to weigh in on her, darkening the room, when Patrick and Jane returned to the table.

"That was fun!" he said, holding the chair out for his wife.

"Yes, indeed it was," she said, taking her seat and grabbing her wine glass.

Everybody had to yell to be heard over the music.

"Too bad it only happens here once a year," Patrick insulted the Roadims culture.

"True," Olivia agreed. "But still it was a wonderful time, and I think it's best if I start heading home." Glancing at her watch, it read 11:48 p.m. "I can't believe I'm not asleep!"

"Yeah, that's the same for us," Jane agreed, "we're normally in bed by nine thirty. The sign of middle age, huh?"

"Sure is." Olivia picked up her black clutch purse by its gold chain, which was laying on the table in front of her. "I've enjoyed sharing the table with you, and hopefully it won't be the last ball we attend together."

"It was a fine evening, and let's make it a tradition, each year!" Patrick suggested, and Jane was nodding in agreement.

"Oh, hey, what do you think of the new President?" Jane asked.

"I don't know, he seems to have a good spiel. What do you think, Patrick?"

"It's wait and see, the guy doesn't seem to have a brain of his own."

"Oh?" Olivia wanted to hear more.

"Yeah, we'll talk about it later," Patrick deflected, gesturing cutting his throat.

"Okay, sounds good. I'll see you on Monday, Patrick. Jane, take care, it was good to see you as always."

"Always good to see you, too. You'll have to come over for tea and tell me about your trip to France."

"Okay, I'd like that," Olivia slid to the end of her chair and stood up in the most lady like fashion and walked away. She wasn't going to hold her breath waiting for Jane to actually invite her.

*May 2008*

It was her first formal meeting with Arnie Williams. She sent the agenda for the meeting to his secretary after dinner with Harmony.

"Hello, Estelle, how are you? I'm here to see Arnie."

"Hello Dr. Clarke, yes we have you on the calendar. He's on the phone right at the moment but we'll be with you shortly, please have a seat," she smiled.

"Thank you," Olivia took one of the sitting chairs. The last time she was in this office was for her interview, but she didn't remember the secretary's outer office. She picked up a *Western State Alumni* magazine, flipping through it nervously. Bored with that, she reached for her phone and started checking email and reading news articles. After ten minutes or so, he came to the entry way between his outer office and Estelle's.

"Hello Olivia, nice to see you, com'on in," he turned around and walked back in.

"Hello Arnie, thanks," she followed him in.

"Please sit down," he motioned her to the couch. Nothing had changed in the office that she could tell. He closed the door, she sat where she sat when she interviewed, and he sat where President Fontecillo sat. He wasn't wearing his suit jacket, but his blue cotton shirt was tucked into his pants, pulled way up over his belly held up by a belt. The tie matched his shirt but only came to the top of his belt. You could see clumps of his hair sticking together with little flecks of white sprinkled through.

"Thank you for taking time to meet with me today, but I wanted to get a head start on the fall semester, and go over some of the issues the faculty are facing." Olivia pulled her skirt as she crossed her legs and sat back on the couch. She rested her left arm on the back of the couch but made sure her jacket covered her.

"Not a problem, hey it was good seeing you at Rotary. I need you to sponsor me. I mean, I'm a member in good standing at my home Rotary club, but I'll have to transfer here to Roadims."

"Sure, that's not a problem, it's a great Rotary group."

"I'm looking forward to working with the senate next year. We have a lot of problems you know, the way Luis ran this organization into the ground with deficit spending." He leaned in and whispered to Olivia, as if there were other people who could hear him. "We're facing at least a five million dollar shortfall, and our reserves are seriously low. I can't believe he was allowed to run this institution the way he did." Arnie bobbed his left leg from the ball of his foot, making the little coffee table between them shake.

"I don't know anything about that, I didn't get involved with him really."

"Oh, Lordie, what a mess, and that … what they call it? A *Piano Competition*, what the hell's that all about?"

Olivia couldn't believe his disrespect, and she tried not to show how much it hurt her. "Michelle Fontecillo directs that, and she is a member of the Rotary group. You could talk with her about it if you want to know more. I don't know that much, as my involvement with it was minimal, only having hosted one contestant at my home a couple of years ago. But it is internationally acclaimed, and attracts lots of big names around Roadims."

He grunted. "This university is a regional college and doesn't need that kind of thing, especially with the problems Luis created. I hear we give them office space, and all kinda freebees. People around here don't want to see their tax dollars going to that."

Olivia didn't say anything. She was dumbfounded by his gall.

His eyes watered involuntarily, he was constantly wiping and sniffling. "So, we have a faculty meeting every month?"

Yuck. She wanted to make sure she didn't let him touch her. Did he need a doctor or what? Where did they get this guy? Didn't he have some Claritin or something, Jesus.

"Yes, we do. And we will want to make some changes as we move forward, particularly with faculty governance, and with the report we received from the HLC accreditation visit last month. We are to implement a shared governance model and strategic planning, the findings of the report indicate that there will be a follow up visit in two years to ensure those two changes have been made."

"Right, I have talked to Dan about that some, and it's his area so you should talk with him about that. I did read the *Faculty Handbook* and I don't see why the President is a voting member, and I want that changed."

"That's fine. We've already changed the meeting somewhat to dismiss the administrators after the discussion of Old Business takes place. That way faculty feel they can freely talk about issues that are important without censorship. I also want to formalize and update the process, professionalize the documents, things like that."

"The faculty need to know they aren't special, and they aren't any better than anyone else on this campus. It takes the custodians, the secretaries—everyone—to make this campus run and it's not the faculty who are the main voice." Olivia was sure she wasn't hiding her shock. What did he think, the custodians were gonna teach physics? She uncrossed her legs and moved to the edge of the couch.

"Right. So, I thought maybe we'll meet the week before the senate meetings, and I'll meet with Dan before I meet with you, so that all the bases are covered."

"That's fine. Just schedule it with Estelle. She keeps my calendar, I just wake up every day to see what I'm doing, see where I'm supposed to be," he laughed and his belly shook, and he wiped his eyes and snorted.

"Great, I will. I hope your summer goes well." She slid her arm through her purse straps, it hung at the crook of her right elbow.

"That reminds me, I'm going to hold an economic summit this summer, next month, and I want you to come. Renee Gruber, you know she's now the Senior Vice President for Business Affairs, and her JD comes in handy for us. Anyway, she and her staff, Rob Boost, and the rest of them, will prepare some data, and I'm going to talk about the problems we're having. Did you know that Luis authorized cash spending for the new Banner software? That was over five million right there. Boy he was something. Renee said she was always afraid of him, apparently he had a temper." He was shaking his head like he was in disbelief after witnessing some awful traumatic accident.

"No, I didn't know him that well," Olivia repeated.

"Anyway, yes, we're going to do that. And I want you to come to the monthly Board Meeting, and have lunch with us. Estelle'll get you a nametag made, and you'll get all the agendas and relevant documents. By the way, who else is on the senate Executive Committee? I will want their names so I can make sure to invite them to dinner at the end of the year, to thank them for their service." He talked to the window, squinting, leg bouncing uncontrollably.

"Oh, okay, sure. The EC for the 2008 2009 academic year includes Veronica Sanderson as Parlimentarian, Eric Robertson member at large, Wes Phillips president elect, Frank Wirts is secretary, and Mike Frazier is past president," Olivia rattled off the names.

"Yes, I have met all of them. Mike is a great guy, he and I became good friends during my interviews for this position. I have him over to the house all the time, we like to drink beer," he threw his head back and laughed so Olivia saw his black fillings. When he was somewhat composed, he wiped his eyes.

"Well, I think I've taken enough of your time today, Arnie. I should get going, I'm sure you have a lunch meeting to attend," she picked up her notebook and added it to the crook of her elbow, crossed her arm in front of her so she wouldn't drop it. That arm movement reminded her of the tragic events of that day, back when she'd gone to the small library in Los Angeles. She pushed the thought back into its box.

"It was good seeing you—hey, did you buy any furniture the other day? We saw you in the furniture store, and Carlotta was really impressed with you."

"No, I was just window shopping mainly." Olivia stood up.

"We got a lot, we have this new house now that the university bought for us, and it needs a whole lot of furniture!" He stood up, put his hankie in his pocket.

"Yes, I can imagine," Olivia said, trying to get out of his office.

"Great, thanks for the meeting and we'll see you over the summer at the economic summit," he extended his hand for a handshake and Olivia automatically extended hers. "Carlotta will look forward to having lunch with you sometime?" he probed.

"That'll be good, you can give her my number." No way I'm having lunch with her, she thought.

"Oh I'll get Estelle to do it," he said, waving his hand as Olivia was out the door.

"'Bye, 'bye Estelle," she waved to them both and headed straight for the ladies' room to wash him off her hands.

<hr/>

After lunch, she went back to her office and started preparing standardized agendas and minutes templates, putting together a notebook for all the paperwork, making tabs by subject. These documents hadn't been updated since God knows when. She calendared the meeting dates for the EC, the senate, and deadlines for meeting with the President and the Vice President. She emailed the EC letting them know those dates. She wouldn't have to think about this now until the fall.

It was the end of May, between the spring and summer sessions so the halls were empty when she left around four, but Patrick was in his office, she took the liberty to stop in to talk with him on her way out.

"Hey Patrick," she said, knocking on his door. The secretary was already gone for the day.

"What's up?" he smiled, pushed himself back from his chair. "I'm just working on the MBA Program we have coming up. Have a seat." He gestured her to a chair.

"Oh, great. Our faculty have agreed to teach?" She sat down, put her purse on the corner of his desk.

"Yes, we have several who are academically and professionally qualified, not enough, but some. Here, let me show you." He started searching on his computer, found a file and opened it. "Here's a listing of who's teaching what. You aren't qualified for this because your degree is out of field." He watched Olivia's face for signs of disappointment.

"Cool. I had my first meeting with Arnie today." Olivia crossed her legs, hooked her thumb over the opening of her skirt pocket.

"Oh, did he blame Luis for everything again? Seems that's the tactic Darnell is using, defame Luis for everything." He clicked his document closed, pushed back from the table where the computer was and faced Olivia from behind his desk.

"Is that it? That matches what I just heard from him." Olivia didn't say he'd already told her that.

"Yup," he said, emphasizing the 'p'.

"Wanna be the MBA Program Director? We'll give you an administrative contract to do it. Not much but something. This way you can participate in the program too." He reached forward, leaned on the desk with his right elbow, pulled a pen out from under a mound of papers.

"What do I have to do?"

"Mainly answer questions from people calling, reply to email, put together the marketing plan, go to meetings, get the faculty to comply, not that much." He laughed a little.

"Right, not that much. I don't know Patrick. It may be too much for me with the senate stuff coming up, with Bob not being replaced, and with Claire being new. Grady's gone and Nancy, bless her heart she's sweet, but she doesn't know what she's doing, she relies on me to tell her what to do. Then I've got all my classes, and the committee work—"

"You'll do fine, and this will help you get in line to become the next Dean when I retire. That's not that far away."

"I'm sure there are other people here who want to be the Dean, and who feel they deserve it. As I have said before, I don't want to step on any toes." Olivia grabbed her purse from the desk, reached in and got her keys.

"Don't worry, that's not for two more years and everybody will be on board with it by then. Besides, you're the only person here qualified to do it. As I look down the halls, no one else has your background and skill." He knew he had her, and he needed to make sure this MBA Program succeeded. Olivia was the only faculty member he could count on that would see to it.

"Thanks, I appreciate that. Well, I gotta go. Oh, it was great sitting with you and Jane at the St. Thomas Ball last week. Are you guys going to the Hudson Arts Opening Reception this Friday?" Olivia stood up.

"You bet, and yes we enjoyed it too, although we can't dance as well as you!" He laughed out loud, showing all of his teeth, leaning his head back rolling his eyes.

"That's to be expected, given the circumstances," she walked to the doorway, turned around to face him. "See you Friday if I don't see you before then," she waved at him for a second, and walked out.

"Brock's brother has decided that Elizabeth gets everything, since Brock didn't have a will." Harmony said, putting the binoculars to her face. "Ooo look at that!" she pointed to the bird in the tree.

Olivia looked but didn't see anything.

"No will? So what does this mean?"

"Elizabeth gets, everything, even Brock's half of the interest in our house. Isn't it a gorgeous day out here?" She paused, looking up and breathing in deeply, closing her eyes and smiling.

They were on the windy wooded path that wandered though the Nature Center Reserve. The air was crisp, the light reflected on everything, making the colors of the flowers, leaves, moss, the rocks, and the bluer than usual sky intense and magical. The water in Shoal Creek was above its banks. There were only two times a year when the weather was like this in Roadims.

"Yes, this is awesome. I love this season, right after the thunderstorm tornado season and before the humid hot sultry weight lays down on us. So Brock didn't name you as beneficiary on anything? Did you guys have any kind of agreement?"

"No, and he was so young, nobody expected, I mean come-on, a stroke? We figured we'd get to that—wills and stuff—later. You know, when we were older, I don't know, we just didn't think about it. Hey, can you hold these for a sec?" She handed the binocs to Olivia, paused and zipped her jacket.

"So Brock has some assets though?" Olivia gave back the binocs.

"Yes, and he pointed them to Elizabeth. She's getting everything." She turned to face Olivia. "Even when I ask Jeff about having some of the money, he says the law says it goes to Elizabeth because she's the sole heir. He wants to come and clean out Brock's closets at home and at the office on campus, wants to make sure all of his royalties and rights accrue to Elizabeth. He even wanted the body to be shipped up to Chicago, but I put my foot down on that one."

"Right, I remember. I'm glad you did. Do you think you maybe need a lawyer?" They continued walking, Olivia noticed the waterfall over the cave, and pointed at it as they passed it.

"Yeah, it's beautiful. For what, I mean, we weren't married, there's nothing I can do."

"Are you sure, is Arkansas a common law state?"

"No, it's not. I don't know, maybe I should, especially with the house. The mortgage is in both our names, and I know Jeff is trying to squeeze the money out of it. I mean, he's *such* a lawyer."

"I get it, I know, my ex-husband was a lawyer. That's why I'm saying you may need one too. Jeff doesn't have to do what he's doing." Olivia slipped a little on a rock. "Whoa!" she raised her arms to keep her balance. "That's all I'd need, to slip and fall." She straightened up.

"Careful Liv." Seeing she was okay, Harmony continued, "True, and if I had a lawyer, he could talk to him and I wouldn't have to, right?"

"Absolutely. I'll email you the name of the guy who set up my trust. I know firsthand what happens in these cases."

"Right, with your Dad."

"Exactly. We had nothing after he died, not that we had anything before, but it made me know that I had to have this taken care of for my son, in the unlikely event."

"Okay, yeah, I'll contact him, send me the stuff. But I wanna know, so, how was the meeting with Arnie?"

Olivia was embarrassed and ashamed about the mess Brock left her in. She wondered why Brock hadn't left her anything. Maybe he didn't love her, maybe Olivia was wrong about him all this time. She watched Harmony put her binocs up to her face, as they stopped on the path, and looked up at the trees. Olivia wondered if Harmony'd had allowed herself these doubts about Brock, but decided not to bring it up. Olivia being sensitive to her situation, just went along. "Oh, boy, I don't know Harmony. Are you on senate this year?"

"No, but I took Brock's place as Chair of the Faculty Welfare Committee, which is a standing committee of the senate. We take up issues related to faculty welfare. So, I'll take up whatever you need me to."

"Great, thanks. I'm sure I'm gonna need all the help I can get. I think Kevin is on senate this year, representing Science and Engineering, right?" They continued walking, Olivia reached in her pocket for a tissue, and blew her nose.

"As far as I know, I think he is because he was nominated to replace someone from his department who left for another job."

"Oh, okay. Well that's great. And Ree agreed to be on the EC and so did Eric. The only wild card I have is Wes." She put the wet tissue in her pocket.

"He's definitely a wild card. I've had students tell me he shows up to eight o'clock class drunk."

"Wonderful, that's all I need."

"But I think Arnie's gonna do good things for the campus, I'm leaving the jury out for the moment." Harmony took the strap holding the binoc from around her neck, wrapped it around them and put them in her fanny pack.

"I don't know, I don't have a good feeling about him. But maybe you're right."

"How's your son? How's Jonathan?"

"Sebastian is fine, he's graduating from boot camp here at the end of the month, so I'm goin' down to Georgia for that. Jonathan's fine, he's coming to visit in June, after I get back from my three weeks in Europe so he can meet Sebastian, before he gets stationed in Seattle. He's so great! I can't believe it's been almost a year since, finally I met someone who is everything opposite what I'm used to."

"I'm happy for you. He seemed really nice when we went to dinner a couple weeks ago. Justin really liked him. I wish Brock was here to meet him."

"Oh Harmony, you had such a great thing with Brock. I know this is hard for you, the fact that he's gone. I know, I know."

The two paused on the path, looking at each other with tears in their eyes. They hugged, lingering long in the embrace. Then instinctively they turned to the direction of the sound of water rushing and stood together in silence staring at the creek. When they'd both settled down, they turned and continued their walk.

Even though it was the middle of the night, Olivia started opening her email and snail mail when she got back from her trip. She was glad to be home, tired of overpriced European hotels, trains, planes, speaking French and German, academic conferences, lectures. It was a good trip, great for her career since she'd taught in northern France and in Austria, and on the way back she presented a paper at a prestigious conference in Boston. But now she just wanted to slow down so she could spend time with her son before he left for Iraq in two weeks, and rest before the semester started in less than six.

An email said Arnie was going to hold his Economic Summit on Tuesday, July 15, 2008 at ten o'clock in Koger's Auditorium. Another email from Patrick was asking her to come in to see him as soon as she got back. She replied to him and said she'd see him Monday. Her spirit was tired and she felt unsettled.

Kevin sent an email with links to newspaper articles, one where Arnie was quoted as saying President Fontecillo led the university to the brink of insolvency, and said cash reserves were way down. She clicked on the link to the article and read it. Apparently it was one of a series of interviews he was giving to the press, letting the community know what was going on at Western, starting back at the end of June.

'Why on earth would he air this kind of idiocracy in the newspaper that's stupid, God,' she said out loud. In the next article he said people in the community didn't think the university needed the International Mission and that was something Dr. Fontecillo set up to his own glory. "We're simple folks here, we don't need that kind of thing. Most of our students come from our local area and have no interest in international travel.

"Sure, if some students want to travel, they should, but we have heard of faculty taking students on these junkets and drinking and partying on the university's money."

She couldn't believe what she was reading. On impulse she clicked on the last link, and the headline was "We can't go into bankruptcy!" What in the world? How could a public university go into bankruptcy? 'You can't go bankrupt you idiot!' she said and quickly did a Google search and found that this was nearly impossible because the state would come in and take the organization into receivership before it went bankrupt.

"This university is facing serious economic problems, based on years of deficit spending. The previous administration did not handle the finances correctly."

She closed her email, fighting the nausea welling up in her throat, and walked back into the kitchen to get the mail. A big stack accumulated after nearly four weeks of being gone. Sorting through the junk and keeping the important letters, she found one from the university.

> *Effective July 2008, any faculty member with clients or work outside the university that compensated them over and above their annual salary needed to get approval to engage in such relationships and the compensation had to be disclosed to the Vice President for Academic Affairs.*

The letter was under Dan Fogerty's signature, whom Arnie'd appointed to the position shortly after Dr. McAllister resigned. Dan's career with the university began some thirty years ago, he was the Dean of Arts and Sciences for a long time, with a PhD in biology.

Olivia thought about the ramifications of this new edict for a few minutes, with the growing feeling that something important had been taken without permission, her pulse increased and heart pounded from anger, piled on top of the nausea she already felt. Her shoulders were tense and she felt fear. How was she going to manage the expenses if she had to close down her clients? Up to now there was no approval needed to do consulting, and that was a great source of income especially in the economic environment of no raises now or forever more.

Standing in the empty house in the middle of the night, she began to feel the edges unravel, knowing this wasn't what she wanted.

*The accusations*
*really say more about the accusers*
*than that of the accused.*
*—Roderick Macleish*


*Do you see men and women*
*who are wise in their own eyes?*
*There is more hope*
*for a fool than for them.*
*—Proverbs 26:12*

# Silent Revolts

*Mid July 2008, Summer Term*

It took Olivia a few days to settle down but she had to hurry because Jonathan was coming to visit and so was Sebastian.

Jonathan arrived on Thursday night. Olivia opened the garage door for him as he pulled up in the rental car. He got out without turning off the car, and kissed her deeply. Olivia felt tingly and perspiration seeped out of her in the humid night.

"Hello darling," he whispered in her ear.

Instantly she was taken back to the tickle she felt from her father and melted into him. "Hi sweetheart," she responded to his touch. It was pitch black outside, and every star in the Arkansas sky was visible.

Inside, they left a trail of clothing between the garage door and the bedroom.

"Are you hungry? I've got stuff in the 'fridge, or we can go out to Country Kitchen."

"Let's go to Country Kitchen, since I'm still on California time."

"Okay, let me get ready," Olivia pushed herself out of bed. It was 11:38. "I find this to be a treat because I don't get to go out like this very often. And you know I never sleep this late." Olivia walked around the bed to him and kissed Jonathan's cheek.

After breakfast, she and Jonathan were out for a long walk around the Nature Center, holding hands and smelling the lust of the summer.

"I told you Sebastian and his girlfriend Kristan were coming tomorrow, right?"

"Yes, you did. I'm looking forward to getting his ... permission — no, no, approval. It's important that he like me."

Olivia didn't know what to say. Sebastian didn't like men she loved. Actually she was certain he *wouldn't* approve. "I'm sure he'll like you," she assured him.

"Great. Uh, so. What do you think about marriage? I mean, in the abstract?"

"I think marriage is the way men and women should be because we weren't meant to live alone."

"Would you take the man's name, if, say, you were to get married again?" Jonathan had practiced saying these two lines at least a hundred times.

"Yes, I would." Olivia kept her eyes on the path.

"Would you wanna work, should you ever marry again?" Jonathan glanced over at Olivia without turning his head.

"If I didn't have to work, that would be fine. But it would mean that my husband had enough money to provide for the lifestyle I want."

Jonathan thought about where he was financially, and in his mind he'd calculated that he had enough money to cover her, at least until she got a job. He had determined to get her to California and see how it went. Then ask her to marry him.

"But I'm not moving out of Arkansas, leaving my tenured position, without being married," Olivia took a drink of her water. "Isn't this such a beautiful place? I just love the sounds and smells."

It was the first time Jonathan had ever heard her say something so firmly to him.

"Yes, it's very nice, this is where you and Harmony come all the time, right?"

"Right. Well, anyway, Sebastian will come over on Saturday, I'm going to cook, fry some chicken, make some greens and cornbread. Get a peach cobbler. He told me he was getting married next month, and we're invited to his wedding. I hope you'll come. It's right before he leaves for his new station in Germany."

"Of course, I'll be there. That's a big deal. Have you met her family?"

"No, not yet, and frankly, I really don't want to be friendly with her in-laws."

"I understand. Hey, it's really hot out here. Let's go get a cold drink. And about that marriage conversation, it was just hypothetical." Jonathan formed an escape route. He didn't know what he was going to do and he didn't want to leave her with the impression that he was going to ask her to marry him any time soon. She was so eager and there were things he needed to tell her, but just hadn't found the right moment.

"Right, hypothetical," Olivia mimicked. "We have tickets to see *Tango Argentina* tonight, so why don't we go home, get cooled off and cleaned up. Then we can head on over to Little Rock. I know a nice place we can go for dinner too, and I made reservations."

Jonathan was used to eating at Arby's and Taco Bell. And he hardly ever went out for an evening, except when he was trying to impress a woman, which he hadn't tried with her.

"All right, that sounds like a plan."


"Sebastian! Hey, how are you honey?" Olivia hugged her son. "Hi Kristan," and then she hugged her soon to be daughter-in-law.

"Hey Mom, what's crackin'? Oh this must be Jonathan. What's up?" Sebastian extended his hand. "This is my fiancée, Kristan," he pointed to her.

"Nice to meet you both, your Mom has told me a lot of great things about you." Jonathan returned his handshake and held out his hand to Kristan.

"Hello," Kristan said nearly inaudibly.

"So, you guys are staying here tonight, right, I cooked — "

"Well, Mom actually, we're going out dancing tonight, and we're supposed to meet a friend of mine in about an hour."

Olivia hid her disappointment and wondered why she had expected anything different. She set the table anyway, and held back her urge to cuss at him.

"What time do you think you'll be back? Tomorrow I'd planned to make breakfast and then we can go over to the movies, see—"

"I'm not sure what time we'll be back tonight, but I know it'll be late. And tomorrow, we gotta head back to Little Rock so..."

Kristan was busy looking in her purse and rearranging the trash bags of clothes they brought in.

"Mom, can we do some laundry?" Sebastian started separating clothes on the kitchen floor, just outside the laundry room. "So Jonathan, how long you here for, man?"

Olivia stopped listening and tried to stop her emotions, blinking hard to keep the tears from falling, which didn't work. She helped herself to a plate of food, poured Dr. Pepper into her glass and sat down and ate. Jonathan followed suit.

"Till Monday, I fly out Tuesday morning."

"Too bad we won't get to spend more time with you," Sebastian peeked his head out of the laundry room for a split second. "Kristan, get you some food," he motioned.

Kristan did what she was told and sat down across from Jonathan at the square, bar-height dining room table and put a wing on her plate, then a teaspoon full of greens. Weird portions, the kind that made you think she didn't eat much but you could tell that wasn't the case by looking at her. She gathered her thin blond hair in her left hand, held it at the nape of her neck so it wouldn't waft as she moved.

Jonathan didn't say anything; he took Olivia's hand under the table, and stroked it.

They ate in silence, as Sebastian came out to the table and got some food and put it in a napkin.

"Hurry up Kristan, we gotta go," he took a bite of chicken.

"Oh, man Mom this is good. Leave the food out and I'll eat some when I get back later tonight."

"Thanks, I'm glad you like it."

After a few minutes of eating in silence, he kissed her on the cheek.

"Okay, we'll see you guys later," Sebastian motioned to Kristan. They went out the door into the garage. "I'll make sure to come in the side door, leave it unlocked like you used to Mom."

"Okay, 'bye."

And they were gone.

"You wanna talk about it?" Jonathan didn't know what to think.

"No, I really don't."

"Okay, but you know I'm here for you if you do, anytime."

Nodding, Olivia got up and put the food in Tupperware and stacked it in the refrigerator.

"Here, I'll load the dishwasher," Jonathan started putting plates in.

"I have a movie we can watch tonight. Have you seen *Babel*?"

———

Jonathan's visit was such a wonderful distraction; it was like she was in a different life. But during the next week, staff, students, community business people, and the Press, filed into the School of Business auditorium eager to participate in the Economic Summit, leaving standing room only. The President's Council, Arnie, Dan, and Renee sat in the front row. Faculty who could make a mid-July meeting time attended, but the majority of them weren't there. All the administrators were present, naturally, since they carry out a lot of unpleasant university work over the summer, while faculty are gone. But still, energy, hope, and excitement buzzed through the air as people believed in the possibility of a new positive direction for Western, even though Arnie's record so far was, well, not exactly stellar.

Patrick considered this to be a room in "his" building. He was moving around quickly with the tech folks to make sure all the equipment was functioning properly. Seething inside, he resented that no one had consulted him before scheduling this event. He brought up Arnie's presentation onto the computer, so that the screen had the Western State logo, with the words "July 15, 2008 Economic Summit" plastered across it. Patrick nodded to Arnie when he was finished with the set up.

Without any introduction, but checking to make sure the remote microphone was working, Arnie began. "Good morning. Can you hear me?"

"Yes, we can," some people reassured him, many of them nodding their heads without looking up from their papers.

"Thanks for coming to the First Annual Western State Economic Summit," he continued, sounding more like an emcee at a church picnic pie eating contest than a chief executive of an institution of higher education. It was middle of July in Roadims, Arkansas, yet he was wearing his black felt fedora hat, along with a heavy wool navy blue suit. He took his hat off and put it on the table next to the lectern, and rubbed his forehead, wiping the sweat off.

"Patrick, where are you Patrick?" he squinted around the room for him and continued, "I hope you got this thing set up right, I'm not a techie," he laughed and the crowd chuckled lightly. People turned around looking for the Dean. Patrick didn't make his whereabouts known, and nobody pointed him out. It was as if everyone knew there was this animosity between the two men.

Patrick's arrogance and reputation preceded him. Arnie was told that he was a Mr.-Know-It-All. In fact he had shown himself this way at the Dean's Council, the only place where Patrick and Arnie formally interacted in a public setting. It was Arnie's goal to drive home one point, to make sure everyone knew he, and only he, was boss. He additionally took a liking to publically embarrassing Patrick and his allegiance with Fontecillo every chance he could. Watching Arnie's verbal attacks on Patrick's loyalty to the former President was like watching Patrick get punched in the face with his hands tied behind his back.

"Well, we wanted to give you an update about the economic situation we're in at Western, and we'll be giving this Economic Summit again this afternoon for those who couldn't make it, for the Board of

Governors at our next meeting, and again in the fall when the faculty get back from being off this summer. I want to thank my financial team, Dr. Gruber, Mr. Boost, and Mr. Libson for their work on this presentation and our budgets, and their efforts in general with this institution. The Board of Governors are particularly grateful for them as well. I understand they operated in fear for a long time and that is no longer necessary."

Patrick thought this was bullshit staging. At least Luis had class; this guy was such an idiot. He inwardly panicked at the thought of having to work with this ass for the remainder of his time at Western.

"As you know Western has an International Mission and it achieved university standing in 2004 because that's what your former President wanted. Western arrived there after many years of being a junior college, then progressing into a liberal arts college with technical and professional education, such as business, nursing, and teaching degrees. We rely on several sources of revenue, the main ones being state appropriations and tuition, along with grants and so on." As Patrick looked at Arnie's slides, he noticed the numbers weren't right. Olivia was sitting in the row in front of him, and he tapped her shoulder. "Yes, I see it," she whispered over her shoulder.

Arnie clicked and a slide popped up showing the tuition history of the organization. "Until this year, 2008, we were free to increase tuition whenever we needed to, but when Dr. Fontecillo signed the ACHEIP agreement, that changed. We cannot increase tuition more than the area's cost of living, and you know that for Roadims that's not much. If we want to increase tuition by more than that, we have to get special permission from the CBHE, the Coordinating Board of Higher Education."

It wasn't that you ass. Patrick wanted to shout this but didn't. He also wondered if other people besides Olivia, who lifted her finger so that he would see she was aware, noticed the errors. It was the kind of propaganda that could go over easy if people weren't thinking.

"In addition, ACHEIP specifies that we need to provide evaluations of faculty and make them public, but that's an issue that Dan will handle in the fall." Arnie laughed, let this sink in, and there was silence in the room.

Patrick knew this would get under the professors' skins. If they hated anything, they hated course evaluations linked to their performance, and the idea of making them public was sure to irritate them. The President was purposely inciting friction, over a requirement in the law that held no threat for professors in regard to their promotion and tenure.

Arnie went on with a slide that graphed tuition and state appropriations. "Here you see that we have had declining appropriations from the state, and declining tuition. Western has the cheapest tuition in the state of Arkansas, but when the tuition was increased in 2004, the total revenue increased, even as enrollment decreased. Fearing another drop in enrollment, the decision was made—a wrong decision and I don't know why Fontcello allowed it—to decrease tuition in 2005, and as you can see, enrollment didn't increase, and tuition revenue decreased again. After several years of yo-yoing with tuition, the revenue has stabilized but the problem is still there: tuition lags behind other comparable institutions in the state, at least according to the financial team's estimates."

Patrick couldn't hold back any longer. "Arnie?"

"Yes, Patrick?"

"With all due respect Arnie, the reason that the tuition was changed was because the Board required it. We, the Dean's Council, the VP AA, Dr. McAllister, and President Fontecillo all recommended that tuition be increased." Patrick saw Renee nod her head.

"Thank you for that clarification, Patrick. I didn't know that, but will take this up with the financial team."

Of course you will, Patrick thought, you blame shifting moron. Patrick threw his pen down on his little arm-desk pull-out that each of the auditorium chairs had.

"Now, let's focus on the state. You can see that this line here, this shows the decline of state appropriation, and I'm told that that number is going to decline even further over the next several years, especially as we are in the worst Depression since the nineteen thirties." Arnie wiped his forehead again, rubbing his damp hand on his pants leg.

He clicked the next slide. "So here you can see the expenditures, graphed over time since two thousand four. You can see that they have been increasing, and if we overlay the revenues, as in the next slide, you will see that revenues are not keeping pace with expenditures, and math isn't my strong suit but I know numbers in red with brackets around them aren't good. You have been deficit spending since two thousand four, much of that expense coming from salaries, travel, and the installation of Banner." He clicked again, and the income statement and balance sheet stood on the screen, the bracketed red 'Total Loss' number seeming to jump off the screen and into the audiences' laps.

Even with this financial situation, the university had recently gone forward to sell bonds to build the new building, and their institutional rating was so low that the cost of the building was double what it was quoted. Why didn't they wait until things were more stable? Arnie could blame Luis all he wanted but Arnie was the one who pulled the trigger on the bond sale last month.

"Along with these problems, the institution doesn't have a strategic plan, never has, and there is little shared governance, historically. We have been tasked with putting together both of these by the HLC and our success at this will determine our accreditation status upon their interim visit in April two thousand eleven. So, Dan'll be responsible for putting together the strategic plan, and within that we'll incorporate a model of shared governance. We want to complete this by the end of this year. Are there any questions?"

Patrick thought Arnie had sufficiently torn down Luis, and believed Darnell would be happy with his initial, publicly-verbal, destruction of Luis' character. It was as if Arnie was tasked with depicting Luis as incompetent.

Unbeknownst to Patrick, or anyone else really, Darnell made sure he emphasized to Arnie that he would need to do this when he called asking him to apply for the position. Arnie agreed to do it as long as he was guaranteed the job for a minimum of seven years, regardless of what the written contract would say. He'd been trying for his first Presidential appointment for years, but his track record got in the way.

"You say there is a deficit, how big is it?" Gilbert Asner, a member of the Press who often covered campus stories, shouted out.

"It is difficult to say exactly but our cash reserves are low, and we're behind in maintenance on our facilities and infrastructure. We would like to have fifteen million in cash reserves but right now I think we have around two. Talk to Renee about that she's got the numbers." He inclined his head in her direction.

Arnie took a white hand kerchief out of his back pocket and blew his nose. He folded the handkerchief and wiped his eyes, folded it again, and wiped his sweaty forehead. He didn't turn away from the audience while he did this. When he was finished, he put the handkerchief back in his pocket, and took off his jacket and lay it on the table next to his hat. His shirt was soaked from underarm perspiration.

"Does the deficit take into account depreciation set-aside?" Francis, an accounting professor asked, without waiting for Arnie to acknowledge him.

"I don't know, but you can talk with Renee about any financial matter and she will be glad to answer your questions," he shook his head, looked up at the ceiling and rolled his eyes, demonstrating his frustration with this line of questioning.

"Is it reasonable to have a strategic plan in place so quickly? Aren't you going to include the community stakeholders and if so do you think it can be accomplished within six months?" Patrick challenged. Patrick knew this guy was in over his head. He also knew that he had to control Arnie, otherwise he wouldn't get to do the things he needed to do to move on with some kind of glory from this undecorated hell-hole.

Patrick sensed the bitter taste of imagined failure and it couldn't come to pass. He couldn't let it. Not with this clown.

"Sure, I do," he paced back and forth in front of the screen, hands in his pockets. 'No way Patrick' he thought, 'I'm not going to argue with you, you self-satisfied elitist. We'll see how you generate the audacity to challenge me like this in the future.'

"What are your plans for the university, what's your vision?" Kevin asked.

"Well, that's up to the Board, not me, and the first thing we have to do is get our financial house in order, and the strategic plan will help," Arnie scanned the faces in the room but didn't focus on anyone. "Any more questions?"

"Yeah, could we get a copy of the financial statements?" Francis wouldn't let it go.

"Sure, those are public record, you can get them from Renee's office. Just give her a call." When there were no more questions, he said, "Thank you for coming, please contact my secretary if you want to talk with me," and he picked up his hat and coat and went over to sit with the other members of his President's Council, as people filed out of the auditorium.

———

Olivia went up stairs to her office, right after Arnie's presentation and before she could get settled good, Patrick came in, took her keys out of the door lock, handed them to her and sat down in the chair, rocking it back and forth as usual.

"That was the second stanza of the 'Blame Luis' song, not an 'economic summit'," he said with his brows wrinkled. "Everything that's wrong with the university they can manufacture will be his fault. You know, I can't get anyone to either say yay or nay to my hiring new faculty, and I'm protecting my budget from them."

"Wow, have you talked with Dan? And why'd they put him in there as VP AA? You're better qualified." Olivia turned her chair around to face him, and sat down.

"Yeah, he doesn't have any power and you know Dan is a farmer, he just thinks we should work harder. He never bucks anything, just comes in at the crack of dawn, and stays until way late. I'm sure Darnell felt he would be easier to push around." Patrick put his left hand in his pants pocket.

"Hmm, maybe you should talk to Arnie?"

"No, no, we're dealing with station WDDW." He knew Olivia didn't understand what was happening. She was too married to the idea of this being a haven for her, which made her the perfect pawn in this new chess game. He had to be careful because everybody used Olivia to get what they wanted. She was smart, and only had one agenda: to research, write, travel with expenses paid, and publish. As long as she could do that, she would agree to do almost anything if she didn't sense it being unethical. He had to make sure she stayed on his side and prevent Arnie from moving her to his.

"What the hell is WDDW?" Olivia sighed. She crossed her arms and leaned back in her chair.

"What Darnell Douglas Wants," he laughed a little. "They don't ask the Dean's anything. Vincent took over for Dan, he says that they don't ask him anything, and the Dean of Information Technology, Caitlin, she said the same thing. They just sit around, Dan, Renee and Arnie, on Monday mornings in their President's Council meeting making each other feel good and not getting any input from anybody on critical decisions."

"Yeah, that's no way to lead an organization. Executive leadership has to take the input of the lower levels if it's to be healthy, or at least bought into. Why don't you go talk to Arnie? Maybe have lunch with him or invite him to your house for dinner? And do something about it besides complaining to me?"

Olivia was so naïve when it came to this, he thought.

"Uh-uh, I'm not getting in bed with that guy" he said laughing hard and rocking back and forth on the two legs of the chair. "The way

I figure it, we gotta keep our School of Business separate from them, I'm going to get my Advisory Board to apply some pressure, those are the folks in the community that have some clout. We have graduate courses to teach, and accreditations to get. You being the MBA Program Director will go a long way towards us remaining autonomous from the administration."

She took her eyes away from him, looking down at her shoes.

"Hey yeah, I see what you mean, definitely — of course — I'm gonna help out, I just wanna make sure that I'm not overloaded with running the graduate program and the Faculty Senate stuff."

Olivia wouldn't say no even if she wanted to.

"Yeah, I know. The first thing you oughta take up under New Business is the Shared Governance and strategic planning, along with budgeting. Faculty are left out of every decision, and this should be a university governed by faculty. If that were the case, we wouldn't be in the situation we're in now. The Faculty Senate is where these decisions need to be vetted through." He lowered his chair down to all fours. He'd drawn the mental picture so that Olivia could imagine a healthy institution, and give her something to invest in.

"Okay, then, I'll bring that up to the EC and then see what we wanna do with that. Our next meeting is not until after the semester starts."

He studied her face for a moment. "That's fine. Oh, so I hear you have a new book out? Congratulations. That's one of the best ways to stay current in your field."

"Thanks, yes, I do." She didn't like talking about her accomplishments, and she didn't tell Patrick because he would broadcast it out over the Internet to every disinterested member of the Roadims community.

"I heard from the International office that you did great things with our partners in France this summer. Weren't you at a conference presenting a paper too?"

"Yes, I was. And I'll thank you for signing my reimbursement forms, that trip cost a lot," she laughed, reached to her desk to get the file and handed him the forms. He signed them without hesitation, and gave them back to her. "I'll be here the majority of the day today, but then I'm going to be working from home for the rest of the summer, so send me an email or call my cell if you need me. I need to rest before the semester starts," she sighed.

"Sounds good, keep me posted if you hear anything," he got up from his chair, and saluted as he walked out the door.

"Will do, for sure."

Olivia got started working on the agenda for the first EC meeting and the first Faculty Senate meeting for August 2008. By around 4:30 she finished her work, turned off everything, and left for the Little Rock airport. With these tasks completed, her excitement grew as she focused on going to visit Jonathan for a week. Her bags were in the trunk of her car, and the house was all taken care of so she didn't have to go home to it to face the emptiness and loneliness thank God.

On the drive to the airport, her mind visited the pain she used to have about her life, her house, her son. She had conflicting feelings, loving being able to provide the house, but hating the memories of Sebastian not living up to her expectation in helping her with it. The cost of the house and the weight of the whole responsibility, but then there was a divine presence in it. And while she bought the house so she could feel some stability, give Sebastian a home after her divorce and losing the house in Grass Valley, now she felt this house shackled her to the ground. She spent thousands of dollars bringing the house up to par, and then there was the ice storm last winter. It was the worst ice storm in the history of southwest Arkansas, and when the trees snapped all night long sounding like military gunfire, it told her she was a fool. On top of the six inches of ice, eight inches of snow settled on the house. Sitting there alone in the living room watching television that night, she heard the loudest boom come from the attic. By the following spring with the first big rains, when she sat there in the same spot, she noticed water was streaming down the glass windows, inside the house. "No, it wasn't storm damage" the insurance adjuster said "but you do need a new roof, Ma'am." He could have told her to take ten thousand dollars and drop it over onto the railroad tracks it would have been the same difference.

Alone in the house most mornings she woke up — actually it was the middle of the night but she called it morning. Three-thirty, four, make coffee and cry. She would feel her family, how they only wanted her to pay to make up for the past. It was her younger sister who shouted "It's because of you that Daddy's dead." That accusation was finally voiced thirty-five years after he was murdered. Until then it was their perpetual elephant.

But no, her sisters didn't know about the sexual abuse, yet and still it was true they'd all been a victim of the violence. One therapist told her she needed to cut all ties with her family, that's how destructive they were. At the time, she couldn't imagine doing anything like that. Like trying to get a piece of corn kernel out of your teeth and just missing, she would then go on to mentally probe the spot that contained her ex husband Tyler. She didn't have anything against gays, but didn't want to be married to one. She felt deluded and betrayed by the divorce, him asking her for palimony, getting the woman-hating divorce attorney to make her out to be the villain. Next she wondered if the divorce was due to the massive loss of her life style when she became redundant. She relived the scene and asked herself why she had been so stupid.

She walked into Dick's office and Mallory was already there. Mallory was that person she could never have been. Cold, calculating, cutting. She had no compassion for anyone, focused only on the bottom line. She wore black pants suits, and gave lesbians a bad rap. Mallory sat with her computer and cell phone, was just as enmeshed with her boss as Olivia was with Shane. He'd say jump and she'd ask 'how high?'

"Hello Dick, Mallory," Olivia acknowledged both of them. Dick had taken over Shane's office. And while Shane was greedy and very egotistical, he always had people's best interest at heart. Dick was not that way.

"Hello Olivia," they both chimed without any affect. She knew this wasn't going to be good. With the recent sale of the company, her role as Chief Exeecutive Officer was undefined, she had no golden handcuffs, and no stock.

"You wanted to talk about this market analysis for a new profit center?" Olivia began.

"Yes, have a seat," Dick said. Olivia began her presentation, and all the while feeling sick to her stomach. But she continued, giving the highlights, and the revenue to be expected, the profits. Where the company should start, what the personnel needs would be, and so on. She explained how she could lead the project, handed them the document, professionally bound, with the charts, tables, and appendices.

"Olivia, we wanted to tell you," Mallory started as she handed the document over to her, "we wanted to tell you we are letting you go today. We have prepared this severance check for you, representing three months salary. We are happy to give it to you provided you sign this statement which basically says you won't sue us for terminating you because you're black and female." She traded her the paper with the legalese for the project plan. "After you sign it, we will give you the check." Olivia had never felt a knot so big in her throat, she could hardly swallow.

"Okay, you mean to tell me I give you a plan for earning three million dollars a year and you give me a severance check for fifty thousand dollars?" trying to keep the crack in her soul from letting her cry.

"Yes, that's right. Please clean out your office today before five, and let us have your keys," Mallory stated as if asking for someone to pass the potatoes at the dinner table while watching television. "We will call a company meeting in a half an hour and announce it to everyone." It was a Tuesday morning in June 2000. Olivia just got up and walked out of Dick's office.

After the staff meeting and all the tears, everyone saying it wasn't fair, that Olivia was the best person running the company, and by the time the fear hit them that they could be next, she finished packing her office into boxes. She made several trips from the office downstairs to the parking lot, some of her employees helping her load. Shane was gone. Patricia, David, all the top execs. They were no longer associated with New York. It was over. When she drove away from the building she pulled the car over and called Tyler. "I'm so, so sorry," he kept saying. She was scared, she cried spastically into the phone, tears and saliva getting all over, staining her silk blouse. They'd been married for less than three months. Just bought the house, and Sebastian was still in high school.

It was in during these mornings that she used to feel her grip on reality slip, and looked to the Lord to help, mainly asking to be let out of this life, but that prayer wasn't answered. The angels in the house led her to intense prayer and meditation, memorizing mantras to give her mind something to hold besides the past, allowed her to live in the present, to deny the desire to lay fetally. The angels reminded her of her purpose on Earth. She argued, and said the burden was too heavy. They soothed. She learned to bring down the light into her. By the time she needed to show up for class or a meeting on campus, she would have fought off the demonic beings that nearly crippled her along her veins and synapses.

"Oh m'God them was some *sad* days," she muttered as she noticed she was on the just a few miles from the exit for the airport. "Ain't nobody gonna send me there again, specially not these crazy folks here in Roadims it ain't that serious. I'm okay." She turned on the CD player and opened the sunroof. The flight was not until close to seven p.m. which she could easily make.

———

Jonathan was waiting for her when she got to baggage claim. He saw her through the glass, walking down the upper level towards the escalator that fed passengers down to the street. He couldn't believe she was coming to see him, and couldn't imagine why. But somehow he'd managed to say enough, to do enough, to keep her with him for the last year. Neither he nor his friends and family ever imagined he would attract such a woman, but they did figure he'd get someone by online dating since that was his life. That she was black was a different issue, but again, not surprising. One day he would tell her the truth, but for now he left it at their compatibility being based on what he'd written in his profile.

"Hello my darling," he kissed her on her lips.

"Hello love, it's so good to see you." She let go of her roller bag, and embraced him.

"Good flight?" He turned toward the door, trying to avoid hitting the people milling around.

"Yes, very good, nonstop, so no problem," she handed him her roller bag handle.

"Oh, sorry," he took the bag. "Well good. Hungry?"

"As usual, no food on the airplane, and the last I ate was lunch, central time. In & Out?"

"Works for me," they walked out of the terminal towards the car. He could smell her cologne, and he remembered he didn't shave and forgot to get a haircut. Oh well, he thought. He ran his fingers through his hair. Maybe I should have worn something besides shorts and a WWDC tee-shirt, and these sneakers, he thought.

"So, how's everything?" they stood behind his Range Rover, while he opened the cargo door, put her bag in the back.

"Things are fine, crazy stuff at work, you know, new president?"

"Oh, yeah, I read *The Globe*, saw his comments, boy," he whistled, "that's bad."

"Right, it's weird, and at the same time, Patrick asked me to be the MBA Program Director, in anticipation of me taking over the Deanship for the school."

"Great, that's fantastic. How's that gonna impact you?"

"Not sure yet, but we'll see," Olivia walked from the back of the Range Rover to the front passenger door.

He was nervous about the new position making her less available. "Maybe you can get them to open an office in San Diego?" he asked, his voice carrying the impossibility of it.

"Ha! That would be funny."

They got in the car.

"You could work at one of the universities here," the parking radar beeped as Jonathan backed out. He mentally kicked himself for saying this. She'd already dropped the hint that she had no intention of moving without getting married first.

"Well, maybe, but the competition is fierce to get a tenured job at any of 'em, and I'm not young anymore, at least by their standards." Changing the subject, she asked "What are we doing this week, anything special?"

"No, I don't have anything planned. I figure we could go to the Apple store, look around. I have to work tomorrow and Friday, and of course next week."

"Hey, no worries, we'll just play it by ear. The week is gonna fly by." Olivia settled down in the car while he navigated San Diego using his built-in GPS. It didn't take long for them to get to In & Out.

They ordered, and sat outside. Olivia was grateful to be back in southern California. It was warm, the air was crisp, not humid, and it was beautiful. But mainly it was home. There were people, all different types of people, close enough to touch. Nobody looked like farmers or inbred relatives, and she didn't feel afraid.

After they ate their hamburgers, they drove to his house, holding hands in the car. Jonathan chatted nonstop about the latest technology, Olivia half listened. She was tired, it was way past her bedtime, and she suspected he was covering up for his nervousness, remembering he was afraid that spending seven days with her at his house was going to be a disaster.

"You got coffee makin's at home?"

"Oh, damn it I knew I forgot to do something!" He ran his fingers through his hair again, grimaced a little. "I can stop at Vons."

"Okay."

"Sorry, I completely forgot."

Actually, Olivia figured he'd gotten caught up in playing *World of Warcraft* and lost track of time, though he didn't admit this.

"Not a problem, I'm just glad I asked, the morning will be something we don't wanna see without me and my coffee," she joked a little, trying to cover up the disappointment.

When they finally arrived at the house, it was close to 11:30 p.m., she felt that dizziness that jet lag brings as they got out of the car. He opened the garage door, turned off the alarm and was holding the door open for her with his back.

"Love, could you get my bag?"

"Oh, yeah, sure." He got the bag out of the cargo area, brought it in. She followed him.

"I need a shower and I'm dead tired. I hope you don't mind."

"No not at all. You can take a shower in the upstairs guest bathroom, you know, the Orange and Red bedroom." He put his keys in the hall drawer.

"Okay," she started following him up the stairs. "Oh, can you bring my bag?"

He turned around and got her bag, carrying it all the way up. She went upstairs, stopped on the middle level, put the cream in the fridge, the coffee on the counter. Then she went up the last flight of stairs to the master bedroom. This week she would sleep with him, in spite of his fear of them sleeping in the same bed.

———————

That next morning they let the day take them, it was beautiful and Olivia wanted to be outside.

"Why don't we head over to La Jolla for breakfast, then go over to UTC and take a look at the Apple store? Does that sound good?"

"Absolutely. Gosh, it's so great to be able to do that and enjoy this weather," she was happier than she'd been in a long time.

University Town Centre was about five miles up the freeway from the restaurant in La Jolla, where they'd had scones and espresso in the sidewalk café style Olivia loved. When they finished, they headed right up to the mall, going along scenic La Jolla Village Drive instead of taking the highway. Olivia gawked at her surroundings.

Once they got there, Jonathan parked the car and they headed down to the open shopping area.

"We have to stand in line? Wow, well let's go over and look in the jewelry store for a minute," he said, steering her out of the crowd of people waiting to get into the Apple store.

Olivia got excited. Maybe he's going to get an engagement ring, she thought, her heart pounded and she found it hard to breathe.

"Let's look at wedding rings," motioning her to the case and they walked over to it.

"May I help you?" The salesclerk asked. She was tall, and very sexy looking, her blouse showing all her cleavage.

Jonathan stared at the clerk's chest, but managed to say, "We're browsing, thanks. Which one do you like Olivia?"

She pretended she didn't notice Jonathan's fixation with the clerk and looked at the rings in the case, "I like these," pointing to the bands with diamonds.

"Umm. Those are nice." After standing there for a few beats he said, "Oh, no, no, don't think I'm getting ready to ask you, to propose, oh, no, this is not a surprise engagement. Let's go back to the Apple store and see what the line looks like."

Olivia felt heat rising from her armpits, and the sweat of anger forming on her forehead. All he'd talked about for the last three months was getting married, at least when he wasn't talking about his jet setting lifestyle. Oh yes, he used to have an airplane. Yes, he used to fly first class to London on a whim. Yes, he commuted back and forth to Asia. Oh, yes, he loved the top quality name brands. Yes, he wrote a check to the IRS for $250,000 one year.

"Right, far be it for you to backpeddle."

"I'm not back peddling."

"What do you call it then? Evil?"

They walked silently back to the Apple store. Olivia wished she could just leave and go home, Jonathan was disappointed that she was too smart to put up with his games. They'd worked on countless women over the years but not with Olivia. She called him on his bullshit each and every time.

"We'd like an iPhone," he told the geeky looking chubby guy at the Apple store, and they went back and forth talking between gigabytes and data plans. "Honey, you have AT&T now, right?"

"Yes, I do." And within the next few minutes, he handed her his first gift that cost more than $40. She figured, from his point of view, it was as close to an engagement ring that he was capable of giving.

"Here you go."

"Jonathan, thank you." She kissed him on the cheek. "This is very sweet."

"You'd been sayin' you wanted one and I wasn't sure if you were gonna buy it yourself but I'm glad to buy it for you."

"Thank you, I really appreciate it." Olivia smiled, avoided telling him that it was mighty white of him to do that for her, especially since he always bragged about his money.

'What's two hundred dollars to you? Mr. I'm-having-a-house-built, trips to London just cause you can, travel in first class because you're platinum for life, paid cash for a brand new Range Rover.' He thought back on his telephone conversations with her over the last year. He must look like an idiot to her, or at the very least, she had to suspect he was not exactly forthcoming with the truth.

"Not a problem. Let's go. We can go look around the mall for dresses for the trip to New York next month." They started walking again. Jonathan grabbed Olivia's hand and snuck a peek at her. He never dated anyone like this before. He was used to cheap stupid women who were impressed with his lies who he could easily manipulate. In his opinion women wanted his money, his babies, and tried to control him through sex. He'd learned long ago how use them to his benefit. But Olivia was different. She read him like a book so when she looked at him he felt exposed and vulnerable.

"Yes, that sounds like a good idea," she took his hand and remembered he still needed to buy their airline tickets for the trip, and wondered how long he would wait before he did that. He'd invited her to his uncle's wedding, but really he was taking her to meet his family but he couldn't say that. 'Whatever,' she thought. It didn't matter.

Olivia lay in bed that Monday morning when he left her alone while he went to work. Saturday had been great—except for the wedding ring thing—and Sunday was wonderful, full of leisurely hiking in Mission Trails, after shopping at REI for hiking stuff for her. And he paid for everything. Well, except for the ticket to visit him. But he did buy the tickets for their trip to New York, and she was going to meet him in Kansas City and they would fly together. She started crying. How could she deserve all of this? Such a wealthy man, emotionally stable and so well adjusted? It was the first time for her and for a moment she wanted to run. "God, am I ever going to get over this?" she asked.

In the shower a few minutes later, she reviewed her relationship

Jonathan, looking at his inventory of strengths and weaknesses, the way they got along, their commonalities. True, he was odd, and proclaimed to be atheist, but Olivia determined that she was going to marry Jonathan, no matter how long it took him to get up the nerve to ask. He'd been honest with her, he had no children, and no ex-wives. Most importantly, he wasn't ever going to be the type that would hit her. Olivia laughed as she thought about this, as these weren't attributes out of the ordinary. They were what any normal person should expect from a loving relationship.

When she got back to Roadims, she'd show off her iPhone and make Patrick and Nancy jealous, and get ready for the semester to start.

*When you find
yourself in a hole,
stop digging.*
*— Will Rogers*

# Bored of the Governors

*August 2008, Fall Semester*

"Olivia, this is Arnie."

"Oh… uh, hi, how are you?"

"Fine, fine. Listen, I need you to cancel the meeting scheduled for Thursday morning."

"You mean the community meeting on the International Mission?" Olivia couldn't believe this, and tried to understand.

"Yeah, that's it. I won't be put on the spot, forced to answer stupid questions from a bunch of misinformed faculty, paraded around like their freak in a circus. If people don't like the fact that the international budget was cut, too bad. I'm President of this univ'rsty and the Board of Governor's is behind me. I take orders from them, not the faculty."

"We talked about this meeting last week when we met, and you were okay with it then. What happened?" Olivia tried to understand why he was scared.

"I know, but now I think it's the faculty trying to exert their power with that shared governance. They didn't have shared governance for the last twenty-five years and now all a sudden they think they can run this institution. What're they *thinking*?"

Olivia remembered how she'd seen him contort his face worse than an ugly baby's when he said 'thinking.'

Even though she wanted to, she couldn't tell him that Patrick was behind the faculty uproar. She thought about her other colleagues and friends who were recruited to protest the cuts. "Faculty want a voice in decisions, but that's not to say they want to run the university."

She had a nine a.m. class she would be late if she didn't wrap this call up. Damn it, why did I answer, she thought? But ever since she became MBA Program Director, she had a phone with caller ID on her desk. She saw it was him and picked up the phone instinctively.

"Whose that Anne Paeth person? I hear she's drumming up angst, getting students to write letters, and who is it, Chris over in your area? I hear he's gone and got Brown and Schiller's CEO to come over. What do they think they're doing?"

Olivia decided that Arnie wasn't mad; he was crazy.

The first thing he set out to do was cut the international budget before the beginning of the academic year. A move like this would tear at the heart of the institution, going a long way to tarnish Luis. Making Olivia cancel the meeting would discredit the faculty. The meeting was agreed upon in the first Faculty Senate Meeting, back in August, and Olivia suspected he waited purposely until today to call her. He had no intention of attending in the first place.

"This is the kind of thing normal universities do when there needs to be discussion," she tried to remain professional, but felt there was something wrong, like why did she have to tell him this was normal university stuff? He was the President, she was only an elected faculty member leading the senate for one academic year.

"Do you think they're mad because I didn't give any raises this year?"

Olivia thought how could people be mad at that if it was the financial team's decision not to give raises? That's what he had always said up to this point. Pompous idiot.

"People are upset about that yes, since it was the first time in thirty years that no raise was given. They're used to at least a one percent increase." Olivia hoped her voice would carry her disdain for his insulting her intelligence.

Olivia had a line of faculty at her door from all across campus the first week of the semester when they found out they weren't getting any kind of raise. They were even more P.O.ed when they found out about the international budget not being *cut*, but rather *re-appropriated* to the football team. Oh they were hot all right. These issues were raised in the first senate meeting, which went down in history as the longest senate meeting ever held at Western State.

"What's wrong with them? Don't they know that Luis ran this organization into the ground, nearly putting it into *bankruptcy*? I think we should hold the Economic Summit for the faculty."

Olivia's stomach felt as if he'd kneed her personally each time he put Luis down. But even putting that aside, she wondered how could he consider this a solution? It wasn't a "summit" but more like a vaudeville show that people, except the performers, had no interest in. He was the one who wasn't 'getting' it. Faculty treated him like the Emperor in his new suit.

Besides, any budget meeting would be a day late and a dollar short, Olivia thought, "we" ain't gonna do nothin'. He'd promised to hold that during September, but didn't.

"Why don't you do the presentation at the Faculty Senate meeting next Monday?"

"That's a good idea, I'll have Renee set it up." He yawned demonstrating clearly that he couldn't have cared less.

Olivia heard his phone ringing.

"Hold on a minute, Olivia." He pushed his hold button.

"Hey Darnell, how's it going?"

"Fine, how you doin' this *fine* morning?"

"Great, great. Carlotta's having lunch today with your wife, I take it."

Yes, I do believe that's the case. Did you cancel that International meeting?" He held a cheap cigar between his teeth.

"I'm on the phone with the Faculty Senate President right now."

"Oh the pretty black thing? She reminds me of my favorite one when I was growing up." He puffed hard on his cigar.

"Yeah, the one you like." Arnie chuckled.

"She's in close with Patrick, so watch her."

"Don't worry, got her where I want her, we'll win her over. Hey, lemme call you back."

He pushed the hold button, "Sorry Olivia, that was Darnell."

"No problem. So. I'll put you and the Economic Summit on the agenda for Monday then." She picked up from where they left off and felt a glimmer of victory.

"Yeah, that's fine. Well, you email the faculty, let them know International meeting is cancelled and I'll let you know when I want to reschedule." He waited.

Olivia didn't protest. "Will do. See you later." Olivia hung up the phone. She heard him saying good-bye as she put the receiver back. She had about twelve minutes before class started, but wanted to get sending the email over with.

*Dear Colleagues:*

*I trust your Monday is off to a good start, and you had a restful weekend.*

*Arnie Williams has asked that we reschedule the International meeting calendared for Thursday at 10 a.m. in Roger's Hall. A new date and time has not been announced yet.*

*Please note that he will give the "Economic Summit" presentation as part of his remarks at the October 6, 2008 Faculty Senate meeting.*

*Warm regards,*

*Olivia*

She forwarded the message to Andrea, the secretary for the Vice President of Academic Affairs, asking her to blast it to the faculty.

Andrea replied by email with her chipper "You bet!" and the next thing she saw was the email in her inbox "From Olivia Clarke to All Faculty." It took two seconds after that for the replies to start coming in, but she closed her email without opening any, logged off the computer, got her stuff for class and left. Before leaving the faculty offices suite, she looked over at Nancy's, right next door to hers, and remembered she needed to talk to her. It would have to wait; Nancy was never in before ten, even though she was supposed to be in by eight. "Whatever" she said out loud, turning to go to teach her class.

Students and faculty moved quickly through the halls, typical for a Monday morning. Half-way down the stairs to her class, she felt it, remembering she'd forgotten to go to the bathroom. She went into her classroom, put her stuff down on the table and went to the restroom, knowing there was no way she could hold it for an hour. Back in her classroom, she saw that she picked up the wrong set of papers, and grabbed them, ran back upstairs quickly to her office. As she was switching the files, the phone was ringing, it was Arnie, but this time she didn't pick up.

By the end of the day, the wave of anger from cancelling the meeting had reached tsunami proportions all over campus and the community. Faculty emailed, called, or physically intruded on Olivia's space voicing their discontent.

Anne Paeth called and yelled, "Why didn't you tell him he couldn't cancel?"

"How would I tell the university President he can't cancel?" Olivia was hurt by the verbal attack.

"Just tell him!" Anne shouted into the receiver. Olivia was discovering that faculty were rude and blistering when they were crossed. Their verbal attacks felt like praises compared to the emailed ones—they were ten times worse.

"Why don't you call him, see what he says?" It was hard for Olivia to believe what she was hearing. Anne and Olivia struck up a nice conversation at the President's thank-the-EC-for-their-hard-work-dinner last May. She and Kevin were in the same area, and Anne's husband lived in Chicago, so they empathized with each other having to travel to see their significant others. She commuted to Chicago, and gave Olivia ideas about how she and Jonathan would handle this long distance thing.

"That's not a bad idea." Anne's voice was back to conversational tone, the one Olivia knew and cared about.

"Call me back, let me know what he says." Olivia hoped this would show Anne she wasn't the bad guy, that she was on the faculty's side.

"Have you heard from Harmony about this?" Everybody on campus knew that Harmony and Olivia were close.

"No, I haven't. But you're right, maybe she should be the one to call, since she's the Chair of the Welfare Committee." Olivia hated putting Harmony in the hot seat. But by definition, chairing the Faculty Welfare Committee meant she *volunteered* for it.

"I'll call Williams, and let you know. Thanks Olivia."

Within minutes, Anne called back.

"He said he'd hold the meeting as scheduled," Anne sounded excited.

"Oh really?" Olivia felt a glimmer of hope that she just might make both him and the faculty happy.

"Yes, he said he was going to call you in a few minutes, so I'll let you go. Tell Jonathan I said hello. When are you going to New York?" Olivia had forgotten that she told her about his.

"That was last weekend. It was great fun. I met his family—his parents—and we went to Niagra falls." Olivia's voice was soft with love.

"Somebody's getting married soon?" Anne questioned playfully.

"Seems like it won't be long now, he keeps talking about marriage, got a trip planned for Santa Fe over the Fall Break in October. I can't wait!"

"That'll be fun. At least something good came out of this fiasco bullshit when Renee was Interim. We're going to Orlando for the break."

"Well, you have a nice time. Listen, let me go so I can call Arnie." Olivia looked at the clock, 5:12 P.M., she would initiate the call rather than wait for him.

"Okay, thanks again Olivia."

"Not a problem, see you soon."

Olivia took a deep breath as she pressed the button down on the phone, released it and listened for the dial tone. He answered on the first ring.

"Hi Olivia, what are you doing here at this time a day; faculty go home at noon, don't they?" He didn't laugh when he said that, and Olivia decided to consider the source. She wondered if he knew how irritating he was or if he was just stupid is as stupid does.

"Hello, I don't know, but I just got off the phone with Anne—"

"Yeah, she's a piece of work. She and Harmony were driving Estelle crazy with rescheduling the meeting, but anyway, we decided, the President's Council, to go ahead with the meeting.

"Great, that's wonderful."

"So, you'll be there right?"

"Yes, I plan to be." Olivia had no intention of coming. She would figure an escape route before then. The only reason she had agreed to be the Faculty Senate President was to work with Luis. But now, he was gone and she really wanted to step down.

"Good. You sit with me, Renee and Dan."

Olivia felt a knot in her stomach. If she sat with him and the President's Council, that would give a clear message to the faculty that she was siding with them.

"Okay, when I get there I'll look for you." Olivia planted an opening, giving herself room to sit somewhere else if she changed her mind.

"You won't miss us. We'll be down front."

"Are you going to send an email letting everyone know the meeting's back on?" Olivia changed the subject.

"I think Anne and Harmony said they would do that." Arnie coughed loudly into the phone, and blew his nose. "Excuse me, my allergies are acting up."

"No worries. I'll send an email out letting people know, and whatever they decide to do will be up to them." Olivia figured it was her reputation that was important.

"Whatever you wanna do, fine with me." He sniffed.

"Okay, thanks, I should get going. I'll see you Thursday."

"Oh hey, are you going to Rotary on Thursday?"

"Yes, I believe so." Olivia grimaced, rolled her eyes up to the ceiling, shook her left hand back and forth in frustration next to her ear, and stood up. Gotta get off da phone witdis muthafucka! she shouted inside.

"Let's go together. We can leave right after the International meeting. I'll drive."

Caught in his web, but not bitten, Olivia said, "Oh, that's nice of you to offer." She kept her distance.

"Since we're going to the same place, no need to take two cars, and the university pays for mine," he laughed.

"Thanks Arnie. I'll see you Thursday then."

"'Night, have a nice evening." Arnie snorted before he hung up.

Olivia sat there for a few minutes in the silence, rubbing her face trying to wipe off the tired like day old make up, then rested her hand over her mouth and propped her chin in her palm. Papers needed to be graded, she still needed to put together her midterms for four classes, her MBA program inbox had 97 unread messages from prospective students who wanted information. The message light was flashing on her phone. Why did he want her on *his* side?

"Your mailbox is full," the automated secretary said when she entered her password. She listened to the messages, mostly students wanting information on the program, or students wanting to let her know they wouldn't make it to class that morning, with the time stamp being after class was over. She played the phone tag game well, and so she returned all the calls at 5:40, leaving voicemails.

Her calendar had meetings scheduled all day the next day, Strategic Planning at seven thirty a.m., IRB at ten; Sustainability at one p.m., Honors Committee at three, Core Curriculum at four. She hadn't read a single word of any of the thick packets of materials stacked on the corner of her desk for any of the meetings. She gathered them up and took them with her so she could read them when she got home.

*October 2008*

"Did you see the article in *The Globe*?" Nancy stopped at Olivia's office, leaned on the door jam.

"No, I haven't seen it yet, why?"

"Apparently we're under a hiring freeze, and faculty extras for teaching online and writing intensive courses were cut," Nancy stood there holding her hand out, admiring her French manicure, and then adjusted her rings.

Olivia rubbed her neck between her shoulder blades. "Okay, let me take a look at it online. I think I have the link in an email from Jim."

"Wanna grab some lunch? Bunch of us are going to the Mexican place."

"Nah, I can't, I have a one o'clock on Wednesdays, so I need to get ready for that." Olivia couldn't stand the food at the Mexican restaurant anyway. They didn't know what "Mexican food" was around there.

"We can bring you something back if you want," Nancy tried to help. She saw Olivia was under lots of strain.

"Thanks, but I think I'm just gonna go around the corner and get a sandwich from Jimmy John's. Their drive thru is fast, and I can eat while I prepare for class. Let's get together this afternoon and talk. You got time around four?"

They were overdue for their meeting. Last week completely got away from them. She often needed Olivia's advice to help her run the department.

"Okay, that works. Just come on in when you're ready." Nancy walked away, "we'll see you later," as she went.

Olivia turned to her computer, opened the email from Jim and clicked on the article's link.

*Wednesday, October 8, 2008 1:15 a.m. .... Dr. Williams, President of Western State University told* The Globe *last night that he, at the direction of the Board of Governors', instituted a hiring freeze for all non essential positions, and positions would not be filled when staff or faculty separated from the university. All position requests would have to have full Board approval before recruiting. Faculty replacements, when they occurred, would mainly be filled with adjuncts. He also said that incremental faculty income above their contracts from teaching writing intensive or online courses was eliminated, effective immediately. "I think this is something we have needed to do for a long time," Williams said. Dr. Harmony Schwab, Professor of Anthropology speaking for the Faculty Welfare Committee spoke to us about these changes. "Wow, how does he or the Board think we should operate the campus? Faculty pay is already set at eighty-five percent of middle range, and they need the incremental pay to make up for already lagging salaries," she explained.*

*Western State recently cut its International budget, and....*

Olivia clicked the article closed, and got up to go get her sandwich. What a mess, she wished Arnie would shut his trap. Why couldn't he, or why didn't the Board get any input for these decisions? Why in the world would he air dirty laundry in the newspaper? She felt embarrassed like she used to when her parents fought. The first rule of branding was control of public relations. Obviously he was following George W. Bush tactics instead.

A week earlier they had the International Budget meeting but Arnie didn't show up. He "was called away at the last minute for a meeting in Washington DC," Estelle's email to the campus lied. Olivia didn't go to the meeting, and she was grateful she didn't have to ride with him to Rotary. Faculty felt betrayed that he wasn't there to hear their concerns, and they were even more pissed off at the Economic Summit he presented at the Faculty Senate meeting two days before.

"What does he think, that we're as ignorant as he is?" Anne ignited the firecracker as soon as the administrators left the senate meeting room.

"We want him to tell us why the budget was cut, why the depreciation is included in the deficit, and we want to be included on budget decisions," that was Eric.

"Who can we ask to present the financial information so it's not smoke and mirrors?" Ree piped up.

"Francis Jones up in accounting can do it for us," Claire volunteered.

"Olivia, why don't you ask him to do it for us? He's in your building," Wes suggested. The senators were nodding their heads at this idea.

"Sure, I'll ask him to do a Special Presentation at the November meeting, before the Administrators are excused?"

Someone quickly moved and seconded the idea, and it carried.

"I'll put it on the Agenda for next month," Olivia wrote the item down on her agenda. She felt good about faculty involvement, and she'd be able to tell Patrick that progress was being made.

"Welcome to Jimmy John's may I take your order?" the speaker in the drive thru asked.

Olivia arrived at the restaurant by autopilot.

"Uh, I'll have the Totally Tuna, no sprouts, chips and a lemonade," she spoke to the speaker, distracted with thinking about what she needed to do. When she got back to the office, she'd schedule the meeting with Arnie to discuss Francis's upcoming presentation. She snapped her fingers, "Oh, yeah, the next Board of Governors' meeting is coming up too. Third Fridays get here way too soon," she said to herself. Oh God, the last meeting was a joke. The Board members consisted of retail business owner, one doctor from Roadims, five lawyers from Roadims, Springfield, Smithville, and Langer. Darnell served as a Judge in Smithville, a contract gig through his law practice. He and Judith

Townsend struck up a conversation at the last meeting. She was as much of a Southern Belle as he was Boss Hog personified.

"Darnell, thanks for sending those hoodlums to jail, they nearly *destroyed* one of our gas stations." She turned to Olivia, who was sitting next to her, "We own several convenience stores around town, in addition to the House Beautiful store on Lenard Street." She had the sound of someone who knew that work was for 'those people' and certainly she wasn't one of them.

"Oh, you own that? I love that store! You have such nice things in there."

"You're welcome, they ain't gittin away wit it as long as I'm judge a Jackson County," Darnell bragged, laughing and his stomach shaking as he put a fork full of roast pork in his mouth.

"I'm so glad we can rely on you, Darnell," Judith flirted with him, her southern drawl matched her southern bell demeanor. She was dressed like Olivia was accustomed to, leather-soled pumps, wool-lined blue narrow pinstriped and tailored business skirt suit, and understated pearls. Her jet black permed hair caught the light from the art gallery where they routinely had these luncheons, and her nails were tastefully done.

"Let me know the next time you're in the store, I mean it now," she told Olivia as if she was talking to her hired house girl. Judith took out her mirror, replaced her red lipstick, and powdered her nose.

"Thanks, I will." Of course Olivia had no intention of doing such a thing, she didn't want her throwing her no bones.

They finished lunch, and the meeting moved to the "Television Room" where the formal board meeting was tape recorded for later playback on the local cable station.

"That'll be six dollars and twenty-seven cents," the clerk interrupted Olivia. "You doing okay today, Dr. Clarke?"

Olivia gave the clerk her debit card. She swiped it, and gave Olivia her card, receipt and white bag of food. "Thanks, yeah, I'm good Megan." They held each other's gaze for a second.

"You're welcome. Here's your drink. See you next time!"

Olivia took it, "You certainly will." Olivia put the bag of food on the seat next to her, popped the wrapper off the straw and stuck it in the lid of the cup. She drank, realizing she hadn't had anything to drink all day.

---

After her class was over, Olivia sat down to prepare for her meeting with Nancy.

"Knock, knock, knock," Francis said, smiling at her, standing in her doorway.

"Don't take up all her time, she still has to meet with me!" Nancy came up beside Francis, and pinched his arm.

"I won't, Nancy, I'll make sure I leave her plenty of time for you," Francis's stomach pooched out above and below his belt. His voice reminded Olivia of a smooth jazz radio announcer.

"You better!" Nancy click-clacked away and on down the hall.

Francis was way up on Olivia's list; not many people were. He was straightforward, and spoke his mind without being abrasive or inconsiderate. Slightly balding and about six-two, his clothes were always pressed, he wore a tie every day, and carried a leather brief case. His agenda was the same no matter whom he was talking to: what's the right thing to do. Francis was from St. Louis, and had that east coast flair. That could explain why he never implied racism towards Olivia, or why he was always professional in his conversation. He was a safe place to go to for advice and brainstorming. Being a CPA, the head of the accounting department, and a partner in his own private firm gave Olivia that unfamiliar feeling, like she was dealing with a sane individual.

Francis came in to Olivia's office and closed the door. They had a very private conversation about the situation on campus, and he confided that the Faculty Welfare Committee was hearing bad things about the Administration, and how the Board was acting beyond its constitutional jurisdiction making decisions that violated the *Faculty Handbook* with hiring and firing faculty, making program changes. Olivia knew this was the case, but felt completely powerless to do anything about it directly. Her solution, she told him, was to involve the faculty and make changes to or institute missing procedures for faculty governance. In essence, she explained, because the faculty had been so silent for so long, many procedures that were needed in communicating with the Administration were missing.

Francis believed hers was a good strategy, because "it codified changes and issues," he said.

She asked him if he would do an economic analysis presentation at the Faculty Senate meeting, using language faculty would understand, along with simplified financial statements. He agreed to, gladly he said. He knew he could get the information he needed on enrollment from Delores in the Assessment Office, turnover information from human resources, and budget information from Renee's office. Olivia told him she wanted a draft of the presentation a week before the senate meeting so she could run it by the President. Francis thought that was an outstanding idea, and he asked if she would make the final presentation available for public view. Yes, she would, she said.

"Thanks for coming by, Francis." Olivia opened her office door and yelled, "Nancy, you in there?"

"You're welcome Liv." He said, "She's all yours, Nancy!" poking his head into Nancy's office. "Oh, she's not there."

"Not surprising," Olivia waved at Francis as he walked away. If she hurried out, she would miss Nancy for the night.

---

They *rendez-voused* in the Albuquerque Airport. Her plane arrived from Little Rock late Thursday night. She made a promise to herself that she was not going to talk about work during her time with Jonathan. Well, she had to concede, as much as she didn't trust Renee, that the Fall Break *was* a nice perk.

Jonathan's plane came in after hers. Since she was already in the gate area, she just waited for him. God, this was great, she closed her eyes for a moment to think about him. All of the obvious stuff was checked off, like not gay, not addicted, not violent, and had a bachelor's degree. But she also knew lots of times people hid things, or more to the point, she ignored red flags until she had to start waiving white ones. Since her surgery, she understood the decaying hip was as a manifestation of her lifetime fear of being who she was, and not knowing how to be. She'd decided to put herself out there and attract the love of her life full knowing she couldn't live without him.

Some people said you could live alone and be happy — what a crock of crap.

A few months into this decision, she went ahead and conceded to herself that in moving to Roadims she'd moved to a foreign country. She didn't speak the local language, wasn't familiar with the customs, was the perpetual outsider. People halfway respected her professionally, sometimes, and socially they tolerated her. The eligible and desirable men that she would consider were all white. But you would have thought Olivia was some kind of exhibit in a show for the kind of play she got. It was a good thing she didn't take it personal.

Online dating was all the rage, so why not? She tried it before, a couple of years ago, but no body of substance turned up. This time, though, Jonathan did. Her main concern of course was to make sure he was one hundred-and eighty degrees from her father.

As a child, in Philly they sat the five of them for dinner at the dining room table. Dad always sat at the head, in the formal antique dining room with sideboards and a hutch, a cabinet full of fine china.

"Didn't I tell you not to scrape your teeth on the fork? Use your lips around the fork, darn it. Keep your elbows off the table, and I don't want to see that left hand unless you're cutting meat. You're not getting up from here till you eat everything on your plate," her Dad ruled in perfectly enunciated English.

Olivia looked at the plate of food: potatoes, which she hated; some kind of meat she couldn't chew, lima beans—yuck. You could hear a pin drop, Olivia not knowing if her father was a fuse ready to blow. Last time he was drunk she didn't know it, and misread the situation.

All she said was, "I have to go to the bathroom."

He stood up in a rage, and yelled, "All you do is eat, sleep and go to the bathroom, all of you, you get on my nerves!"

"Oh Lord," you could barely hear her mother pleading under her breath. He got up and before they could blink, he grabbed the bowl of potatoes off the table and threw it into the china cabinet. The antique glass shattered, her mother screamed. Her older sister Karen started crying.

He backed up, away from the table, walked over to the china cabinet, "Raul, please don't, those are my mother's things," and he looked directly at her and held her gaze for a beat, looked away into the distance, reached into the cabinet where the glass had broken and in one sweep sent all the dishes on one shelf flying, crashing to the floor.

Olivia got up from the table and ran up the waxed hardwood stairs, sixteen steps in all, taking every two stairs and holding onto the banister.

She looked over her shoulder, and she saw her mother grab her baby sister out the high chair, didn't bother to loosen the tray and the chair crashed onto the hardwood floor, food splattering, she handed her to Karen, and they followed Olivia. The dining room table chairs tumbled to the floor as they stood up and tried to stop time to save themselves. Upstairs the girls sat on the landing.

"Raul, please stop, please—" and right then, first another crash of dishes, then the sound of flesh on flesh.

Karen and Olivia swayed like autistic children, and Olivia prayed he wouldn't come to her room later that night. She wondered how she could get to the phone without him seeing. There was no way.

"Flight number 209 from San Diego, now arriving at gate seventeen," the loud speaker bellowed so loudly that it startled her. Olivia was already sitting in the gate area, and she stood up when she saw him coming.

"Hi sweetheart." She reached for him.

"Hello my love. How are you," he kissed her deeply.

"Fine. A little hungry — "

"I know a great place. The Loredo Hotel where we're staying has a wonderful restaurant. You're gonna love it." He grabbed her hand.

"I'm sure I will," Olivia hadn't decided what she should tell him about her father. She told Tyler everything, and she now thought that was a mistake in hindsight, he used the knowledge and manipulated Olivia's emotions worse than her mother did. Sometimes Olivia thought he married her out of pity.

Jonathan knew Olivia's father had been killed. She left out her constant need of expecting men to settle in her favor the argument of whether his death was her fault or not. Her father made his choices, she reminded herself. With her newfound resolve to find the love of her life, she practiced pretending her father's abuse didn't affect her anymore. What did they call that? "Re-parenting" the therapist said. It seemed to work, after all, look how far she'd come.

After checking into The Larado Hotel, he took Olivia to their suite. Inside, there was a wide mouthed, crystal vase containing a bouquet of twenty-four red long-stemmed roses sitting on the table next to the couch. "Oh my God, Jonathan, this is beautiful." She felt like she'd died and gone to heaven.

"I'm glad you like it. I made dinner reservations for tomorrow night, but for this evening we're having a massage, down in the hotel spa, followed by room service. Is that okay with you?" He waltzed her around the three rooms, and next to the balcony overlooking the pool with views of mesas.

"Yes, of course that's great!"

She held him tight, eyes closed, savoring the moment. Finally she'd gotten here. In a split second she remembered Tyler, and how he had wined and dined her, and showered her with gifts. She felt tricked in the end, when she found out he was seeing other men. But she pushed these memories out of focus.

"Okay, so let's get unpacked — we're going to be here for three days. You want this half of the dresser?" He pointed.

"It doesn't matter to me honey, whichever one is fine with me."

Jonathan loaded his clothes into the drawers, and so did Olivia. He came up behind her and kissed her, and she responded.

"What time is the massage?" Olivia asked playfully.

"Oh, right, we better get going," laughed and moved over to the closet, taking down two white robes. He handed her one.

Jonathan led her down to the elevator, holding her hand. His belly was full of butterflies, and he needed a restroom. Looking at Olivia's contented expression made him feel so manly, something he'd never felt before. At the same time, he felt like an imposter because this wasn't his lifestyle. It would have been just as fine with him to stay at the Days Inn, and he never got massages like Olivia did. But she looked at him with such adoration, love and affection, he didn't dare tell her any of this.

"Honey, are you ready?"

"Yes, I'm ready. It looks like it's going to rain." Olivia looked out over the balcony.

"Yeah, it does, but that's okay. We're going to be inside for dinner and the performance." Jonathan checked his jacket pocket for the ring.

Olivia was ecstatic. The whole weekend had been fabulous, this was their last day in Santa Fe. She loved the fact that he was taking her to a ballet performance and she didn't have to do the work of finding or planning anything.

That evening after dinner, he said, "Olivia, let's go down the hall for a moment, I want to look in the gift shop before we head out to the performance."

"Okay, that's fine with me."

Just before the gift shop, Jonathan said, "Oh, look, let's duck in here, and see what they're doing." It was the hotel's grand ballroom.

"Oh, okay," Olivia was confused, but she went in without asking.

Inside, the room was set up with a stage and two round white table-clothed tables with chairs. There were waiters standing nearby holding silver trays with champagne flutes.

"Come this way," Jonathan led Olivia to the tables. He pulled a chair out for her, and helped her with her jacket.

One of the wait staff came and whisked away the jackets. Jonathan sat down.

"We're not going out to a performance, Olivia. I've arranged for the Santa Fe Ballet to perform here for you."

A waiter came over and placed the glasses on the table, along with a bucket and a bottle of champagne. As he was finishing, another waiter came over and placed silver platters of cheese and dessert tarts, and small plates with silver place settings.

"Thank you," Jonathan said to the waiters. They moved into the back area of the room.

"Jonathan, this is awesome, I've never had anyone do anything like this for me before. Wow, I don't know what to say."

Jonathan pushed back from the table, and reached into his sport jacket pocket and kneeled down on the floor next to Olivia.

"Will you marry me, Olivia?" He opened the ring box.

Immediately tears welled up in her eyes, her hands covering her mouth.

"Yes, yes, of course, my love."

He took her hand and put the ring on her finger, and kissed her hand. She pulled him up from the floor, and hugged him tightly.

"I love you, Jonathan."

As she was hugging him, three couples of professional ballet dancers started performing classical ballet to music by Chopin, as the lights dimmed.

*December 2008*

In her studio she faced the aloneness. The space was expansive, completing one huge dream she had in owning a house with her own studio space. The view from the back window she put in that went from nearly the ceiling to the floor was awesome, and the woods in back of her house were blanketed with snow. It was Christmastime, without the Christmas trauma.

"Sweet serenity thank you God," she breathed in, and turned on the space heaters. She had been in the house for four years, but it had been over three years since she danced, only a year since the surgery. Her first ballet lesson was over 30 years ago, when she checked a book out of the library that had ballet positions in it. It was one of the books she checked out the day her father was shot. She tasted the powdery bitter grains of disappointment in her mouth at having the studio but not being able to perform anymore as she started doing her *demi plies*. Dancing alone through the pain, she got to the *grande battements*, and did a little bit of center work. Her hip hurt, she didn't have the range of motion she used to. She tried a little choreography, but then she just sat down on the floor to stretch. She cried.

Ballet used to be meditative for her, she could escape into it and leave the world behind. It wasn't so easy now. She leaned forward, straddled her legs, and tried to put her breasts on the floor. Pain shot up her inner thighs and down her lower back but she allowed it to take her back to her love for performing. Preparing, learning choreography, rehearsing, unlearning, costumes, and makeup. Dancing in tune and in sync with other dancers, all the while hogging the stage. She savored the memories and smiled. Yes, she could get across the stage with one *tombe pas de bourre glissade pas de chat* combo. It made her feel like she was flying free. Yes, she could do *cabrioles* and *fouttees, sauté passé glissade grande jette pique passé contre temps tour jete.* And then the performances, with the after parties and flowers, oh so much fun. Her last performance featured her in two solos *en Pointe*, with newspaper photos. She wasn't sure if it was her dancing or her skin that attracted reader's attention. Did black people do ballet?

Nobody in her family had ever come to see her perform. Well, yeah, Sebastian had seen her in Grass Valley, but not here. He was in the audience that last night here, along with his girlfriend.

He came back stage, and said "Mom, we'll meet you at home in an hour, okay? Then we can go to dinner," he yelled over the other dancers and the fans, the back stage area was jam-packed.

"Okay, I'll see you there." Olivia was so glad he was there, he gave her that sense of grounding you need when you been away from your people, your culture, for too long.

"Great job, Mom. You so good, hey, my mutha," he hugged her.

"Thank you sweetie. Thanks for coming."

"You ought to wear that kind of make up all the time, Mom. You look great!"

"Oh, go on now," Olivia blushed, batting her fake eyelashes and whipping her fake hair back off her shoulders. Her skimpy costume only had black fishnet stockings, and a black felt halter-top leotard, her last piece was *All that Jazz* and it was a sultry sexy *Pointe* number. She felt like she shouldn't be looking like that in front of her son.

"A-ight then, I'll check," he walked away. He was so handsome, standing now at about six-one, he was dressed to impress, going to school at Western, working part time. She was proud of him.

But, by the time she got home, the phone was ringing as she walked in the door. She picked up the note.

*Dear Mom,*

*You were great! But I decided to go over to Chris' house and I hope
you have a good time tonight.*

*Love, S.*

She lay the note back down as she looked at the caller ID. It was
local, but law enforcement. Oh no, now what, she thought, knew in her
inner most core, that this was not going to be good. "Why couldn't he
just wait? Just wait five minutes for me to get home?" she screamed in
desperation and the sound echoed through the empty house. It was the
same question she asked him many a time when he was growing up, like
when he left his keys at home and was locked out. "Why couldn't you
wait until I got home rather than kick the door in? It wasn't going to be
that long."

"This is Olivia," she answered finally.

"Mom, Mom, I've been in a head-on collision and the car rolled
over in the ditch, there were two other people in the other car, they're
going to the hospital. The ambulance and cops are here and they want to
take me to Freeman ER," he was yelling and crying.

"What? Where are you? What's going on?"

"I've been in a car accident and I hit two people, I was going fast
around the curve on Oak Boulevard."

"You're on Oak Boulevard?"

"Yeah, Oak Boulevard."

"Okay, first, Sebastian just stay there. Put the officer on and I'll be
there in a second."

"Hello, Ma'am? This is Officer Doyle. Your son has been in a head
on collision. He needs medical care immediately."

"Officer Doyle, where are you?"

"Oak Boulevard and the curve in the road just past O'hara Road.
You'll see all the vehicles when you arrive. Where are you?"

"I'm in Newhall Springs."

"Okay, well just come down El Camino Road." He was explaining driving directions but Olivia wasn't listening. She knew where it was, and knew that Sebastian had had the accident there because he was going too fucking fast, and was probably under the influence.

"I'm on my way," Olivia breathed when he was finished giving directions. And so, she put her purse down, changed from her ballet warm-ups that she wore after performances into jeans and a sweatshirt. Crying as she changed her clothes, she wondered what she was going to have to do to get him out of her life.

She kneeled at the side of her bed for a moment.

"Now he don't got no car; how's he gonna get to work or school? I ain't gonna be the one chaufferin' him around and be at his beck and call, knowing full well that somewhere in his subconscious, Sebastian wants just that. To be completely dependent on me. But I am tired, Lord, I'm tired, empty, and I ain't got no more to give."

She changed her clothes as the thrill of the performance took a back door out of her mind.

At the scene of the accident, there were ambulances, police cars, and fire trucks. Her heart sank as she contemplated the possibility of Sebastian having killed someone in this accident, and she wondered too if he had paid his insurance. She parked and got out.

"Ma'am, I'm going to have to ask you to park your vehicle somewhere else—"

"Are you Officer Doyle?"

"No Ma'am, I'm not, but—"

"I'm the mother of one of the drivers."

"Oh, Ma'am I'm so sorry, please step this way. What's your son or daughter's name?"

"Sebastian, he was driving the Ford Escort...." she trailed off in shock at the scene. She'd only bought this car less than six months ago, and still owed eight thousand dollars.

"Oh, yes, he's here, on this stretcher" he pointed, "waiting for paramedics to take him to the hospital."

"What's wrong with him?" Olivia was scared to hear the answer.

"We don't know yet Ma'am but as routine handling, all victims are immobilized and placed on the stretchers until we can evaluate them at the hospital. In collisions like this, we have to minimize the trauma, and plan for the injuries that may be internal."

"Oh, okay, can you take me to him?"

"Yes, of course Ma'am, right this way," he led Olivia up the road, past the wrecks, the lights were swirling red, gold, blue, and you could hear radio conversations going on.

"Let me ask you Officer... " Olivia hesitated in formulating the question. "Is anyone dead?"

"No Ma'am, no fatalities." Olivia let out a deep sigh of relief.

They approached a body stretched out, across the width of the ditch, strapped down with the head immobilized, a neck brace on, all manner of medical equipment hooked onto the body and stretcher gurney.

"Sebastian, is that you?"

"Mom, I'm so sorry, I'm so sorry, I didn't mean to do it. I am so sorry. I was going too fast around the curve and I was thinking I should slow down but I was mad and so I didn't, I'm so sorry." He was crying.

"Sebastian honey, that's okay. No one is dead and let's see how you are. Tell me, where do you hurt?"

"I don't hurt anywhere except on my arm."

"No where?"

"No, just my left arm hurts."

"He has a bad burn from the air bag on his left arm, a second degree burn from what I could tell," the officer said. "But he needs to go to the emergency room to be evaluated, because we often see situations like this where the victim is in shock and can't feel anything and they think they're okay." Olivia looked from the officer to Sebastian, and back a couple of times.

"Honey, do you think you can stand up?"

"Yes, I can, I can walk."

"Honey, if they take you to the emergency room that's going to cost a lot of money. What I think would be better is if we get you out of this, and go over to urgent care and have the doctors look at you. That way it won't be so expensive. But if you are hurt, and you really think you need to, we can go to the emergency room, and I will take you rather than have the ambulance take you."

"Okay, that's fine you can take me," he agreed.

"Officer, can you please untie him from this stretcher?"

"Yes Ma'am." And so he disappeared off into the chaos and talked to a paramedic. The paramedic then came over, asked Sebastian some questions about his pain, tried to convince him to take the ambulance to the hospital, Sebastian refused.

"Okay, well then I have to have you sign a release, and I need your phone number so we can get a hold of you, and the officers will want to contact you as well."

"That's fine." Sebastian signed the form. And they walked back to the car feeling their way in the dark.

"Mom, I'm so sorry," he said.

"That's okay, let's go see about that burn."


They got back from the hospital. Olivia fixed him a sandwich, got him a Dr. Pepper out of the fridge.

"Why don't you rest for the night now, and in the morning we can see what we need to do next?"

"How am I going to get to work, how am I going to get to school?" Sebastian talked with his mouth full.

"Well, I don't know but I'm sure you'll figure it out. I can take you sometimes. Maybe you can get rides — "

"How am I supposed to get around without a car?" He yelled at her.

"I don't know what you are going to do, but it'll work out," she said with a soft voice, trying to keep him from losing his temper. "I'm tired now, Sebastian, I need to go to bed so I'll see you in the morning. It's around midnight and I'm way past my bedtime. I usually go to bed at ten," trying to make light of the situation.

"Okay, Mom, see you tomorrow."

"You rest now, here's some Advil, should help some."

"Thanks, Mom."

A couple of weeks, maybe a month later, she told him you need to get your own spot. Twenty-three you old enough. You bringin' Kristan over here and she sleep here all night with you. You ain't payin' me no rent, ain't savin', smokin' reefer and cigarettes, leavin' butts on my driveway. You gotta go.

When he didn't move and didn't change, she had some people come over and move his stuff out her house to a storage unit. She went up on his job and gave him the address and key. My house ain't a option fo you no more, she told him and walked out. He didn't think she would.

The quiet of the studio lulled her. Arms outstretched with hands on her ankles, she noticed her *Pointe* shoe ribbons waving to her from the basket at the other end of the studio. "God, I miss this."

Tomorrow she was leaving for San Diego to spend a month with her husband. The wedding in Eureka Springs was nice and quiet, just the two of them. Olivia didn't want to have a big wedding because she didn't want to figure out where to draw the line on who to invite or where to have the wedding. Jonathan didn't want to either. It would have been an elopement if Olivia had her way but she mentioned it to Nancy. After that, the whole entire school knew. Not long after that, all of Roadims knew.

"You're getting married? Wait, you're engaged and you didn't tell me? So are you leaving?" Nancy nearly screamed.

"Yes he proposed when we went to Santa Fe for Fall Break. And, no, no, we're thinking we're going to live here, especially since now I'm supposed to be the next Dean." Olivia did ask Patrick if she should start looking for another job after Arnie came on board. He reassured her she was not in danger of losing her job, and he was "putting her name in" as his successor.

"Good, I can't function withoutcha."

Olivia loved Jonathan deeply, and he loved her. Since Brock's death, Olivia was a little uncomfortable talking about the relationship with Harmony. She did talk to Kathy about it whenever she got a minute with her. Kathy was so busy with keeping up her house and working now, she barely had time to talk on the phone, and she hardly ever came over. Of course, sexual relationships were not a topic of discussion for her and Kevin.

But a couple weeks ago in Philadelphia, Olivia had a wonderful time with Xena. They'd agreed to meet there, since Olivia was presenting a paper at an academic conference in New York, and Xena had a board meeting in DC.

"Girl, the stars aligned this time for us, didn't they?" Xena said as she embraced Olivia.

"Yeah, they did," Olivia hugged her tight, "it's so good to see you."

"What's that on your finger?"

"I'm engaged. Jonathan asked me a couple weeks ago."

"And you just now telling me? Oh, my God, lemme see that ring!" Xena grabbed Olivia's hand and held it up.

"I'm sorry, I just didn't think it was important."

"Tell me, tell me, how did it happen, what did he do?"

Olivia told Xena all about it.

"Have you set a date yet?"

"Yeah, probably Thanksgiving weekend."

"Wow, that's only a month away. You sure?"

"I'm positive," Olivia assured Xena.

"What kind of wedding are you gonna have? Do you have a dress already?"

"Most likely we'll elope and I'm not getting a dress, it's not my first wedding." Olivia felt ashamed at this fact.

"But you'll regret it if you don't, Livia. At least get a new dress."

"I'll think about it. But we may have a big reception, and invite all the people from the university, family, friends…." Olivia trailed off. She was tired just thinking about it.

"That sounds like a good idea, let me know as soon as you know the date. I'll fly into where ever you're having it. And don't forget to get a registry."

"Really? You think so?"

"Yeah, get a registry. Matter fact, get a couple."

Olivia nodded her head at Xena's advice. Maybe she was right. Up to till then, Olivia just figured it was no big deal. "I'll think about it," was all she could manage.

They spent the day talking, shopping, and being together. Olivia had that feeling of being at home while she was in Xena's presence, and she didn't think about the university.

Olivia got up from the floor, turned off the space heaters and lights, and went inside the main house to pack. Time spent with Jonathan was exactly what she needed to give her an overdue and cherished escape from the stark reality of Roadims.

*You yourself,*
*as much as anybody in the entire universe,*
*deserve your love and affection.*
*—The Buddha*

# Stepping Down

*Spring 2009*

Kathy came over to Olivia's house early on the morning of the anniversary of Brock's death. Harmony decided she wanted to go to his gravesite, so she left the day before driving to Chicago.

Olivia and Kathy sat in the kitchen and drank coffee, talking about the weather, Kathy's grand children in Illinois, and Thomas. Olivia liked Kathy because she didn't read from a smeared political agenda scribbled in her hand. It was regular conversation between fallen socialites.

"Me and Thomas we're moving to be closer to the grand kids, probably by the summer, depending on this one job I'm hoping I get. But we're going, either way. We can't stay here, with the economy and everything." Kathy took a sip of her coffee. "Olivia, where's the cream, this coffee, I forgot, you like it real strong."

"Here, it's right here," Olivia pointed to the counter top next to the coffee pot., and waited for her to pour her cream. "Well, I guess I should tell you. I got married."

Kathy nearly spit out her coffee. "You bee-ATCH! Why didn't you tell me I woulda at least sent a card! I don't believe you." Olivia was so secretive. She never wanted her private life discussed, and she swore Kathy to secrecy about everything. It made Kathy have to think before she gossiped.

"Yeah, I know, but I didn't want to make a big deal about it." Olivia didn't want it in the newspapers and she didn't want people thinking she was going to leave. That wasn't her intention at all.

Kathy told her she'd run into Renee at the Country Club. Olivia felt her stomach sink. Kathy didn't tell her that Renee was thinking of resigning. Up until her conversation with Renee, she thought Olivia was knit-picking Arnie. Kathy'd met Arnie at a friend's house, the owner of O'Brien's Furniture Stores in Langer, who Thomas used to work for before he sold the firm to that Canadian company. To Kathy, Arnie seemed nice enough. She did notice he drank quite a bit, and the way he talked to Carlotta. She wouldn't have put up with it. But when Renee told her he was hell on wheels and walked around intimidating her staff and the other administrators, Kathy started to think maybe Olivia was right, and she changed her tune. Apparently he told Renee what he wanted, and if she protested he'd punish her by telling her he would say that it was she who made all the financial and budget recommendations. Renee said he was a hundred times worse than Luis and most days she wished he was still there. Kathy had asked her about the Board and why they didn't do anything.

Renee laughed, "The *Board* doesn't do anything, *Darnell* calls the shots and they're so scared of him they do what he wants."

Kathy studied the articles in *The Globe* like they were holy scripture, the most recent one she remembered, said he'd cut a child care program that the campus community used, and the men's soccer team. Then he changed his mind on the childcare program, saying "staff miscalculated the loss it produced before they suggested it be cut." She asked Renee about it and she told her "It was all him and Darnell. They didn't ask staff for any analysis or anything, just went in and cut. The after the fact analysis on the daycare center showed it made a profit, so they put it back." Kathy decided not to bring any of this up to Olivia.

"So how's your marriage gonna affect you being Dean?" Kathy hipped herself up on the barstool.

"Jonathan and I talked about it, and he's moving here. You know that's been a dream of mine anyway, to find a husband who isn't threatened by my success so I keep my tenured job." Olivia stretched her neck to look out the kitchen window to the street, the thick glistening snow cover mesmerized her. "Did you park in the drive way?"

"No, I walked over. I need the exercise what with this last storm we had. Course you wouldn't know about that being that you were in *California*." Kathy pulled her sweatshirt away from her boobs and let it pop back to her chest a couple of times. "Hot flash," she said, and then fanned herself.

"Don't even start that. I know, another ice storm, and I was thinking it wouldn't happen two years in a row. But at least I got my trees taken care of."

"That's a relief. Did I tell you Thomas got a job?"

"Now who's the bitch?"

"Right, we'll see how long he lasts. It's like he can't get motivated. He's had two jobs since your surgery, and hasn't kept either one of them.. That's why I said 'Screw it, we may as well move to Illinois.' You have a good time in California? I know you did."

Kathy missed living in California where she met Thomas twenty years ago. He told her if she married him she wouldn't have to work. She followed him out to Arkansas when he got that VP job back in the early nineties. Now look at her, she supporting him at sixty-six, savings disappearing faster than you could swing at and miss a fly. She felt like a fool.

"California was California," Olivia looked at Kathy in the eye, knowing she didn't have to say anything else.

"Okay, I'm leaving now. I hope you don't just MOVE OUT without telling me!" Kathy walked over to the dishwasher and put her cup in. Olivia walked her to the door.

"Love you Kathy."

"Love you too even if you are a bitch," As Kathy was leaving they hugged, promised to be in touch. Kathy knew Olivia well enough that, even if Olivia didn't know it yet, Olivia was gone. The university prostituted itself when it divorced Luis and married Darnell. Olivia would not be able to tolerate it and still look in the mirror.

Monday morning, she passed Francis and Chris in the hall, standing having a cup of coffee, "Have you seen Patrick yet?" Chris' face looked troubled.

"No, not yet, why?"

"I'll come talk to you in a minute."

Francis just stood there, he seemed paler than usual.

She got to her office at about 8:30 to be ready for her 9:00 office hour. This semester she had an administrative leave for being Faculty Senate President, so she only had two classes. This wasn't a codified compensation for the position, but since it was precedent, she got it.

As Chair of the Committee on Committees, she drafted and submitted the senate-approved Resolution of getting the course reduction privilege added to the *Faculty Handbook* to the President's Council. Arnie denied it. The memo from Dan Fogerty said it was the prerogative of the VP AA to fund the course reduction and since it was a budgetary issue, they preferred to evaluate it each year. Translation: if they liked you they would give it to you. Olivia thought it was total bullshit like every other nickel and dime ounce of flesh they took out of faculty. A course reduction cost them at best $1,800 a year, as that's what they had to pay for another faculty member to take a course overload. Rumor had it they were going to cut summer school pay, so that it depended on enrollment and salary rather than give folks seven percent of their salary for teaching one class. People taught two classes usually to make up the loss of the already below eighty-five percent of the market's average salaries. Olivia was sick of her intelligence being insulted.

Patrick was waiting for her when she turned the corner down the hall to her office. He stood with his weight on the left leg, with his hands clasped behind his back, Patrick's characteristic stance when he was waiting.

"I resigned as Dean, effective June 30th." As Olivia opened her office door, he leaned against the wall, crossed his left leg over his right foot, resting it on his toe, left hand in his pocket.

"What?" Olivia couldn't believe what she was hearing. What would that mean now to her and the Deanship?

He'd just come from Arnie's office, where Arnie'd told him he was "not going to be paraded in front of your advisory board like I'm a jack ass. Who do you think you are?"

Patrick told him that it was his "Advisory Board that suggested you get a different approach to the Strategic Planning process. You can't do it the way you were planning and keep credibility in the community." Patrick kept his distance like he kept his distance from rattlesnakes. He knew he was a fly in Arnie's ointment.

"Yeah, well I'm the President of this University and I report to the Board of Governors, not your piss ass make pretend Advisory Board."

"Fine, I just wanted to tell you that I'm stepping down as Dean, effective at the end of this contract." Patrick looked at him because he knew that Arnie, as much as he despised him, needed him to stay in the position. "We don't have anyone qualified to take over for me either." It was quite arrogant of Patrick, and he knew it.

"So what do you suggest?"

"You could go out to national search, but unless you're going to pay them at market rates, you won't get anybody. In that case you could appoint an Interim Dean."

Patrick didn't care what he did, as long as he got to retire in August 2010. Stepping down and going back to teaching would give him the contract he needed to do that. His eldest son was already in college, and the younger boy would go in a year. There was no disappointing Jane, either. She had to have the upper class life, and if Patrick was impoverished, well he couldn't bear the thought.

He saw the writing on the wall, the pending implosion of the School of Business and if he stepped down before it came to pass, he couldn't be blamed for it. The faculty were lazy about publishing and teaching. The few who were productive would soon find that they were not going to get anything except intrinsic satisfaction, especially since the "Moratorium on Travel" was set. The university wasn't reimbursing any faculty travel. Oh come on! Everyone knew people got reimbursed when Arnie said they should. Patrick couldn't give any incentives or punishments. How could he be expected to lead the school with no resources? Arnie had taken over fundraising, requiring it all to be done through his office. As Dean, it was a major function of his job. Patrick already had no say over his budget, having to go to the VP AA like a little boy for every little thing. In fact, after Luis left, Patrick had no idea how large his budget was, or what happened to money that came in ear marked for the School of Business, or whether his budgeted allocations for faculty positions were shifted to other areas of the campus. He did know that the money was not being used to his benefit. It vanished into some black hole he could never find, and they denied ever existed.

"Patrick, who do you recommend? Olivia?"

"I think several faculty have aspirations for the position, but none of them are qualified, so I don't have any specific recommendations."

The two men looked at each other and they both understood they shared a very intimate moment. They were the only two who knew that their souls were composed of nothing but desperate greed. It was an ugly, embarrassing awareness that neither of them intended to expose, and certainly couldn't hold in their conscious minds for long in front of another human being.

Patrick repeated to Olivia, "I stepped down as Dean, effective June 30."

Olivia motioned him to come into her office but before they could sit down, Francis came up with a piece of paper.

"Have you seen this email?" He handed it to Patrick.

That vindictive asshole, Patrick thought. He didn't say anything to Francis, just handed the document to Olivia.

It was the first time Olivia saw any inkling of anger coming from Francis in the entire five years she worked with him.

"Wow, can he just fire a professor without talking to you about it first, Patrick?" Olivia's heart was beating fast.

"He could have at least talked to me about it before he fired a professor in my department teaching a class with fifty-five students in it. The class starts tomorrow for God's sake!" Francis took the email back from Olivia.

"What are you going to do?" Olivia looked at Francis, her brow furrowed.

"This is why I'm stepping down as Dean. I can't get my positions filled, I can't—" he trailed off. Patrick looked defeated. He sat down in his chair in Olivia's office, shoulders slumped, heart full of bitter resentment.

The game he played with Luis he'd lost when he was fired, he painfully conceded to himself. He had pegged his pace to the beat of Luis' retirement, which had the Board not gone crazy, would have coincided with his own. The new childlike game of cops and robbers he played with Arnie kept him off balance. It was complete with lying, bullying, cheating, and not playing by the rules. All he'd worked for was blown. He wasn't going to leave in glory, ride off in the sunset with Jane in a white BMW and a fat retirement check to a new prestigious position.

All the jobs he applied for resulted in the 'thanks, you have great qualifications but you're not good enough' letters. He hadn't counted on a worldwide financial meltdown just at the time of his exit, either. Patrick did count on the accomplishments he needed to make at the School of Business, but they fell like sand slipping through his fingers away from him just as he had grasped for them. He hated that he failed to consider the political players more carefully, a strategic blunder he could only lament. And now, the Dean also realized there was a gap in his employment contracts, and if they weren't renewed, he would lose his entire retirement. Since he was tenured, he felt the jeopardy diminish with the idea of a teaching contract. Stepping down as Dean, Patrick could also indirectly signal the Board and let them know things weren't good. Maybe that would get their attention.

"Francis," Patrick pulled himself together, for a moment, "let's call a Department Head meeting for 10 A.M. in the Dean's Conference room. I'll be right over to your office."

"Good idea," Francis walked away.

"How was California?"

"Great, had a nice time. Relaxing. Thanks for sending the boys over to rake the leaves while I was gone. I mailed them a check. Did you have a good holiday?"

"Yes, it was nice. My step-children and grandchildren came down from Kansas City, and Thousand Oaks, out by you, we had a house full." He clasped his fingers together, rested his hands in his lap, crossed his legs at the ankle, and adjusted his butt on the edge of the chair. "I drank a lot," he laughed, but then he felt self-conscious, remembering Olivia never drank. She also held meditation groups on campus. He racked his brain to remember what religion she was. He couldn't think of it.

Olivia ignored his drinking comment, "Great, sounds like you had a fun time with family. Oh, I got your emails about going to Dean's conferences. I'm looking forward to it. Jonathan is excited about it too. We're planning to set up our lives so I can be here, and so can he."

Patrick got up and closed the door.

"I don't know who is going to be the Dean." He stared past her, looking out the window.

"What? I thought you were stepping down in 2010, not 2009." Olivia couldn't believe what she was hearing. "Did you tell Arnie you wanted me to take your place, that you would take over the MBA Program and teach? How am I going to get up to speed by July 1?" Patrick told her a couple of months ago that it would be him changing places with her if he didn't get another job. Her head was spinning at the ramifications. "Did you at least recommend me?"

"Yes I did," Patrick smiled.

Olivia didn't believe him. After a moment of sensing that, knowing he was lying, she said "Listen, I've got to get ready for my meetings with Dan and Arnie, and I still need to get my syllabi copied for my classes. So, I'll come see you a little later. I know you need to go talk to Francis." She put her purse in the bottom file drawer next to her desk.

Patrick got up to leave, "Hey, do you have some meditation websites you can send me?"

"Sure, I'll email you a couple links, right now, you'll have them when you get to your office." Yes, you definitely need some spiritual guidance, but you need more than some website links, she thought. Sitting down, she turned to her computer and he walked out.

---

She was almost to the door and thought she was going to avoid talking to him. The Rotary meeting had just ended. This week it was held in the St. John's Hospital conference room, different from the usual location at the Country Club. She was putting on her coat when Arnie walked up.

"Olivia, hey, how are you? How's California?" All he could see when he looked at Olivia was Patrick.

"Fine, fine, I had a nice time."

He didn't care about California, or the fact that she married a white guy, or that she was commuting, or anything like that. What he cared about was making sure he did what he set out to do, tearing down the façade of this university, taking it back to being a regional college, if not a junior college. "What's going on in your department, what are you people *thinking*?" His face was red and twisted from anger.

Olivia felt his blow, but didn't want to cause a scene. "What do you mean?"

Arnie didn't say anything. He stared at her, grinding his teeth, his jaw bones moving.

"What do you mean?" she repeated.

"Who do you people think you are sending over the memo saying you want to talk to me about my decision to let Ryan Burns go? You don't know what you're doing, and you don't get to call the shots. We don't need to get your approval to let anyone go."

"That's not something I'm involved in. I think that was the department heads, following your directive to talk with you and the President's Council if they have concerns. And they are concerned about the way Ryan was fired right before classes started with no warning." Olivia took the risk of telling him the truth, and tried not to show she was scared. She wrapped her scarf around her neck, took her gloves out of her pocket.

He stepped up to her. "Don't fuck with me. You tell them that. So I'll see you at our meeting tomorrow? What's tomorrow, Friday?"


Olivia remembered this feeling from a long time ago, when she had only asked for something she wanted.

"Could I have some more rice — please?" Olivia asked.

"Got damn it you don't need no more rice, no more food at all!" her father yelled.

"Raul, please — "

"Don't 'please' me. She needs to eat more rice like she needs a hole in her head look at her!" he raged.

"I know but it's just a phase," her mother begged, and with that he picked up the bowl of rice and flung it across the room.

"Oh, Lord, not again," her mother said, breathing heavily.

He got up and hit her mother so hard she fell with the chair when it tumbled.

Instinctively, Karen and Olivia moved from the table and pulled Faith into the living room.

"Stop Daddy, stop!" Olivia yelled. "You said you weren't going to hit Mom anymore, you promised and you just went back on your word!"

And for a second there was silence and stillness. As if he was observing himself, he looked at his hands, looked at his wife, turned and looked at his children. He walked away from the table, away from the dining room and to the coat closet across from it in the living room.

He opened the door and got his coat, "I'm going out," and left without saying goodbye.

They huddled together for a few minutes, shaking, wanting to make sure the storm had passed.

"Let's get this rice and stuff cleaned up, Karen, get Faith's bath going," and Karen obeyed.

Her mother brought her hand to her cheek, swollen and bloody. She went to the refrigerator, took out some ice trays. She ran the water over the ice trays, twisted them and popped out the cubes. Made an ice pack with a dishcloth and sat down in the chair.

"Oh Lord," she sighed, shook her head, held the ice pack to her face.

Bang! Bang! BANG! The noise got louder and louder.

"What in the world?" her mother wondered out loud.

Another bang, another, and another. Next, a corner of a piece of metal pierced the door. It shook on its hinges, the deadbolt vibrated, the knob reacted to each hit. More metal emerged until the door was fully broken, the inside of the apartment exposed to the stairwell. He stood there, holding the tire iron and changing base in his right hand.

"Get in the bedroom all of you," he ordered. They cried, whimpered, sat down on the floor. "I'm going to kill all of you tonight," and Raul grabbed his wife by the arm and pushed her.

"Karen, Olivia, Faith, come in here."

The three girls marched into his bedroom and stood at the foot of the bed.

"You love your Daddy?"

They didn't answer.

"You love your Daddy?" he asked again, and this time he stood up and took off his leather belt, sliding it from the loops. His pants were open and unzipped already.

"Yes," they said in unison, starting to cry again.

"Good, now go on and sit down on the couch, and don't move till I tell you to, or I'm going to beat your behind." They turned on their heels, and ran quickly out of the room so he couldn't hit them with the belt on their backs.

Olivia peeked around the corner. She saw her mother when she went to the bathroom and watched her father go to the bedroom closet and get his gun and put it under his pillow. When her mother came out of the bathroom, he was sitting on the edge of the bed pretending he hadn't moved.

"You girls come on back in here, now." They went, like lambs to a slaughter.

"Sit down on the foot of the bed, and Joanna, you don't move a muscle I'll be back in a minute," and he got up and went to the hall bathroom. Blood was coming out of her mother's ear.

Olivia whispered "Mom, Mom there's a gun under the pillow!" She didn't say anything, like just looked at her in disbelief, shaking her head with furrowed eyebrows and bruised face. "Mom, there's a gun under the pillow, on his side of the bed, look!" Olivia whispered louder.

Summoning courage from somewhere, she reached over and lifted the pillow. She picked up the gun like it was a dirty diaper overflowing and you couldn't get it closed, and tiptoed backwards and around to the open closet where the clothes hamper was, lifted the lid, and placed the gun in the hamper. Quickly, she moved back to her side of the bed, put the pillow back, just in time, as he was coming into to the bedroom.

"You all are going to die tonight," he said, even here perfectly enunciating in his deep voice. He lifted the pillow. At that very moment, Olivia ran to the kitchen to call the police, past the bludgeoned front door, half-off the hinges fully open to hall stairway. Karen and Faith ran to the neighbor's apartment, across the hall, ringing the doorbell frantically, and violently banged on the door. Olivia walked with the phone to the middle of the living room where she could see the master bedroom and the outer stairwell, holding the phone in one hand, the cord trailing behind her with its own life. She held the receiver with her shoulder while she gave the address and the crisis.

Her mother was still sitting on the bed "Damn it Joanna, what you do with my gun," and she tried to get up and run but he grabbed her by the neck, locked her in a chokehold.

The neighbor Larry took only one look at the girls. He looked through the door at Olivia. Olivia pointed him to the bedroom. He just went.

A few seconds later, her mother came out, bloody, tears smeared, not meeting anyone's eyes but focusing on the floor. She touched her neck to survey the damage, with her left hand on her hip. Larry and Raul remained in the room until the police came.

Someone was walking up the stairs and you could hear the sounds of a walkie-talkie.

Her mother went to the door as if it was a cue, thankful she could.

"Ma'am, we are responding to a call from a little girl?"

"Yes, that's right. That was my daughter Olivia."

"Ma'am is what your daughter said true?"

"Yes it is, officer."

His partner joined him in that characteristic way that police stand, no display of emotion and always expecting black people to shoot. Their arms stuck out sort of because of the gear they wear. Their mere presence garnered control of the situation, which gave Olivia a sense of safety. The two officers exchanged looks.

"How long have you been married Ma'am?"

"Thirteen years."

"What's your name?"

"Joanna Gonzalez."

"Has your husband ever done anything like this before?"

Sitting down on the couch, she said, "Well, not like this."

"How old are you Ma'am?"

"Thirty-two."

"How many children do you have Ma'am?" The officer made notes on his pad.

"I have three, Karen, Olivia, and Faith." He looked around at the girls, one by one.

His partner who was standing over by the shattered door asked, "Which one is Olivia?"

Her mother pointed at Olivia, who was sitting at the dining room table. Karen and Faith huddled on the love seat.

"Ma'am, I ask you again, has your husband ever done anything like this before?"

"He's gotten violent before but he never threatened to kill us," she lowered her eyes, clasped her knees, and rocked back and forth.

"How many times has he gotten violent Ma'am?"

Olivia's mother thought for a moment. She started counting with her fingers. Olivia wanted to say 'Everyday!' but she didn't.

"I don't know. Often, but he's a good man, he just has some problems."

"Ma'am how many times have the police been involved?"

"Just four or five, but none here in California. Those were all in Philadelphia."

Like that makes a difference, Olivia rolled her eyes.

"How long have you lived here?" The officers kept asking questions and writing notes down.

"Ma'am, so you moved here a year and a half ago when you left him, took him back, and now he's here?"

"Yes."

"Do you want to press charges? We can't arrest him unless you do.

If you don't, we will remove your children from the home because you are placing them in an unsafe environment by having them watch you repeatedly be beaten, themselves being beaten, and having them held at gun point. I will have to call child protective services."

Olivia's mother just looked incredulous, like she didn't believe what she was hearing.

"What? Well when would he be back? He just got a job and was doing—"

"Ma'am he'll be processed through the system and we can't guarantee when he'll be released. I'm sure the judge will set bail at the arraignment tonight. You will want to make sure your children are not placed in jeopardy if he is bailed out." The walkie-talkie squawked and the officer turned the knob so it was silent.

Joanna knew this was the fundamental dilemma. Him, or me and my children? Him, or my career goals? Him, or my dignity? Any answer, other than "him," were nails in her coffin.

"Okay, if that's the way it has to be."

"Whatever you say Ma'am. However, another distress call for domestic violence will have your children taken so you will want to make sure you look after this." He turned to the other officer, nodded.

"Mr. Gonzalez, we're coming into your bedroom..."

Olivia's mother went and stood in the kitchen as they escorted her husband out the splintered door.

Before the officers left, Officer Bryant, the lead officer told her, "Ma'am you'll want to get that fixed tonight or you won't be able to stay with your children here. The door won't lock or remain closed sufficiently to provide a barrier."

Larry went across the hall to his apartment and got some plywood, nails, hammer. He proceeded to repair the door best he could, on a Sunday night, himself having done no work with his hands. He was an architect, standing about six-five and weighed well over two hundred and twenty pounds. Larry was dark skinned, and had short gray steel-wool hair.

At the moment she was standing there looking at Arnie, listening to him, Olivia verified an impression on how Carlotta looked when she saw her at Arnie's Christmas party last month. Carlotta carried that beaten woman look in her eyes and mounted no defense for Arnie's constant verbal abuse disguised as jokes he told there in front of the guests.

God bless you, Arnie and this place, Olivia thought. You can find someone else to abuse.

Without backing up, she stared him in the eye and made no attempt at disguising her disgust. "I think you should talk with Patrick and the other department heads about the memo, and yes, Friday at 4:30 we're meeting. We have a lot to talk about. See you then." Olivia held his gaze for a moment until he looked away, then she turned and walked away, down the hall past the gift shop.

"Uppidty black bitch," he muttered under his voice. "She's gonna regret this." Arnie turned, smiling, and started glad-handing with the Rotarian business folks.

Clearly he didn't understand whom he was messing with.

Olivia wasn't gonna stand for no disrespect like this. He was lucky she didn't have her son here to send a posse for his ass. But at that moment Olivia knew it was time, that what she needed to do at this place was finished. It was a lot like knowing when you're finally going to leave the unconscious love of abuse.

When would she find time to send out position application packets? From what she'd heard, the world had shifted — there were no open positions. But Olivia would not accept that as her reality.

Patrick read the terse email from Dan Fogerty, which was copied to all department heads in the School of Business. He wasn't going to reinstate Ryan Burns, but rather Patrick should direct Francis, who heads that department, to find an adjunct. Unfortunately, further, they were going out to national search to find a dean. Patrick would be made aware of who was going to comprise the search committee, and when the ad would be placed in *The Chronicle*. The President was not interested in meeting with him or any of the faculty from the School of Business regarding these issues.

He printed the email and at the same time, he looked up Wes's number, over in chemistry. Taking the paper from the printer, Wes answered the phone. Patrick told Wes the faculty needed to hold a vote of no confidence against Arnie.

Wes agreed wholeheartedly, "but I'm not senate President until the end of May. That I will have to run by Olivia."

He and Patrick talked for a while, as Patrick filled his ear with allegations against Arnie.

"You know Patrick, I'm not particularly fond of you because of your self-serving and backstabbing greed. But I hate Arnie worse, as I have said publicly at the EC meetings.

"Yes, I know, I've heard. So?" Patrick wanted to know if he was going to move or not; he didn't care what Wes thought of him, and he knew he was unpleasant before he called. But Patrick was glad he had an ally against Arnie.

"I'll talk to Olivia about it,"

"Fine, please keep this between us," Patrick asked. The last thing he needed was faculty thinking he instigated anything.

"Do what I can," Wes hung up and immediately dialed Olivia's office.

"Olivia, Wes here. Yeah, we need to talk, I'm getting hundreds of calls from all over campus about doing a vote of no confidence against Arnie."

"Yeah, I know people are sick of the nonsense. I just walked in from being at a meeting where I ran into him, and I'm not putting up with this nonsense."

"It's bullshit, not "*nonsense*" Olivia."

"I was trying to be polite."

"No time for that." He was matter of fact.

"I like that you are direct and to the point Wes. Great, an item for discussing the procedure to hold a vote, it's on the agenda for Monday's EC meeting at four."

"Thank you Olivia. Most of us despise the man, and can't wait to get rid of his ass. Have a good weekend, I'm goin' to, got my beer all chilled."

"Thanks. See you Monday."

Immediately after talking to Wes, Olivia went to see if Patrick was in his office. He was usually gone by 4 P.M.. She saw him sitting there, and walked in without knocking.

"Patrick, people are asking for a vote of no confidence against Arnie. I don't think that's a good idea, since we really don't have evidence against him for that, and, we don't have the procedure set up." She stood in front of his desk, leaning with both hands on the back of one of the sitting chairs.

"No, a vote of no confidence is premature, I agree. I mean, the guy doesn't have any culpability on his hands since he blames everything on everybody else, and makes other people do his dirty work."

Patrick rolled his chair around behind his desk and started loading his briefcase, getting ready to leave, thoughts racing. Did Wes call her already? Did he tell her I called him? Olivia didn't give him any clues.

"I'm not holding a vote against him Patrick. It's not happening on my watch, not on my dime. If Wes wants to hold it when he's President next year, fine."

Patrick was surprised at her resolve, but smiled as he nodded his head in agreement. It was what he did when he couldn't do anything about an uncomfortable situation.

"Okay, I need to go, I have a meeting with Arnie. I'll see you later." She walked out. Patrick left almost right behind her, his mind already fixed on his glass of wine.

Olivia started the walk across campus to the Administration Building, being careful not to slip on the ice. The wind blew hard as she put on her coat, buttoned it, and then her gloves. She saw her breath as she walked, and her eyes watered from the cold.

She picked up her pace since her meeting with Arnie was in less than fifteen minutes. Her phone was ringing, and she fumbled with her purse to answer it.

"Hey Kevin, what's crackin'?

"Dr. O-livia, what you doin' this fine Friday? We still on for dinner at Jack's Place tonight?"

"Absolutely. I need to talk."

"Tell me about it. Did you hear about what happened over here in Poli Sci?"

"No, what?"

"Girl, they cancelled all our searches and hired this JD lawyer woman from Little Rock to teach."

"Oh, no... but hey, I want to hear all about it but I'm meeting with Arnie in a few minutes."

"Okay, that's cool, so I'll see you then around six?"

"Yes, I have a reservation for us."

"Very cool. I'll see you there."


Kevin ordered a gin and tonic and Olivia ordered hot herbal tea with honey. She looked around the restaurant to make sure there were no spies or would be informants. It was such a small town, but only the upper crust frequented Jack's Place. It was the most upscale restaurant for at least a 70-mile radius of Western. Once inside, that good old sideshow of Roadims ended, and Olivia felt like she had come back to reality. People dressed normally, wait staff acted like they weren't freaked out from seeing a black woman. Needless to say, Olivia went to Jack's Place as often as she could.

They talked, shared horror stories about the situation at the university. Olivia confided in Kevin, and he in her. They never betrayed one another, both of them understood what they wanted, but couldn't have.

"Kevin, we need to set up the process for a vote of no confidence."

"Sounds good to me. We gotta get rid of this yahoo. You know I hate Arnie with a passion. His whole approach to the presidency and fucking leadership make a farce out of my credentials, and I didn't get a PhD to come somewhere and be treated like a god-damned second rate high school teacher who babysits truants in detention." Kevin was mad, madder than Olivia had ever seen him.

"Right, but we have to do it so that when the vote is held, it's bullet proof. And we gotta be careful we don't get fired."

"I don't give a shit about getting fired. I got money in the bank and can find another job." He took a sip of his drink. "Let's, see. Who's on the team? Everybody from my department, and the Anthropology department. I know Wes will be. What about the business school?"

"Yes, most folk in the School of Business want him gone too."

"I'll do some research on it, and send you the info."

"Use my private email," Olivia took out a piece of paper and wrote it down, slid it across the table to him. "They monitor the campus email servers."

He took it, folded it and put it in his bag. "Thanks, and Olivia, don't worry."

Olivia drove home in silence. She got home and went down to her basement, her meditation room. She thought about Kevin, and believed he was at home taking tranquilizers and drinking as he said he would. That was the reason she could not date him, and it was something she never said out loud.

Tomorrow she would have to call Harmony and warn her about what Arnie said when she met with him today. But for now, she needed to sit in the silence and hear. Her basement was painted soft earthy green, and the carpet was thick with a crochet pile. There was a door that opened onto the bottom patio, and a window that cranked outward. In the center of the room was a supporting column, painted white to match the crown molding. It was her meditation room, her sanctuary.

She closed her eyes.

*We set out walking to the library.*

*"Which way should we go?"*

*"Let's go this way" Karen said. "Walk down Santa Rosalia to LaBrea and then down LaBrea."*

*"Okay," Pam and I agreed.*

*So we started, walked though several apartment complexes and meandered through until we reached Santa Rosalia. Past Dorsey High.*

*"Let's stop at Thrifty's and get an ice cream," I said.*

*"Do we have any money?" Karen asked.*

*"I have a dollar."*

*"Me too" added Pam.*

*"Why don't we stop at Newberry's on the way back instead. We can look at sewing stuff and you can get an ice cream cone," Karen said.*

*"And I can look at earrings!"*

*"Yeah!" agreed Pam.*

*So we walked along, talking and laughing. It was a hot day in April.*

*At the library we entered and went our separate ways. This wasn't the real library so it was small. The real library was downtown and it was big, with lots of tables and an elevator. But this building was only one floor and had four large rectangular tables like you see on Perry Mason, and they were put in the center of the library. The place where you checked out books was directly across from the door, behind the tables. And the bookcases were standing around the space. It didn't matter that this wasn't the real library. I was always able to find books I wanted to check out. I looked in my purse, the one I made on the sewing machine yesterday, to see if I had my library card. Seeing it was there, I sighed in relief that I hadn't forgotten it or lost it on the way. I walked around the bookcases and I looked at books and pulled some off the shelves. I got the ones I thought were good, and carried them to one of the tables. I was allowed to check* out ten. So I did. Pam didn't check out any books and neither did Karen.

Walking back, we were near Newberry's in the shopping center on La Brea and Rodeo. The sun was shining, and I was sweating. I was really looking forward to going inside where it was cool. The walk to the library was always shorter than the walk back. I walked in and as I opened the door, you could feel that blast of cold air hit you right in the face. Ahhh.

"I'm going to look at the fabrics and stuff you guys," Karen said.

"Okay," I said.

And Pam and I wandered.

"Ooo, they have dolls here," Pam was excited.

"I don't want to look at dolls, I'm going to look at the earrings."

Olivia wandered off. There was a whole table full of earrings with the sign "$1 a pair." That was really cool because I, had just got my ears pierced — finally. I was the only one with pierced ears in the family.

I walked up to the table, it was one of those big bargain tables that sit out in the isle. I still had all ten of my library books, and was holding them, cradling them rather, like you know when you have lots of books. So I was looking at the earrings and picked up a pair, and just at that moment the books started to slip and I sort of hunched over and re-scooped the books so I wouldn't drop any of them.

At that same moment, a man came up next to me and said "Please step to the back of the store, young lady."

I looked at him, he was white, short, slightly bald, and I knew immediately what he was thinking of me. My entire body was scared to death it felt like I had to go to the bathroom and in a split second I thought the last thing I needed was to get arrested. Dad would kill me.

The man was pushing me by the right upper arm, and I was trying to stay close to the table to drop those earrings back on the table, but they were stuck to my palm and wouldn't fall. So I carried them with me as he pushed me real hard to a room at the back of the store. I didn't see Karen or Pam anywhere.

Hours had passed since he'd brought me into that room, and when I came out, my sister and Pam were standing by the front door looking around, like *when you try to find your Mom in Fedco or Gemco. We saw each other and I was so glad they hadn't left me.*

*"Where were you," Karen asked me, concern in her voice and on her face. "Let's go home, and let's go quick,"*

*We left the store, and on the way home I told them the whole story.*

*"Where have you been?" Mom demanded when we walked in the door.*

*"See you later, Olivia, my mother is wondering where I am and I don't want to get in trouble."*

*"Bye, thanks for going, it was fun."*

*"Bye," and Pam left.*

*I told Mom the story about the security guard. I showed her my books. Karen didn't say anything.*

*"Come on, get your jackets, we're going down there." It was late in the afternoon, starting to cool off in the characteristic Los Angeles manner.*

*"Where's Dad?" I asked.*

*"He's in the shower, but we'll be back before he knows we're gone," she promised.*

*Mom, Karen, Faith and me all walked down the stairwell, out to the car and drove back to Newberry's.*

*When we got there, "You stay in the car, I'll be right back."*

*She got out, slammed the door. She had a nappy afro, and was tall and skinny, pockmarked face from bad untreated acne. She was wearing a purple dress that came just above the knee, and was fitted with a criss-cross across the breast, tan sort of ribbing, zipped up the back with a hook at the top. The fabric was textured, and her sandals were purple too. She didn't have pierced ears because she said only fast girls got their ears pierced.*

*She came back to the car.*

*"What happened?" Karen asked.*

*"I told him we would never shop in this store again, and that he ought to know better than to harass a child."*

*I didn't say anything. She drove us home, were not in the mood to talk.*

*"Where have you all been?" That was the first question he asked when we walked in the door.*

*I didn't say anything, but Mom said "Come in here for a minute, Raul."*

*And so they went to the bedroom. I couldn't hear what they were saying. He came out.*

*"I'll be back," he said, and got his jacket from the living room closet.*

*"Can we turn on the television, " I asked.*

*"Yes, but after you get yourselves ready for dinner."*

*We were sitting down, watching television, when Dad left. He looked too calm and my stomach started to cramp like I had diarrhea.*

Olivia opened her eyes, blew out her candle. "I'm not gonna be the scapegoat anymore. And I ain't fixing nothing else, things will fall where they will, and I am leaving," she said to the room, tears streaming down her face. She blew out the candles and started up the stairs just as Jonathan was calling.

She wasn't going to tell him that Arnie said she could apply for the Dean's position, and that Patrick had not recommended her. Nor was she going to tell him that she told Arnie she wouldn't stoop so low, that if they wanted her to be the Dean, if the search failed, they could appoint her.

No, she would tell Jonathan that Patrick stepped down prematurely and that other people in the School of Business wanted the job and were willing to apply for it. There was no need for any more discussion on him moving to Roadims.

"Hey love, how are you?" She breathed, feeling love and warmth as she answered the phone.

"Fine, my darling, how are you this evening?" He still needed to tell her something that he'd left out of his profile. He kicked himself for not doing it sooner.

"I'm good, but, I'm not going to be the next Dean of the School of Business. I'll tell you about it when I see you."

*People are like stained glass windows,*
*they sparkle and shine when the sun is out,*
*but when the darkness sets in,*
*their true beauty is revealed*
*only if there is light from within.*
*—Elisabeth Kubler-Ross*

# Cast Your Vote

*March 2009*

People in the School of Business went crazy. It was like the place was hit with a demolition ball they couldn't see. Patrick walked around with his head down and shoulders slumped over, Nancy pled ignorant, but she always followed that by saying she "might be interested, I don't know, we'll see," outwardly maintaining she didn't want the job as Dean if it meant working with Arnie. Abe, Francis, Brian, Mark, and Alex vied for the position but were scared to say so. Come to find out that Patrick previously promised each of them the position at one time or another. They became each other's prey, the men exposing their rabidity with each bite at the other. Olivia gagged every time she saw it, like when Brian strutted around in his best suits. He'd never worn suits before then. Or when he told all the secretaries that he was going to be the next Dean, and so ordered them to do more than his department chair work. He had them doing his grading, posting on Blackboard, his budget estimates, and even his faculty reviews.

Olivia and Brian were friends by virtue of being black. He'd been at the university for some fifteen years, and his wife and two boys were deeply entrenched in the community. But Brian and Olivia had a code of communication, an unspoken understanding. He came to her office often and sat in the chair by the door. And Olivia confided in him about Jonathan. So when she heard he wanted to be Dean, Olivia immediately stopped pursuing the job, which wasn't hard after she found out that Patrick had promised it to Brian long ago. After Patrick announced his intent to step down as Dean, a few days later she and Brian were coming out of an honor's committee meeting that they served on together. Well, he was on the committee but like all his other service commitments, Brian volunteered to do everything and followed through on nothing.

"Hey," he came up to her.

"Hey, what you up to?"

"Do you think I would make a good Dean?" They started walking back to the business building.

Olivia was dumbfounded. Stumbling for composure all she could think to say was "Sure, I think so."

"Great, so I have your support?"

"Well, I don't think you should apply for the position, Brian." How could she tell him that Arnie had no intention of letting him be Dean? He'd as much as told her that at their last meeting. Nobody on campus liked working with Brian because he was a social loafer, and always denied when he'd dropped the ball on something.

"Why?"

Oh God, now I'm in trouble, she thought. "Because I just don't think you should. I mean, you'll have to work with Arnie." Olivia shivered from the wind.

"No problem, I can handle him." He stared at her, grinning, as he walked. He wore a black beanie on his head, and his dark skin was hard to differentiate from it.

"Oh—uh, okay!" Olivia looked at her watch. "I've got a class. Let's talk later this afternoon?" They stood in front of the double glass doors of the building. Someone was smoking and this annoyed Olivia. She reflected on how she'd stopped smoking years ago, and coughed from the smoke.

"Maybe, I gotta get the boys at 2:30."

"Okay, I'll see you tomorrow then, my class doesn't end until 2:15." Olivia not only wanted to get away from him but from the smoker too.

Brian gave her a hug. "Thanks friend."

"You're welcome," Olivia felt icky as she watched him walk to the parking lot.

Topping this all off, she remembered that on the Monday after her Friday meeting with Arnie, he called her and said, "Oh, yeah, Olivia, I was wrong. Patrick *did* recommend you and you were the *only* one he recommended."

What a bunch of two-faced treachery. Naivety gone and not willing to play the scared of the bully game, Olivia had taken to only meeting with Arnie once a month now, since there was no point. She'd lost all respect for him. Last month she told him that the faculty were investigating holding a vote of no confidence, but that she wasn't going to allow the vote to happen. He launched into his venomous tirade of how the faculty don't know what they're doing, using his favorite phrases "Are they *crazy*? What are they *thinking*?" Olivia avoided the temptation to answer "No, but *you* are, and at least the faculty do think," while at the same time resisting the urge to roll her eyes, turn her head, and suck her teeth in the most supreme Sapphire way.

"Thanks for letting me know that, Arnie," she hung up and was grateful she didn't have to try to conceal her total disdain for his idiocy permanently showing on her face when it came to him.

Nobody smiled about anything anywhere anymore on campus, and many just went through the motions. After a strategic planning session where Patrick again, in front of everyone, told Timothy, who led them and formulated the process of defining key success factors, that his strategic planning approach was all wrong, Renee stopped Olivia in the hall.

"Olivia he's awful." Renee stood still looking at her, but her fat kept giggling.

"Patrick? Oh, you know he's always like that. I agree with him though, Timothy doesn't know a key success factor from a door key."

"No, I mean Arnie. He's vindictive, threatening, like something's wrong, ADD, bipolar or I don't know, not right. He and the Board.

Darnell..." she trailed off, tears coming to her eyes. "I'm going to step down and go back to teaching. Do you think you could talk to Patrick about letting me teach business law?"

Looking down at her feet for a second, and then raising her head to look directly into Renee's, "I'll talk with him." Olivia couldn't believe what she was hearing. First of all, A: She and Renee weren't *even* girlfriends, they ain't had a cup of coffee together: why she now talking to her like she her best friend?; and B: why didn't she just talk to him herself instead of regurgitating this victimization story all over her? Patrick had told Olivia before, more than once, he didn't want Renee in the School of Business because he didn't think a JD would look good for AACSB accreditation, and he didn't want an administrative mole in "his" building. That was back when Patrick had an agenda; Olivia wasn't sure what he would say now.

Renee and Olivia stood in the hall. Faculty walked by and didn't acknowledge the two women standing there as Renee recounted her desperation with what seemed to be nonstop breathless stories about Arnie for at least twenty minutes. Olivia finally had to make up an excuse to get away from her because she couldn't endure how embarrassed she was for Renee. The stories she told made Olivia want to ask her why do you allow this? Why do you let people treat you like that? In typical fashion of an entirely self obsessed person, Renee never once asked Olivia how she was doing, just stood there making that loud sucking sound "Feeeeel sorrrrrry for meeeee." It made Olivia sick, it reminded her of her mother, pathetic narcissitic martyr. It was that closed in feeling all over again that people like them projected, amoeba spreading and gobbling up anyone who'd listen. She wanted to tell her so bad, you made your choices and your choices got you here you fat lying bitch.

Renee, like other people on and off campus, didn't want Olivia to betray her confidence and she agreed not to, and never expected reciprocity since people talked. All of them though were scared of Arnie's retaliation. It was in talking to each other that relief came, most of them couldn't talk to anyone outside the university. So even as much as Olivia hated the way Renee was wrapped in her co dependent and food addictions, she agreed to keep the conversation between the two of them when she asked her to.

"Renee wants you to call her, she wants to talk to you about teaching in the fall." Olivia passed by the Dean's office on her way to hers right after she left Renee, popped her head into his office. Seeing him there behind his desk, she walked in, but she didn't sit down.

"Okay, I'll give her a call. We can't hire a real faculty member, and since Arnie fired Ryan Burns, we're short. She can teach business law, that was what he was teaching." Patrick climbed up on his soapbox and lectured on the benefits and features of a vote of no confidence and how the faculty should do something.

Olivia recognized that everyone was gung-hoe on the idea, but they all wanted to hide behind her, happy to sacrifice her worse than Abraham was willing to sacrifice his son. Olivia intervened on her behalf in this case, getting a clear message from God that she no longer had to rescue anyone but herself.

"I'm not holding the vote Patrick. I'll make sure the senate has a process for doing it next year, but no vote is going to happen, not this academic year. Besides, real change will need to come from the Board anyway." She didn't smile. She felt the squeeze of Arnie's manipulative threats and the pressure of the faculty's cowardice. What about me, she whispered inside, and felt guilty for it. Standing there feeling completely abandoned, she held back burning tears that would roll down her face with the wrong blink.

Patrick wasn't used to her newfound resolve. "True, but getting the Board to do anything is going to take a miracle. Look how long it took them to get rid of Luis."

"Right. I'd love to chat longer Patrick but I can't stay, so I'll catch you later, okay?" It was more of a statement than a question, and she waved good-bye as she left.

"See ya."

Patrick saw Olivia retreating further and further away. She didn't come to the art gallery openings any more, she didn't come to chat with him in his office like she used to. And she didn't apply for the Dean's position. He'd asked the search committee who was in the lineup, and she wasn't. In the event that one of his faculty got to be Interim Dean, he planned to just take their teaching line, and take the MBA program away from Olivia.

Instead, he remembered that she'd recently asked him to write letters of recommendation for her, as she informed him that she was on the market. "Absolutely I'll write letters," he'd told her.

"Thanks Patrick," she smiled.

He knew she wasn't going anywhere. How could she with a doctorate like hers? No business school was going to hire her, especially now with the way the economic and educational policy landscapes were being redrawn.

Patrick turned and started composing an email to Renee.

———

Instead of meeting with Arnie twice a month, since the beginning of the year, Olivia met with Dan Fogerty, and Timothy Jones, who had been appointed to the Assistant VP AA, responsible for shared governance and strategic planning. She decided that they could tell Arnie whatever they felt was important, since she wasn't paid to coach, evaluate, or advise the President on the proper functioning of the University. And, she wasn't qualified to perform talk-therapy—which he needed along with some serious medication in her opinion.

"Hello Dan, Timothy. How are you both today?" Olivia walked hurriedly into the crowded and stuffy office, with her arms full of papers and notebooks, convincing them she cared.

"Fine, Olivia. Thank you." Dan, never asked how she was, and had no affect at all. He was a tall, skinny, old, and gray haired man. Dan slouched behind his desk, which was piled high with papers and books.

"We're handling it best we know how," Timothy was rubbing his temple, standing next to the table in the center of the office. He reached behind him and leaned on the floor to ceiling walnut bookcase populated with zoology and microbiology books. "We have to do something to save this university."

Sliding past the invitation to gossip loaded into the plea, Olivia kept going, "I brought you some information on shared governance from AAUP, some examples of universities that utilize the model, and a survey that you can use to assess the degree of it on campus. You can use this for your baseline KPI in the strategic planning process, Timothy."

He stared at her for a second then exchanged glances with his lieutenant. "Thanks Olivia," Timothy said. For the most part, during these meetings Dan just sat there and didn't say much. "Can you send me this information electronically and I'll disseminate it to the committee?"

"Sure. Oh, by the way, I wanted to let you know so that you wouldn't be taken by surprise, there's talk of holding a vote of no confidence on campus. But, I'm not supporting that. And I told Arnie the same thing last week."

"What? Why?" Both Dan and Timothy now gave their undivided attention as they revealed their utter ignorance of the situation.

Olivia was not intimidated by their quizzical gazes though. "Faculty are not happy with the administration in general, Arnie in particular. They don't think he knows what he's doing. Like I said, I won't allow the vote. I won't be able to stop it though after my term is over in two months." These two were worse than the Pharoh and his advisors in their denial.

"Thanks Olivia, keep us posted on the progress of events. We don't think the faculty have the right to judge Arnie's competency, they only think of themselves and fail to consider anyone else on this campus. I'll look forward to getting your information electronically," Timothy was a company man all the way. He spoke in a modulated almost syncopated rhythmic tone, accommodating his southern drawl.

Olivia stood up, and so did they. "Thank you, Gentlemen," she shook their hands. "I'll make the next appointment with your secretaries," she said as she walked out.

---

Olivia opened her Novell inbox to find an email from Arnie. Now what does he want? Tired, she sighed, "Let me send this information to Timothy before I forget," she composed the email, attached the information, and copied Dan, thanking them for the meeting today. She pressed the send button. Then clicked on Arnie's email.

*March 6, 2009*
*TO:*     *Olivia Clarke*
*FR:*     *Arnie Williams*
*CC:*     *Renee Gruber, Dan Fogerty*

*Olivia,*

*I have become increasingly concerned about what appears to me to be a growing and unhealthy attitude among certain faculty about their role in shared governance. After the Senate meeting earlier this week, I have some concerns, and I have a responsibility to share them and set some guidelines and heuristics.*

What in the world is he talking about?

*My first concern is that faculty now believe the administration reports to them. We have been asked to provide all manner of information, in a belligerent attitude that bespeaks of insistent demand.*

Olivia reflected in an instant on his other emails. She felt tingly under her arms.

*Let me make this clear. Neither I nor the VPs are under any obligation whatsoever to accept recommendations from the faculty for any reason.*

*I think it only proper to inform you that I have no intention of reporting to the Senate or any of its committees. As such, I will no longer allow those in administration to take requests for information from any faculty member. All requests for information must go through me first. I will evaluate the request and if I think it has merit I will forward it on to the correct office. Further, approved information will be provided when the time permits.*

Oh my God! He's sensoring the communications!

*I have given genuine evidence of my desire to work with the faculty. If the Senate has evidence that either I or my administrative associates have intentionally provided incorrect information, I expect you as the President of the Senate to make me aware of those concerns so that I can address them.*

How stupid is he? He has never shown evidence of this, never. Olivia shook her head in disbelief.

*As I have mentioned publicly, this campus is not a democracy. I alone have the final say in decisions. That is not because I have extraordinary power but because the university is structured that way. As such, I have an obligation to listen to concerns. I will not foster any notion that any faculty or group thereof will conduct a tribunal where I am called to account for my decisions. If that attitude continues to persist, you can be assured that I will interpret such a posture as a violation of the social contract I assumed we had of advice and consent in a civil environment.*

Nausea and bile rose up to Olivia's throat. She swallowed hard to keep it down.

*The Faculty Welfare Committee has asked for information, but I am unwilling to be put in the position that I am required to defend decisions*

*as though some ill motives are afoot. So, I will send you the information*
*they requested from me. You can present it to them in lieu of my meeting*
*with them on March 9. That committee insinuates that my administrative*
*team is not competent. These are assaults on character. The Faculty*
*Handbook clearly says that final decisions are made by the University*
*President and/or approved by the Board.*

No leader of any merit demands to be followed. Olivia's hands
shook with fear and the awareness of her powerlessness.

*Faculty believes it has taken the brunt of the cuts. I am willing to*
*discuss cut backs but not willing to defend my decisions.*

*If the Senate desires an adversarial relationship, pitting faculty interests*
*against those of the university, they will do damage to their reputations*
*in seeking their own interests.*

*I resolve to work transparently as possible, and no one can produce*
*evidence to suggest that I will manage the university differently in the*
*future. I will stand against slurs to the character of my administration.*
*If you have any reason to believe I need clarification on any of my*
*resolutions, please contact me.*

*Arnie*

Olivia slumped over and lay her left cheek heavily on the desk, her
arms slipping down between her knees as she felt as if she took a direct hit
in the chest from the blows of the invisible demolition ball. 'That Glazed
Look' took over her face and she walked out of her office. Her skirt and
cowl neck sweater felt as if they had disappeared off her body. She went
to the printer and got the email. She wandered into Nancy's office. Stood
there. Nancy typed on her computer, her French manicured nails clattered
on the keyboard. She looked at Olivia and instantly stopped typing.
Olivia was ashen, as close to colorless as a black person could be. Oh no,
Nancy thought. She knew from talking to Olivia that she was bitter about

Patrick's premature move from the Dean's office. They'd announced it and everything at the Christmas Party at her house. People trusted Olivia and they knew they could get things done with her in charge. She wasn't afraid of Arnie, she was equipped with the savvy to deal with the Board, and keep the School of Business interests first. But now, Nancy knew Olivia wasn't happy, and she was afraid of losing her. She'd been applying for jobs, fellowships, visiting professorships, and had talked about doing a sabbatical. Plus, now she was married. Although, Nancy did secretly wish she could be the Dean because she felt she deserved it and could do a more humane job than either Patrick did or anyone else would. She resented that Patrick offered it to Olivia in the first place.

"What's wrong girl?" Nancy tried to make light of what she knew was a bad situation.

Olivia just stood there.

"Here, sit down," Nancy got up and cleared the piles of files off her sitting chairs and stacked them on the floor next to her desk. Her office was overly decorated with brick-a-brack and knickknacks and crammed full of too much furniture. There was barely any room to turn around, and you had to be careful not to knock stuff over. Olivia sat down but still didn't say anything.

"Olivia, what is it?"

She handed her Arnie's email. Nancy mindlessly took a slow drag of her Diet Dr. Pepper as she read it, but nearly choked.

"Oh, my God, oh my God." Nancy's color drained from her face. "Olivia, I'm so sorry."

Olivia cried unable to hold back, even as she hated to cry at work, in front of colleagues. "Something is wrong with him. We gotta be careful. I want you to put this in my personnel file, and I want you to know that I am not going to forward this email to anyone but you and Patrick." Olivia was hysterical almost. She took a wad of five tissues out of Nancy's designer tissue dispenser to focus on something, anything to get grounded, and wiped her eyes.

"Okay. You haven't done anything wrong and he can't fire you."

"Right." Olivia didn't believe that. "He can do what he wants to do, if he wants to, when he want to. That's exactly what he's saying." Olivia's mouth was full of cotton and her eyes spilled hot tears of anger, that dripped silently onto her white sweater.

"I need to get back to work, so I can be ready for students on Monday." Feeling as if she was a burden, Olivia padded across Nancy's Persian floor rug, out to her neighboring office, but she kept going down to Claire's office. It was unusual for Claire to be in the office on a Friday afternoon; today, thank God she was. Olivia admired Claire so much. They had an instant connection from the first day they talked, with each of their birthdays being February 15, and Claire was a fugitive from her family too. Of course they skirted the particulars, hinted only the lingering sentiments.

Nancy got immediately out of her chair and followed Olivia, Nancy's shoes click clacking all the way. "Wow, Claire's here?" She laughed in disbelief as she held her head down to see over the top of her reading glasses.

"What's wrong?" Claire asked. Her office was two doors down from Olivia's, and was well furnished with a glass-topped desk, an expensive black desk chair flanked by two stainless steel lamps like those seen in a magazine photo of contemporary house living room with vaulted ceilings. *Avant guarde* artwork lined the walls, and a black and brown rug replicating a backgammon board lined the entire floor. She sat there behind her desk with a puzzled look on her airbrushed, perfectly made up face.

Olivia stood just inside the door, feeling inadequate and Nancy stood next to her, holding her psychedelic multicolored reading glasses in her right hand by the crossed over ear pieces.

"She just got an email from Arnie." Nancy told her, putting her wrist on her hip and still holding the glasses.

Claire nodded, "Oh... What'd say?" When she talked to people, Claire made them feel heard.

"Let's call Patrick," Olivia pulled her phone out of her skirt pocket, punched a few buttons. "I'm just getting his voice mail." She pressed the 'End Call' button without leaving a message.

"Here, let me call him," Nancy reached into her jacket pocket and got her cell phone. "Patrick, Nancy, could you call me as soon as you can? We got a serious situation here. Thanks."

"He's terrible, I know. I'm only here now because I needed to print out some stuff for a client." Claire was also looking for a way out. She'd been hired two years ago on a non-tenure track contract, and Patrick wouldn't put her position in for tenure. He'd promised that he would, but because she was an EdD, he said she no longer fit the profile for the School of Business. Knowing that she didn't see any reason to stay, or to do any work for that matter, and she didn't need the headache and embarrassment to her career that Arnie brought. She had plans to leave by the fall, but she kept these to herself, and she did as little as possible. Olivia was amazed that the guilt didn't get the best of her; she found it difficult to get paid and do nothing but she was beginning to see the merit in Claire's strategy.

Nancy knew from Renee that Arnie was vindictive and mean, what was it that Renee called him? Sinister and frightening, she thought it was. Nancy decided she would call a friend of a friend of a Board member and let her know what was happening. Something had to be done about this. She hadn't worked at this place for the last 25 years to see it go down.

"I've got to get out of here," Olivia walked out of Claire's office, went back to hers. She called Arnie's secretary and scheduled a meeting for the next day at 3 P.M., then turned everything off. She got her stuff and left, waved at Nancy as she went, yelling "Thanks Claire," through crackly voiced tears.

"'Bye, take it easy, 'Liv,'" Claire tried to be supportive.

In her car, she called Dan and asked him if he'd seen the email.

"Why yes, I did." He was way too chipper.

"Should I be worried about my job?" Olivia couldn't mask her tears. Inside she screamed, why hadn't he told her about it when she was in his office earlier? He was way worse than Judas.

"Oh, no, no. Not at all." Dan lied. He didn't tell her Arnie wanted to get rid of her and if he could he would get rid of all the faculty he viewed as troublemakers. He felt bad though because Olivia was one of the best ones they had. But he couldn't say that since he was too scared to lose *his* job at this late point in his life.

"Thanks Dan. I'll talk with you later." Olivia was frustrated with his playing it safe all the time. He could stand up to Arnie if he wanted to, but the man was a coward. She had more courage in her left foot than he showed in his pathetic play at being VP AA. All he did was roll over for Arnie.

Her next call was to Arnie. "Hello Olivia, how are you?" He sounded happy and maybe a little self satisfied.

"I'm fine, but I need to cancel the meeting I just scheduled with Sharon to see you tomorrow. And, Arnie, I'm not going to send that email to anyone. If you have things you want to communicate to the faculty, including the Welfare Committee faculty, you'll need to do that yourself."

After a few beats, he said "The email wasn't personal against you. It was meant for you as senate President."

"I appreciate that." She wasn't going to back down. "I'll send Sharon an email to clear your calendar, and make another appointment to see you soon, for our regular meeting of the month to discuss senate issues."

"Hey, thanks for calling. Don't worry about the email." All he needed was another black woman suing him. The case back in North Carolina had cost him, and that's why he wound up in this pitiful and pathetic place after thirty years of academic life.

"I gave a copy of it to Patrick and Nancy so they could put it in my personnel file. I'm also going to document this conversation so it can go with." The light turned green and Olivia continued driving. She didn't know where she was going.

"Fine, fine."

"See you soon, have a nice weekend," Olivia hung up.

Her next call was to Harmony. Weird, she answered. Nowadays, she never seemed to.

"Harmony, it's Olivia. You got a sec?"

"Sure sweetie, what's wrong?" Harmony heard Olivia's voice creaking.

"Can you walk this evening or Sunday?"

"Sunday is great, I can meet at about nine-thirty?"

"Okay, that's fine. At the Wildcat?"

"Yeah, things are really crazy on campus. Welfare is hearing all kinds of shit about Arnie."

"Oh, you don't know the half of it," Olivia held back her tears. "But I will see you Sunday, at the usual spot."

"Great, see you, love you!'

"Love you too." Olivia was turning into her driveway as she hung up.

Inside the house, she put the mail on the desk, and went to her room. She took off her hat, and lay down on the bed, rolling over to her right side. Oh God, I have to find another job and I have to do it quick, she thought. She remembered the movers were coming tomorrow, taking most of her stuff to California. The house was pretty much packed up. Ever since the first of the year, she and Jonathan decided it was best for her to move to San Diego, and she could find a position there. Of course, it was the worst time in the history of higher education in California, with the economic crisis. The public institutions there were on hiring freeze. Olivia saw tenure now as a lifetime job tethered to nothing but low salaries, insults, and administrative battles. Teaching and research were thankless secondary concerns, and these were only important in the fact that they increased and maintained enrollments or endowments, or stroked the egos of politicians. This was what people worked so hard for? Coveted?

She didn't understand but she wasn't going to let the petty bullshit of this small town, JUNIOR COLLEGE they call a university run by FOOLS, break her, or tarnish her academic accomplishments. She got out the bed and started getting ready for the movers. Jonathan would be calling pretty soon, and she wanted to have dinner with him while they were on the phone.

---

"Harmony, I have to tell you about a meeting I had, and an email I got from Arnie." Olivia approached the subject after they'd been walking for about an hour.

"Yeah, he's something, he never faces the faculty. I don't like him one bit, mainly because he's a coward." Birds chirped in the distance, and you could hear water rushing down the creek.

Olivia took a deep breath. It smelled like mulch, green, and wet tree bark.

"Well, he was complaining to me about Faculty Welfare. I said 'Talk to Welfare,' and he asked me 'Isn't Harmony your friend?' and I said yes. Then he said, 'She's hell on wheels, I hear that she yells at administrators, and she's stirring things up.' I didn't say anything, but then he said 'I would hate for her to get hurt in this process.' That was in the context of him telling me he was going to use the economic crisis as an excuse to clean house. Harmony, I want you to be careful of him."

Harmony started to laugh, and laugh hard. Gasping for air laughing, bending over, and holding her stomach, then turning around in circles, after a few moments Harmony got temporary composure of herself.

"What? He can't do *anything* to me, I'm tenured, full professor, and I only have five more years before I'm retiring." She started laughing so hard, she leaned backwards, and Olivia started laughing watching her. They stood there, in the middle of the nature preserve laughing hysterically. Tears were rolling down their faces. The sun was shining through the trees that were budding, some were flowering, and the air was crisp.

After about what seemed like an eternal laughfest, Olivia continued, "I got this email from him that was extremely threatening and hostile. I don't want to share the details, but I did give it to Nancy and Patrick to put in my personnel file. Patrick called me at home last night to talk with me about it."

Harmony looked at Olivia. Now she was getting the clue that something was wrong. Most of the time she ignored Olivia's premonitions, but she remembered the ones that came to pass, including Brock's death.

"So what are you going to do?" Harmony's face was serious, and inside she felt a tinge of fear.

"We're going to set up the process for a vote of no confidence. But, we're not going to hold the vote. The process includes gathering data, information, and documenting actions so that when and if there is a vote next year, there is hard evidence to point to. And by the way, Patrick is totally in favor of it."

Harmony thought about her colleagues in the Anthropology department and she knew that a vote would succeed if it was held. She didn't understand why she wouldn't hold the vote now.

Olivia read Harmony's mind and said, "I'm not going to hold the vote now because I am leaving the university soon." She waited for her to let this sink in.

"What do you mean?"

"I'm on the market. And I don't want the political smearing that is bound to occur with a no-vote. Wes is fine with letting that be on his record, since he'll retire soon. But I have twenty more years to work, and can't afford the tarnish on my record."

Harmony allowed herself to think about leaving. It was a fantasy she stopped torturing herself with years ago. Justin, Brock, her life at the university just took over. She hadn't published anything, didn't write anymore, or done anything for years now, except teach. Now Brock was gone, Justin was in Philadelphia. For an instant she felt she could make a change. Then she thought about how hard that would be, and she retreated back behind the closed door of acceptance.

"You'll find another job, this place hasn't gotten to you yet."

*San Diego, California*

Even though she normally didn't, Olivia checked her office voice mail messages while she and Jonathan were driving around San Diego.

"Oh, no, I have a message," she looked over at Jonathan, and he held her hand. "It's from Judith Townsend, one of the Board members asking me to call her." Olivia fiddled around in her purse, got a piece of paper and a pen.

"Hello Ms. Townsend, this is Olivia Clarke, returning your call from Western State. What can I do for you?"

"Hello Dr. Clarke, thank you for such a quick response on a Friday evening."

"You're welcome." Olivia waited.

"I am hearing rumors about Arnie Williams' handling of the campus. Would you know anything about that? I figured I'd call you since you're Faculty Senate President."

"About what?" Olivia was unsure, since she had only met Judith at the Board meeting a couple of months ago. It was strange that she was calling out of the blue.

"Since you asked, many of the Board members are concerned that he's not doing such a great job. I wondered if you would be willing to come over and bring with you the emails he's been sending out? I hear that he sent you a doozie."

Oh God, not this. Olivia wondered how she "heard" that. But there was so much of this clandestine closed-door conversation going on right now. "Sure, I can meet with you but you'll have to agree to keep everything we discuss confidential and not disclose where you got the emails." Olivia couldn't believe she said that.

"Well, let me get back to you… I'm going to ask around from some other people. I'll call you on Monday, will that be okay?"

"Sure, we'll be back from spring break. By the way, let me give you my cell number; that's the best way to get a hold of me." Olivia gave her the number, Jonathan still holding her hand.

"Thanks Dr. Clarke. I'll call you Monday. Have a nice weekend."

"Thanks, call me Olivia, Ms. Townsend, talk to you soon."

"Who was that? Bad news? Good news?"

"Judith Townsend, Board member from Western." It was taking a moment for that to sink in. Olivia began getting a picture that the situation might change, maybe the Board would do something? Pushing those thoughts to the back of her mind, reluctant to let any hope surface, she dropped her phone in her purse.

"What did she say? Is there anything I can do?" Jonathan wished Olivia would talk more about what was going on. She was so reserved about the whole thing. But of course he didn't want to do anything except what he needed to get her to California. He sure as taxes and death wasn't going to Roadims.

"She wants to meet with me about Arnie. You heard me say the whole confidentiality thing. As soon as I said that she started stammering. Now she's gonna call me Monday, supposedly."

"Hmm. Interesting. I know it's hard on you. But in a way, it's kinda good because it makes it easy to make a decision. We can always move to Arkansas if that's necessary." Jonathan didn't know what to say. May was coming and that's all he cared about. Her house was up for sale or lease. They planned for a car company to ship her car, and he was going to drive to Roadims and pick her up and bring back what was left of her stuff. Only two months, he hoped nothing would change at Western to deter Olivia or interfere with what he always maintained was *her* decision to leave.

"So, where are we going?" Olivia changed the subject.

"The plan for the evening is, dinner in the Gas Lamp District, and then *The Shrew* at the Old Globe. After the play we go to 'Just Desserts' restaurant, which I know you'll hate," Jonathan knew she loved French cakes and pastries.

"Oh that sounds like exactly what I need!"

"Then, tomorrow we'll go out to Idyllwild, have lunch and go for a hike. The weather's supposed to be excellent."

Ug, a hike? "Oh, all right, I really enjoy Idyllwild, and I haven't been there is such a long time. I think the last time I was there, Tyler and I went when Sebastian was a teenager," she half-heartedly engaged in the conversation but her mind was back in Roadims.

"We don't have to hike if you don't want to," Jonathan sensed something was wrong.

"Okay, we'll see. I don't have hiking shoes or clothes, and I sure don't wanna take on something that will cause me to injure my hip — but I would love to be outside in the California sun." She didn't want to sound like she was whining.

"No worries, we'll go get the stuff we need. And the place I have in mind is more like a walk in nature, not really a steep hike. But you'll feel like a million bucks afterwards, I promise." Jonathan looked over at her. He knew Olivia wasn't going to tolerate the great outdoors. Her idea of camping was staying in a cabin with a king-sized bed, running water, and heat, or at the very least, a fully equipped and modern 35-foot RV.

Olivia rubbed the front of her neck and slightly nodded her head, looking out the window.

"I promise," he repeated.

"Okay."

"Help me find a place to park," he diverted the conversation.

"We're here already? Cool."

They had been married now for four months. She mainly came to San Diego and Jonathan was glad. Their accounts had been merged, and she took care of the finances. Jonathan felt bad because his net worth had plummeted since the economic crisis and this worried him. He'd promised her that she could leave the university and not work, or do what she wanted to do. Now he had kept his secret that he had schizophrenia from her, and on top of that he didn't have the resources he'd claimed to have. 'God,' he thought, 'I don't have life insurance or even long term disability.' And there was no venture capitalist or interested party banging at their company door to invest in the firm.

"Yup, we are."

"There's a spot," Olivia pointed across the street.

Jonathan made an illegal U-turn and swung into the parking space. They got out of the car, and he clicked the key-lock button four times. "I just love the Gas Lamp District," he beamed as he put his arm around her shoulder and started walking.

"You always push the button four times?"

"I do. That way I know it's locked. You in the mood for steak?"

"Sure, whatever, well, except, you know, Wendy's, Mickie D's, *Jacques dans la boite*," she laughed and so did he.

"Yes, well that's my normal fare when you're not around but I know you won't eat that kind of food. Let's go to the *Blue Dolphin*. I think you'll like that."

They walked under the gas lamps of San Diego with the lights of the hillsides twinkling, the buzz of people milling in the streets and standing in line for bars, the blare of bands filling the streets, and a distant plane flying overhead. Olivia sunk into pillows of emotional relief as she studied Jonathan's wire-rimmed spectacled face. He looked just like an intellectual, with the chiseled nose, the perfect jaw line, and somewhat disheveled short brown hair. Sure he was a bit quirky, but who wasn't when you got right down to it? She'd made the right choice in marrying him and she was sure of that.

"Nancy, I just got off the phone with Judith Townsend. She wants me to provide her with documents showing Arnie's incompetence. Can you gather all the emails you have about Ryan Burns?" Olivia poked her head in Nancy's office, standing in the doorway.

"Wow, you betcha I can. When do you need them?" Nancy was happy that her phone call to her friend Anne, who was a close friend of Judith's, got the wheels spinning.

"By five o'clock would be great if you could."

"Good deal."

Olivia went back to her office. Today was Monday, she was meeting with Judith tomorrow at ten in the morning. Olivia called Patrick at home last night, after she got the second call from Judith.

After explaining what Judith wanted, Patrick blurted, "Are you tenured? You shouldn't be talking to the Board members and giving them information."

"Yes, I am tenured Patrick how could you forget that? Anyway, I am not sure if I'm going to meet with her, but I told her to call you in any event."

"Did she say what they were going to do for a president when Arnie leaves?"

Olivia was dumbfounded. "What? N-No, we didn't talk about that. But you can bring it up with Nancy when she calls you. I'm sure you'd make a good president."

"Sounds good."

"You think I should meet with her then?"

"I don't know, it's a dangerous position to put yourself in. But do what you think is best."

"See you later Patrick. Thanks, and enjoy the rest of your Sunday."

That night she determined to meet with Nancy, but she was going to have her sign a confidentiality statement, a point she didn't raise with Patrick.

By the end of the day on Monday, Nancy and other people came by her office leaving documents like wealthy people making donations to disaster relief victims. Olivia was given all kinds of emails, newspaper articles, statements from people who were all too eager to see Arnie go. Hopefully the meeting with Judith will make a difference, Olivia prayed.

———

Needier than she'd like to admit, Olivia called her friend Xena in New York. She had to talk to someone who she could trust, someone not connected in any way to Western, and Lord, somebody black.

"Hey girl, how you doin'"? Olivia was so glad to hear Xena's voice, with the 'New Yowk' accent and all.

"Hey, 'livia, girl, I'm fine, what you up to?" Xena felt so close to Olivia because she could let it all hang out with her. Olivia was just plain old black folk, never judged. You know, how black people don't look when they know something's not right, or how they don't say nothing when something's gone wrong.

"Nothing really but these folk down here 'bout to drive me crazy. Girl it's like being back in the 'hood with drive by shootings and a ghetto bird."

"I know that's right, and they use different kinda bullets in they guns, don't they?"

"Sho nuff do. We got the neighborhood gangster terrorizing, he got everybody scared to go out, scared to talk to anybody. Now I got the Board calling me asking me for information."

"Oh, so why they call you? They shouldn't be calling you they should call some administrator, not you." Xena was already angry.

"That's what I thought, but I gotta tell you 'bout this email I got." Olivia told her about Arnie's threats, what she did about it. Xena responded, so that Olivia felt the warmth of someone listening to her who heard and saw from the same experience as Olivia's. She needed that and could never get it from anyone in Roadims.

"So what you gonna do 'livia?"

"I'm gonna give her the stuff I have, but before I do I'm gonna make her sign a confidentiality letter saying I had agreed to meet with her but I changed my mind, and she didn't get anything from me."

"That's right. You gotta watch them cause they don't care nothing 'bout you or nobody but theyself. It's all about them, girl. They will use you until ain't no more a you left, I'm telling you, I am *telling* you. I seen a lot a stuff in academia. These folks girl ain't got no life, all they have is their jobs and the job define them. It's like they have no identity without their place in their institutions, and Lord the ones with PhDs and no real world experience are the worst." Xena laughed, she had a low melodic voice.

Olivia and Xena talked until the batteries in their phones wore down.

"Girl, I gotta go my phone is dying, but you know it was good talkin'." Xena hated to hang up from Olivia, she loved her so much.

"Yeah, me too, plus it's getting late and we gotta go to work in the morning. I'll keep you posted, and you take good care." Olivia loved Xena, and wished she'd spent more time with her when she lived in Kansas City.

"Oh, hey, I almost forgot, I'm going to be in New York for a conference next semester. Maybe we can hook up?"

"Yeah, girl of course. Just let me know and I'll make myself available to come see you."

"All right, then, I'll talk at you later."

"Okay, good luck tomorrow."

"Thanks, 'bye Xena."

"'Bye."

Olivia sat down at her computer and started typing the letter. She would see just what Miss Judith had to say tomorrow.

*Thou shalt decree a thing*
*and it shall be*
*established unto thee:*
*And the light*
*shall shine upon*
*thy ways*
*—Job 22:28*

# Roger That...

*April 2009*

A s Olivia was leaving, Judith thought maybe there was a chance the Board could get Arnie out. From what Olivia told her, things were bad on campus. Of course she knew that employees were greedy and selfish, never taking the owners into consideration so you couldn't trust them. Mainly what she wanted to garner from Olivia was whether or not she was instigating strife. It seemed more likely to her that Arnie was out of control. Not that the Board hadn't seen it, and she'd experienced him intimidating her — well trying.

"I flatly told him that my contributions would only be voluntary, and at the level I wanted. After that conversation, Olivia, you know, I promptly rescinded an upcoming hundred thousand dollar contribution. Please don't repeat that," she waved her hand.

"Repeat what?" Olivia played dumb, like she didn't hear anything Judith had said.

"Yes and you know that I only took the Board seat as a *personal favor* to the Governor. I know absolutely nothing about running a university but the Governor said it needed *business* minded people on its Board. O'course, at the first meeting I *instantly* detested Darnell Doolittle, with his Napoleon complex."

"I can imagine," Olivia encouraged her. She sat opposite the desk in Judith's office, just off to the side of the store.

"And, when the Board was calling for a more transparent recruitment, Darnell was adamantly opposed. Like with Little Bo-peep, all the Board 'sheep' followed. I simply don't understand the *ho-old* he has over them." She chuckled in her Southern Belle sarcastic politeness.

"I for one am not going to be bulldozed into giving more for a medical school partnership where Western only receives a pass-through from the building lease. The entire building needs to be built and the capital campaign calls for ten million dollars minimally. Not to mention their mis*management* of funds so far. They have lost their ever-living minds." Judith was shaking her head in disbelief.

"Yes, I agree with you," Olivia found her to be quite charming and refreshing.

"Now, Olivia, thank you for coming over to see me t'day. I will call Patrick and let you know if we need you at the special meeting."

Her voice completely southern, Judith stood up from her desk and regarded herself in the mirror that hung on the wall just opposite her. Her nails were painted with blood red nail polish to match her lipstick. Her haircut was impeccable and her skin was flawless with her foundation make up. She wore a country apron over her fine black wool pants and beige cashmere pullover.

"I don't know what we're gonna do if we don't get his you know what out." She smiled showing her perfectly implanted white teeth as she checked her hair placement.

"You are most welcome, Judith. I will look forward to your call." Olivia admired Judith's Rolex watch and her diamond earrings.

As she was walking out of Judith's office through the back of her store, she felt a twinge of jealousy. You couldn't buy anything in there for less than $100 and that was *with* the liquidation sale Judith was having because she was moving to the east coast. How many times had she had been in that store and left empty handed? Every time but once last October, when she bought those love bird bookends as a birthday present for Jonathan.

"Please keep that between us," she studied the shelves full of merchandise. "My husband told me he was ready to retire, and I had to sell the business. Just out of the blue he brought this up. He's quite wealthy, old enough to be my father...." She trailed off. After a silent moment to herself, she continued, "Olivia, do you think I'm being selfish because I don't want to go, giving up my store that I've built from scratch? I told him I would sell it but I'm just going to close it." After a moment she added, "It is Ashton, after all."

The only response Olivia could come up with was, "Well, I see your point. It's difficult to leave something you've created and built." Olivia knew how that felt but she didn't want to go into any detail with her.

Judith looked at Olivia with pleading desperation in her eyes, staring out from a face surrounded with perfectly finished salon-styled hair.

"You have my confidence, Judith." Olivia assured her that her candor was well placed, and never to be spoken or implied to another soul.

The two shook hands and communicated across their vast social divides that some sad things just come with being a woman no matter her station in life.

Olivia was turning out of the parking lot when Patrick called.

"Hey Patrick, I'm on my way to campus now. I thought about what you said and decided it was best to meet with Judith. I'll tell you all about it when I get there."

"Okay, I've got a meeting at eleven-thirty, so we should have plenty of time."

Olivia looked at the clock on the dashboard. "Yes, I'll be there by quarter of."

As she was sitting there in his office telling him about the meeting, the phone rang. He answered it. "It's Judith Townsend," he mouthed the words and covered the receiver with his hand. He was smiling, something he hadn't done for months.

Olivia sat for a few minutes, listening to his end of the conversation.

"Yes, that's right. I intend to step down as Dean in a couple of months, at the end of June." Patrick listened. "Yes, we did, nationwide, and it was declared a failed search. We got good candidates, but the shortlisted ones withdrew after they heard we were going to pay eighty-five K for a School of Business dean." Patrick laughed. "You can't get anybody good for that kind of compensation," he was doing his selling routine.

Olivia half whispered and half motioned with hand signals to Patrick that she was going to her office, and to come by when he was done. He nodded, motioned her to close his door, and turned to look out the window.

Hope pulsed through Olivia's body as she walked down the hall to her office.

That hope sprung eternal when Judith called Olivia later that day, she said "The Board is going to have a special meeting."

"That's great news," Olivia nearly sneezed the words out she was so excited.

"Yes, a closed-door session to vote to have Arnie terminated, in about two weeks, on April 17 in the evening. We have to do it so that a quorum of Board members can make it and the requisite time for announcing the meeting is met."

"I see."

"Can you come to the meeting?"

Olivia was shocked at the question.

"I think Patrick should be there, and that ought to be sufficient. He's better informed about the situation than I am." Olivia was more than willing to give him the stage since there may be a hidden guillotine behind the curtain.

"So will the faculty hold the vote of no confidence at the the April 29 meeting?" Judith came to the point.

Olivia felt shocked. Inside she screamed, What? We aren't having a vote of no confidence, don't you get that?

"What do you mean? The meeting on the twenty-ninth is the

annual faculty meeting where faculty vote for next year's senators and *Faculty Handbook* changes. I told you that earlier." Olivia wanted to make sure this was clear. "But if the Board doesn't take action to remove Arnie, then the vote of no confidence will go forward next fall, probably around September or October."

"Oh yes, you are correct, you did make that clear. Well you have my number, let me know if you need anything from me. Do NOT hesitate to call. Thank you for everything, Olivia."

"You're welcome, and good luck with all your endeavors."

Olivia hung up and went directly to Nancy, "We need to tell Dan to put Patrick in as Dean until someone is appointed Interim." Nancy had been christened 'Acting Assistant Dean' when the search had been officially announced as failed.

"That's a good idea, let's do it. He's the one who knows what's going on and how to run the place. How was the meeting?" Nancy didn't want to pry but she was dying to know.

"Fine, fine, Patrick's on the phone with Judith right now."

"What a relief! Maybe we can get back to or move into a normal operating mode." Nancy really wanted the Dean's position, and if Patrick was in there as President, they could go back to what it was like "back then".

People looked back, and now with nostalgia, back before Luis left. Olivia and Nancy both agreed they didn't have to watch their backs or wonder if what they were seeing was a line of BS longer than the people waiting at Walmart on Black Friday. Everybody had their roles, knew they were stuck but being okay with it. Whenever somebody up the ladder retired or died, the next person in line would take the job, like natural selection. Back then you could just sit and listen to Luis and know it was like getting a lecture from your Dad who only complained and never did anything about it. It was the way he showed he cared, and he wanted you to spend the money and take the car — he felt like he had a purpose. In the regular life of folks, that is, not like Olivia's father.

The thing is that, nobody ever suspects what the answer to prayer looks like and so sometimes people pray these general prayers like 'Lord, make this place grow or make the community more progressive, more modern, less like a good old boy network.' People really wanted Luis gone. And they prayed for it. Even Olivia did. She figured his being gone would usher in a new progressive era.

The thing is God has a sense of humor they say. But Olivia found it's more like a sense of God saying, "I don't know what you mean. Last week you asked for a new boss, this week you want to be a different person but don't want to work at it, and last year you asked for more money. You have no sense of direction, no control over your own will." God gives according to one's specificity, on a watch nobody can figure. And so, somehow this answer to the prayer to get rid of Luis was baffling everybody.

Folks found out the devil they knew was better than the one they didn't. The people were in the desert without a leader. "It was better when…" they lamented their disdain for Luis' velvety dictatorship and searched for a way to turn back.

Olivia definitely wanted out NOW because "back then" it was different. She only had thirty-three days before she changed her residence to California. She knew that wasn't going to be the end. Living there was one thing. Finding another tenure track appointment was a whole other thing.

"I gotta go back to Patrick's office, so I'll talk to you later, Nanc. I know he's not gonna come find me after the phone call is over." Olivia waved and left.

Once in his office, Patrick handed her a little twisted piece of stainless steel with a ball on the end of it. "Here, this is for you." He smiled at her, as she took the little gadget from him.

"What's this?"

"This is your magic wand. You have just pulled off a miracle. Arnie will be gone by the end of the summer, and they're putting John

Bryant in as Board Chairman in place of Darnell, at the June meeting."

Olivia stood in his office and leaned back against the wall, resting herself there with a long heavy sigh. She closed her eyes for a moment to savor that feeling. She'd had a similar feeling before, and she relived the Exodus from Philadelphia where her very own Red Sea had been parted.

Riding in the police car to the airport was the last step in a long secret escape from the house on Stillman Street. Her mother instilled in them that they couldn't breathe a word of the plan to him because, well they all knew that it would be bad. Mom would get beat again; Olivia would have to call the police — again. They would arrest him, put on the handcuffs and escort him in his underwear to the police car. When they got to ride in the patrol car to the airport to catch a plane to California, it was quite a different situation. The policeman was so nice. After He'd left for work that day, her mother pulled out all the suitcases she had packed. She hid them from him and talked the whole thing over with her friend Stella and her sister Doris. Olivia overheard her talking on the phone all the time.

"Yeah, chile I got to go, got to get away from here," she'd say taking a drag on her Viceroy, shaking her head, worry furrowing her eyebrows. Olivia heard her say she would get a job in California, raise the girls by herself if she had to. She could do bad by herself, didn't have to put up with it no more.

That morning they got dressed, Olivia and Karen, and her mother dressed Faith. The old brown hard suitcases with locks and keys remember them? Well that's what they had and they were so huge, no wheels, back when you needed a Pullman Porter. Her mother checked to see if she had the tickets in her purse; she wore a hat, gloves, dress coat and dress suit. The girls did too. It was February in Philly so you know it was cold. Black people dressed when they went somewhere. Dresses were lined, shoes were made of leather, coats made of real wool, and honey look, no faux fur. Her father used to dress well too, the suits and all, how they hung on him right, fitted.

What Olivia didn't know then but could understand now as she stood there in Patrick's office was that those were some really bad times too in the late 1960s and early 1970s. It was right about then that notions of equality for women were heating up, spurred on by the civil rights movement of blacks and the end of segregation. Desegregation broke black communities, but that's another story. That's what prompted her mother to get the guts to leave. And no, she couldn't take the fine wood furniture, the draperies, the china, or the other decorations from the house, she took what clothes she could fit into the suitcases, hopes, dreams, dignity, determination, and left everything else. All Olivia knew was they were getting out finally. And it felt so great like laying down in green pastures and walking by still waters.

Olivia opened her eyes, "Thanks, Patrick. We had to do something to part the Red Sea. But it's not over yet. Anyway, congratulations on being reinstated as Dean." She hugged him.

Hugging wasn't Patrick's strong suit, and he floundered uncomfortably in an awkward embrace.

"How'd you know about that?"

"I have my sources," Olivia chided.

Olivia thought about how Arnie would be recounted and remembered when he left Western. Nobody but his Mama would be sad about it, and she might not at least not when she was honest with herself. But publicly, it would be like any other funeral, nobody saying anything about what an ass he was because it wasn't p.c. However, people could rest in peace.

"Here, I'm going down to see Nancy so I'll walk with you." Patrick walked like a peacock with his feathers spread wide, certain that Judith and the other Board members were going to get rid of Arnie.

In his mind Patrick imagined being called to testify against Arnie, and the triumph of being appointed by the Board as Interim President since they now would listen to reason: take a year and figure out what we want in a President, and then recruit through a professional firm. Patrick could get his experience; he would sail up to his retirement date with accolades and lots of well-done-young-mans.

His first task as President would be to get rid of Renee and bring in a real chief financial officer, and after that he would clear out Arts and Sciences administration. Make Dan retire, get a qualified Dean for the school. He would put Olivia in charge of the School of Business. He counted the faculty, one, two, three, four — four faculty over there would get replaced since they would be coerced into retiring. Finally, he was going to enjoy the limelight he'd worked so long and hard for. It was sweet.

*May 2009*

"It smells different here now," Jonathan said, rolling down the window as they drove out of Arkansas heading through Missouri.

Arkansas smelled like love. Hay bails, thawing soil, fresh creek water, and newly placed mulches surrounding blossoming annuals and buried acorns. It smelled like that in the springtime. In winter it smelled more like neutrality not caring one way or another with sleeping animals in every semi-warm nook, and naked tree branches glistening with ice. Summer smelled like lust, you could smell it whenever you went to the local Shake's for a Concrete, or stopped at Sonic for a root beer float that 'Sonic's got and other's don't.' Musty rain, Cicadas songs carrying on the humidity, as teenagers made out on screened porches and in backseats after a joyride. Fall smelled like hope when Labor Day finally passed and the public pools closed, the men winterized, the kids went back to school, the women grateful for no more trips to the lake this year. Falling leaves drying from winter's freeze, Arkansas smelled like death in the winter, not death in a bad way but in that way when people know it's time to say goodbye. Love would soon return again.

"Yes, it does have it's own distinctive smell, one for each season," Olivia agreed, deciding this was the best answer. She was looking forward to the drive through Colorado. They were going to take Interstate 70, a completely different route than she took when she drove, alone, to Kansas City six years ago.

Jonathan wondered what kind of denial Olivia was in when he arrived three days ago. "Oh, I don't have that much to take back with us," she'd said to him before he arrived. But there was way too much stuff to pack in the back of the Range Rover.

"When did the car ship?" He asked her as they were packing books to take to the UPS Store.

"The car shippers picked up the Mercedes yesterday, and it should arrive in San Diego a couple days after we get there," Olivia said. "Hopefully it'll be in good order, as I don't trust them one bit."

"I'm sure it'll be fine," Jonathan tried to be encouraging. "Can you pass me that small box?" He stood by the pile of books on the floor of her office.

Jonathan grabbed the box and started filling it. At least, finally, they'd sold her house, even in the recession. The difference in the sales price and the closing costs was about twenty-four thousand and he'd given her the money. Well, he'd put it on his credit card, and figured he'd pay it off at some point. It wasn't something he thought he should tell her about, since she was so glad he'd done that.

For the two days that Jonathan was there, they packed up the rest of her belongings, and cleaned up inside and outside the house.

If only they could take the house with them. There was no way he could afford such a house in California, but he wasn't willing to move to Arkansas.

As they pulled away from the driveway for the last time, Olivia was quiet.

Jonathan reached over, touched her. "You okay?" Jonathan watched Olivia. She didn't look back as they drove away. They were at the point of no return, but his fear remained, that she was going to change her mind. He wanted her in San Diego, away from all the turmoil, completely focused on him.

"I'm fine, just feeling a little sad. Hey, did I tell you Harmony got another job?"

"Really? Where? How?" He glanced over at her. Boy, wouldn't it be great if Olivia found work in California? She kept telling him that it was a long shot, her age, her field, and her degree being mitigating factors. He didn't know, but she could find *some* kind of work, maybe not in academia, but something. She could make one or two thousand dollars a month and that would be fine. At least she didn't have any debts and so he figured he could cover the expenses however minimally. But, it would be tight if she didn't work, so he wasn't sure how that was going to pan out. He'd told her she could do whatever she wanted to do, but it had to include income.

"It's at the University of Rochester. Apparently somebody she knows from her work through jimbe and her Entropy music group told her about an opening in the Ethnomusicology center. She was able to get a joint appointment with the Anthropology department there. Starts in the fall. I'm really happy for Harmony; there've been too many conversations when Harmony alluded to suicide. Brock left a gaping hole in her life, and it is swallowing her. Moving on is probably the best thing."

"That's great, good for her. She's closer to Justin too, right?"

It always amazed Olivia when Jonathan remembered these kinds of details. She just assumed he wasn't listening most of the time.

"Yup, exactly.

"What did Patrick say when you turned in your resignation?"

"I didn't resign yet."

Jonathan was shocked. "Why, I thought you said you were?"

"Right, but I'm going to teach summer school online so I can't resign until that's over."

"Okay… but the job search is going well?"

"Not exactly. I've sent out at least fifty, maybe seventy packets to announced positions but so far…." Olivia didn't offer much.

"I'm sure you'll find something," Jonathan encouraged. But he was relieved that she was going to have income at least through the end of July.

They rode along in silence for a while, which Olivia was grateful for. Driving was a good way to make distance between situations, more real than flying. She leaned her head back, "Let me know if you want me to drive," she smiled at her husband, knowing he wouldn't turn the wheel over for hours. He nodded his head, turned up the satellite radio.

She looked out the window at the cornfields of Kansas, the sun bright, wind bending the crops. Rounded bails of hay sat along the road. The meeting with the Board would happen while she was on summer break. Patrick was back in there as Dean. And, most importantly, she was no longer the Faculty Senate President. She passed the baton to Wes with pleasure.

"Here's all the resolutions the faculty voted on, and here's the procedure for holding the Vote next fall. Arnie knows it's coming, but hopefully you won't have to hold it, if the Board does what they say they're gonna do." Olivia gave him two three-inch thick binders stuffed full of papers. "I'll email you the documents I have, and you can get access to the ones posted on line. Just call over to the Blackboard office." It felt like a weight had been lifted off her shoulders.

"Great, 'Livia, thanks. I do expect the Board to take action, I've been in conversation with John." Wes was so gruff. His grey hair and beard were yellowed by years of smoking, his skin wrinkled from that, too much sin, and too much drinking. "I don't care Olivia, he needs to go. I aim to make it so, if they don't." He took her binders and stood up.

"Good luck, Wes. Let me know if you need anything—oh, by the way, I got this call from a guy who wanted to tell me about some illegal activity related to Arnie." She pushed a piece of paper into one of the binders. "You call him, I told him who you are."

"'Livia, we got enough evidence to put the screws to him already. Hopefully the Board will do their jobs."

"Honey," Jonathan interrupted her private thoughts, "Let's stop and get some barbeque before we leave Kansas."

"Barbeque? Sure. Let me get out the iPhone and see what's nearby. I think we can find a place in Witchita. You know, all the faculty—Nancy, Eric, Claire and Patrick—they all got iPhones now."

He beamed, "Very cool, all 'cause of your husband! Oh and uh, we already passed Witchita," he laughed. "Here's a place up ahead, let's stop there." He pointed at the sign on the highway.

He knew she was thinking about Western. It was a terrible sight to see, from the outside. Patrick used her, Nancy manipulated her. Arnie threatened her. Of all the people there, Harmony was the only person who didn't want something from her.

"Hmph, I didn't know we'd come that far," she laughed.

While Jonathan was getting them to the restaurant, she checked her email. "Oh my God, honey, Dan Fogerty stepped down as VP AA and he's going back to teaching. Arnie's putting Timothy Jones in as his replacement. Oh wow, this is bad, this is very bad." Olivia shook her head and laughed.

"When's the Board supposed to act on getting rid of Arnie?"

"At the June meeting, third Friday.

"Oh, I thought they were doing it before classes were over." Jonathan concentrated on the navigation system display, looking for the best way to get to the restaurant.

"That's the meeting where they're getting rid of Darnell, but the special meeting to get rid of Arnie was supposed to be a month ago, you're right, but they decided not to hold it. They're gonna do this "go into closed session" thing at the Board meeting and discuss it." Olivia held her hands up making quote marks.

"You don't believe they're gonna do it?"

"Nope. I really don't, but I hope they do." Olivia put her iPhone back in her purse, and got her lip balm. Rubbing it on her lips, she checked herself in the side mirror and unbuckled her seat belt.

"Sure hope the barbeque is good," Jonathan got out, waited for her at the hood of the car, and took her hand when she got there. He loved her so much, it hurt.

Olivia couldn't believe she was married to him, that she'd sold her house, and moved to San Diego. Her plan was to finish summer school online, and see what happened for fall. She couldn't quit her job, because he didn't have enough money for her not to work. She didn't want to hurt his feelings by saying it that way, but hell, what could she say? She *would* stay at home, but he would have to have a lot more net worth. And when she thought about it, she was disappointed that he lied to her about his finances and mad at the economy — or whatever. What she wanted was to not work or have to think about money anymore. That was the whole point of looking for this relationship. But how would it look if she broke up with him because he wasn't wealthy? So she let it go as best she could but "God," she thought, "I was *totally clear* with you about this. Why did you let me go forward if he wasn't what I asked for?"

Maybe something would open up so she could quit, but things were so bad in the market. Not a single nibble from all those application packets. It was disheartening. Then, Harmony just gets a job with a snap. She was glad for her but a little jealous.

Jonathan was wonderful, and she loved him like she never thought she would be capable of. And most of all she let him love her and she was committed to him and the marriage. Digging down, she wondered why she felt uneasy. Then she recognized it. Olivia felt like there was something wrong but couldn't place it. It was the same feeling she had when they were driving away from the house. Like she was making a huge mistake. She stuffed those feelings down back to her solar plexus, and told herself to relax.

In spite of teaching classes online, which she hated doing, the summer in San Diego moved by in slow motion, surrounded by warmth and love, and Olivia felt wrapped in its cocoon. She and Jonathan went to visit his parents for three days in Florida, taking rides on their sailboat and enjoying the sun of the Florida Keys. Olivia felt like she'd died and gone to heaven.

At one point her luscious summer was interrupted when she attended an academic conference in Ann Arbor to present a paper. The trip expenses were supposed to be reimbursed to her: Patrick told her she could get reimbursed from money he had in some budget somewhere off the radar. Olivia completed the necessary forms and gave them to Nancy.

"Hey girl!"

"Hey, what's going on?" Olivia responded when she called.

"Nothing, same old same old."

"That's good, I guess. They say no news is good news." Olivia tried to make the conversation light, knowing that Nancy wanted to know when she was coming back for office hours, which Western held even in spite of the fact that no students came to campus in the summer.

"True enough. Hey, what was the conference you went to?

"Oh that was the Association of Marketers. I saw that there was a deadline to get the reimbursement forms in, coming up here pretty quick."

Nancy promised she would get it to her, "Oh, don't worry about that, I know people in the accounts payable office, so the deadlines don't matter."

Olivia didn't make any plans to go to Roadims since she didn't want to spend the money on it. But, she never told that to Nancy.

Her phone was ringing, she looked and it was Patrick.

"Nancy, Patrick is calling me on the other line, let me call you back in a minute."

"Good deal. He's got some news for you."

"Hey, Patrick, what's up?" Olivia switched over.

"How's life out in California?" He sounded upbeat and happy.

"Great, we're taking it easy," Olivia was careful because a call from Patrick meant trouble.

"Timothy stepped down as VP AA and is going back to teaching. Did you see his email?"

"What?" Olivia realized she shouted. "Why?" She walked downstairs to her computer, and logged into the email. "I'm looking at my email now."

"Well, let me summarize it for you. He didn't like Arnie's management style." Patrick wasn't laughing.

"Did the Board take action last month?" Olivia hadn't been looking at the news because part of her didn't want to know, the other part didn't want to be disturbed.

"No, they didn't. They extended his contract, and put John Bryant in as Chairman."

Olivia was silent.

"Anyway, Arnie's asked me to take over as Interim VP AA. What do you think?"

"Whose gonna do the Dean's job?"

"I'll still remain Dean, but Nancy has agreed to be Associate Dean."

"So you're gonna be Dean of the School of Business *and* Interim VP AA?"

"Looks that way. We can't recruit for either one of them now, it's July 17, the cycle for hiring for this year is completed. We have to wait until next academic year, 2010."

Olivia wanted to say, that's total bullshit, the whole mess. What about academic integrity and objectivity? "Well, I think you'll be good at the VP position, and it'll get you through to your retirement date, look good on your CV. Just remember who Arnie is. Never forget it, and don't think you can change him Patrick."

"So I have your support?"

Olivia felt Patrick's sting. He was *not* asking for support. He was flaunting his triumph in her face.

"As much as I can give, without sacrificing myself, sure." Olivia had to put some caveats on it. Though she didn't say it to anyone, she was disappointed that Nancy got the job. She could have just said from the get go that she wanted the job, and all this could have been avoided.

"Okay, thanks. Enjoy yourself." Patrick sounded happier than Olivia could remember him sounding in the last year.

Olivia read all of Timothy's email, which was distributed to the campus. Then she opened the online version of *The Globe*, and it was reproduced there in a scathing article about Western. Oh my God, she covered her mouth.

"Thanks Patrick, you too." She hung up.

"I gotta call Xena, I hope she's home." Olivia pressed Xena's picture on her contacts list. After a few rings, she answered. "Hey Xena, it's Olivia. You got a minute?"

"Hey, girl, yes, what you up to?"

Olivia put her headset on, and got her hat and walked out into the sunshine, heading she didn't know where. She started walking towards the park.

"Oh, nothing much, but just the usual."

"How was the conference?"

"Good, you know, academic conferences. The hotel was nice, the Dalton. Very upscale. But I'm still waiting to get reimbursed for that trip." Olivia pressed the "Walk" button while she waited at a light.

"Yeah, I know how that is."

"Can you believe this? Two internal appointments to VP AA stepped down in a matter of weeks, and my Dean, Patrick, has now agreed to take the job." Olivia was on the verge of tears. Reaching into her khaki skirt pocket, she pulled out a tissue. Putting her blackrimmed Oakley sunglasses on the collar of her pink tank top, she wiped her eyes.

"So who's going to be the dean? You?"

Putting her sunglasses back on, Olivia said, "No, girl. He's going to do both jobs."

"What? That's crazy! How can they do that? That's going against the whole structure of the university."

And this was all the validation Olivia needed to hear.

"Yeah, I know. Hang on Xena, there's a plane over head."

When the noise died down, she continued.

"Is the Board doing anything, I mean, don't they get something is wrong if people keep stepping down from the administrative positions?"

"They were supposed to get rid of the new president but instead they extended his contract. Can you believe that?" Olivia stopped by a landscaped area with a running fountain. She put her foot up on the short stucco and brick wall that encircled it and bent over and tied her shoe.

"You know, I'm not surprised by anything in academia anymore. So you think that Judith was just a play now?

"Exactly."

"How's the job search coming?"

"Slow. Not a single nibble. Not one."

"I know girl, it's ugly out there. But you'll find something."

"Until I do, I'm going to commute to Western. I think I'm going to fly in on Sundays and fly home on Wednesdays. At least for the fall semester. And in the spring, I've got my classes online, so I'm not going to go to Roadims at all unless it's absolutely necessary."

"That's right, you're going to France for a couple of months right?"

"Right, but that's not till January or February, but yes, that's why I'm teaching on line. Then, I'm applying for a sabbatical for the following year, so at least I can give myself two years to find a new gig." She stopped in front of the Walmart. Fishing around in her back pocket she found a one dollar bill. Unfolding it she fed it into the vending machine and bought a bottle of water.

"You think they gonna pay for a sabbatical?" Xena asked in her nonchalant manner.

"No, but I'll take an unpaid one, that way I can have an affiliation with the university, health benefits. I hope I get a stipend as a visiting prof somewhere."

"That sounds like a good plan, honey I don't blame you. You gotta work the system to your good."

"Thanks, Xena. How you doing?" Olivia took a sip from her water bottle.

Olivia walked found herself at the park about a mile and a half from the townhouse and felt herself relaxing as she chatted with Xena. She always knew what to say.

"Girl, I'm fine, dealing with these folks too, trying to stay away from the ax man cutting budgets and taking names." Xena laughed.

"I'm sure it's frightening with you being an administrator now." Some children ran by laughing and shouting as Olivia walked around the park, full of trees and playgrounds. It was packed on this hot summer afternoon, as mothers sat fanning themselves and dogs lay in the grass without moving a muscle when people passed by.

"True, but I would trade my tenure again any day, because at least I'm free. You got kids with you?"

"Oh, no, those are children playing in the park. But, yes, I agree with that, tenure is really not all that it's cracked up to be, huh? Well, I'm glad to hear you're doing fine too. Hey, I'm going to be in your neck of the woods in the fall at a conference. Maybe we can hook up?"

"Oh yeah, definitely. Just email me the dates, I'll come down to see you. Where is the conference?"

"Over in Boston, at Bentley College." Olivia headed back towards the house. Her hat provided good shade against the burning afternoon sun. But next time she would think twice about taking a walk in this 100-degree heat.

"That's real close, so yeah let's get together."

"I'm pretty sure the conference is the third week of September. And I'm paying for that myself too. But we'll talk of course between now and then."

"At least a few times," Xena chuckled.

"Let me let you go, I know I've taken your whole afternoon." Olivia wanted to get back home and get off the phone, since Jonathan would be home soon. She didn't like talking on the phone when he was around.

"It's been great talking, and don't let them people get you down."

"Thanks, Xena, good conversation as usual. I'll talk to you soon."

As Olivia opened the door to the townhouse, she had a new resolve. If she went back to Western in the fall, things were going to be different.

*Through persistence,*
*self knowledge, prayer,*
*commitment, optimism,*
*a resolute trust in God*
*and the building of your own*
*personal moral strength*
*you can enjoy the blessings*
*of a deeper faith and*
*face the difficulties of life*
*with courage and confidence.*
*—Norman Vincent Peale*

# The Turn

Olivia sweltered in San Diego's record length one-hundred-eight-degree heat wave. But all the public universities and colleges in southern California put the freeze on hiring since money evaporated from the state budget in the protracted recession. Community colleges were only throwing bones to adjuncts, and only to people the department heads knew. The racket of hiring faculty became clearer and clearer as the recession deepened. Just because there was a position announcement in *The Chronicle*, it didn't mean there was a real position. Colleges and universities hired who they wanted and hid behind the cloak of equal opportunity. Yeah, sure, a few positions were *bona fide* openings but only a few. At any rate, whatever jobs were posted, inside or outside California, the news reported that thousands of people applied for them as universities turned hungry recent PhDs out onto the street.

Olivia lay in bed night after night terrified both of not having a job and wondering about what was going to happen in academia in general. Anger mixed with disappointment as she faced the fact that she wasn't going to be able to quit, and, that she was in a dying industry.

"Jonathan, I have a plan for the fall." Olivia approached the topic with him as they were laying in bed one night, a couple weeks before school was to start.

"You mean, for...?" Jonathan was distracted watching *The Big Bang Theory*.

"Fall at Western." She let her book plop down on her lap, and pushed her pillows up against the handcrafted wood headboard Jonathan made for them. Olivia's hair was piled all over her head.

"Oh, I thought you were going to resign." Jonathan acted surprised, raising only his ear in her direction.

"Yes, but you know I haven't gotten another position, and I don't want to go to France or my conference in New York being unemployed."

"Okay, so what's the plan?"

"I'm going to commute back and forth to Arkansas, leave on Sundays and return on Wednesdays."

Jonathan didn't say anything but he finally looked away from the 42-inch TV. He turned the corners of his mouth down and raised his eyebrows.

"Fly to Roadims, rent a car, and stay in a suites hotel, like Extended Stay. It's just three nights a week for the semester. Then when we get back from France, I'm working online from home. That way, we keep the income and I stay continuously employed."

"That's not a bad idea," Jonathan was grateful she'd come up with it. "When would you start commuting?"

"Classes begin at the end of August so that's what, in three weeks or so? And then I wouldn't do it for Thanksgiving or Fall Break, and of course for the conference in October. So really it only boils down to maybe twelve weeks?"

"Kewl." There's no way he would be able to do that, but if she wanted to, he wasn't going to stop her. Returning his attention to the TV, he said, "Let me know if you need me to do anything to help with that." He had no inkling of how he could help her but it sounded supportive.

"You want a cup of hot tea?"

"Sure, I'd love one."

Olivia flung back the olive green duvet cover and matching 600-threadcount sheets, and padded her way barefoot down stairs. She tied her thigh-length black robe at the waist as she went.

Meanwhile Jonathan sat still in bed feeling guilty about letting his wife commute to Western. Shrugging his shoulders and sticking one navy blue pajama-ed leg out from under the covers, he switched over to the TiVo searching for more episodes of *The Big Bang Theory* using his black, giant universal remote.

Filling the red teakettle with tap water, Olivia whispered, "Oh God, what have I done?" She blinked hard to hold back the tears. Her eyes burned as she put the kettle on the front gas burner, turned the knob. When the clicking stopped, she turned the flame down and leaned against the granite counter top near the sink. Head in hand, in her mind she added up the debt on the properties they owned in Arkansas and California, on what had become valueless dirt. "We can invade our retirement accounts," she said to herself. "That's just plain stupid," she answered.

The teakettle whistled, as she took two mugs out of the cupboard. They were two Monet's that Tyler had given her, from the Guggenheim. Dipping the chamomile teabags into the hot water she put her right foot on top of the other's arch. "Ooo, my bunion is back again, damn."

Drizzling the honey into her cup, she decided that on her way back upstairs she would grab the laptop so she could make her reservations for the first trip back to Roadims.

*Roadims, Arkansas, Late August, Fall Semester 2009*

At the opening address of the faculty for fall semester 2009, everyone endured Patrick's VP AA drone, which was worse than any they'd heard so far. Sure there was the bad continental breakfast, and of course the apathy. Leading up to it though, there were no bets about how long he would talk, and no expectation about a raise however meager. But faculty all over campus tentatively allowed themselves to anticipate finally having a sane person in Administration.

To their chagrin, Arnie was still there.

True to his nature or calling or whatever, Arnie took the stage using it as an opportunity for continuing to drum up panic and nausea in his hellfire and brimstone speech about the financial future of the State of Arkansas and the university.

Perhaps Patrick would be able to manage him. Olivia knew he wouldn't be able to — hell Patrick couldn't manage Claire. In fact, recently she had placed her picture on Facebook, well it was her swimsuit edition that got the students talking and "friending." Faculty, some, well most, resisted getting email remotely but Claire? Now she could do a bunch of stuff online. It was probably because she taught Internet Marketing and used the university as a cover for her real job. Actually, faculty complained that it was people like Claire that gave them a bad rep— she never showed up to meetings, never returned email, and always promised to take the lead on committee assignments. Her point was, "Hey, this is a great gig. I've got my real estate business, and it's worth almost two million even here in Roadims," she once told Olivia.

Envy crawled up all their spines.

Claire came to campus when she felt like it and *some*times that coincided with her class schedule. One day she was wearing a yellow dress with a side-zip, capped sleeve with a white ballet neck border. The dress was some kind of linen blend but if she made one small wrong move people standing nearby would have to duck and cover because at least one of her huge breasts would pop someone upside the head. The split in the back of the dress, the back vent, was spread apart, a few stitches broken from the stress of her hips pulling the dress in opposite directions. Shoes from Nordstrom, sling-backs with pointed toes, tan with white trim, that snapped sharply on the state-issued linoleum floor. Her hair dyed red-brown, limply sitting on her head apologizing for thinning, porcelain teeth flashing below the Channel diamond studded one inch rectangular framed glasses whose reflecting light blinded anyone from seeing her as regular.

At the School of Business faculty meeting that followed that morning's address, faculty denied Patrick's cry of 'WOLF!' when he switched out of his VP AA hat and into his Dean's. Distance learning was pointed to as a tornado coming toward them that was gonna wipe them off their faculty high horses.

"We should model ourselves as 'A Phoenix'" he said, "and this model was going campus-wide." Eric leaned over and said to Olivia, "Why don't you tell him to shut up?"

Olivia told Eric "I flatly disagree with Patrick, but I ain't gonna say nothing to him, not here in public." But she had told Patrick in private one time—when she figured he was in the mood to hear a dissenting view—that distance education was substandard. He didn't disagree with her on that point; he did maintain however, that it was the way to generate revenue.

"Yeah, well there are still students who don't want to take classes online," Brian blurted out. Eric, Claire, Alex, and many of the other faculty nodded in agreement. "Besides, education is not all about making money," he added.

Olivia glanced over at Nancy, now fully appointed to Associate Dean. She just smiled sitting in her chair because she was too far in over her head to say anything intelligible. And anyway, Patrick did all the talking and decision making. Nancy basically served as his gofer and dirty work doer.

At the department lunch in the Smokehouse Grill Restaurant that followed Patrick's bullshit meeting, people ate in silence. Nancy-the-Department-Head tried to drum up enthusiasm without success, mainly because she started with the added point that course evaluations were now going to be equal to advising in promotional considerations. All the faculty knew there weren't going to be too many promotions, at least not for a while, especially those who were already full professors. People who still had a promotion left to full professor knew too that they shouldn't hold their breaths, partly too because they were hardly going to be hanging around waiting for that.

"Who is going for promotion this year?" Eric asked.

When that didn't go anywhere, Nancy tried to shift the tone of the meeting. "Does anyone have any announcements? Eric, why don't you start?"

"What are y'all having today?" The waitress interrupted.

After people ordered their lunches, Eric said, "I don't have anything."

And so it went around the table.

When it came time for Claire to say something, she pointed to her body, "I'm twenty-five pounds lighter than I was last year at this very time," she grinned and pulled up her Facebook page on her iPhone and passed her phone around the table.

"Whoa, you look hot in that swimsuit!" Jim said kind of in disbelief. "Do your students see this too?"

"Absolutely!" Claire had no shame.

"Okay, here we go, I have baby backs..." the waitress reached over, setting the plates on the table.

While doling out a lot of false praise for Claire's photos, the faculty put their faces in their lunch.

"Are you divorced now, Claire?" Eric didn't try to be polite.

"Yes, we're so done, it was easy with the kids being grown, and we have established a corporation for our real estate. I'll tell you more about it on Monday, after my ten o'clock class," she promised.

"What's going on with Arnie, Olivia?" Nancy intervened and changed the subject.

Olivia didn't take the bait. "Hey, I dunno."

"The vote needs to go forward, the Board's not gonna do shit." Eric said, chomping down on his chicken Ceasar salad, some of it falling out of the corners of his mouth as he talked.

Silence swallowed the table, changing the mood to solemn. They all ate and nobody made small talk.

"You all know we still have Program Review to do this semester. It'll be due before the start of winter break."

"We can dust off what we have," Olivia offered.

"No, Patrick said we need to do a new set of benchmarks."

Olivia and Eric exchanged glances.

"That's insane," Eric yelled, the veins poked out of his fat neck. "We spent almost a whole semester on that just a couple years ago. There's no way that business schools like ours have changed that much."

"I'm not doing it," Olivia stated. "I'll do another piece of the Program Review if you want, but not that."

"Whatever. That's what Patrick said," Nancy shrugged. Then she snapped her fingers and pointed with her index finger to the air, "Oh, and Brian is the new MBA Program director."

"So Patrick didn't bother to tell me about that?" Olivia asked. "I mean, not that I wanted to keep being what amounted to his secretary."

"He said he talked to you before he did that!" Nancy said. "Damn him!"

Silence fell on the table again, until the check came.

"Well, I hope you enjoyed your lunch, complements of the business school."

"I'd rather have a raise, not a ten-dollar lunch," Jim slurred.

"Yeah, well you can forget about that," Claire snickered, "Unless you leave here anyway."

"Okie dokie, let's head back to campus, we've got students to advise." Nancy moved out of the booth.

"Sure, there'll be loads of students waiting to enroll this afternoon. Why don't they just say they want us to have office hours from 1 to 4 P.M.? At least that wouldn't be an insult to my intellect," Eric complained as he slid out from the inside of the booth.

It was going to be a long semester.

At the office on the following Monday, Nancy-the-Associate-Dean, not Nancy-the-Department-Head, came to the doorway of Olivia's office and stared blankly at her. Nancy motioned to Olivia to come into the hall. Other faculty were already standing there as Olivia approached, and Nancy pointed to Claire's office. The group moved in unison to peek through the door window. The office was dark and empty.

"Claire disappeared over the weekend, Sunday night campus security recorded her moving her things out. She sent me an email saying she was going to Belgium. Could someone cover her ten o'clock?"

It was 10:20 — nobody volunteered.

"Oh, so that's why she said all that stuff," Eric concluded.

"We'll get through it," Nancy made an attempt at lightening the mood.

Faculty went back to their offices and didn't say anything.

Olivia waited for Nancy, and followed her into her office.

"So Associate Dean? Congratulations. I'm sure you're excited?" Olivia wanted to ask: Why did they appoint you? But she didn't.

"Wanna be the department head? We sure could use you." Nancy sat down in her chair, checked her lipstick in the mirror hanging next to her desk.

"That would be stupid of me now wouldn't it?" Olivia sat down, crossed her legs.

"Oh, so you're saying I'm stupid now?" Nancy knew Olivia thought she was incompetent.

"No, I don't mean that. I'm still on the market, I've got two conferences to attend and papers to present — which I'm paying for by the way. I'm going to France as an invited professor next semester, and I'm planning on applying for a full year's sabbatical next year. Remember? My classes are all online for spring 2010. So it wouldn't make sense for me to go into the department head role. And besides, the twenty-seven hundred dollar annual administrative contract ain't worth it to me."

"Oh, that's right, I do remember. I'm sorry, half the time I can't remember to put my shoes on, there's so much going on. Ken's worried about me 'cause I have no desire, and this weight, I can't get it off." Her voice started cracking. "This place drives me crazy." Nancy started to cry.

Olivia was startled by Nancy's letting down her guard. She never did that, always maintaining her personal distance, gossiping up a storm. "Why don't you retire, you're eligible? You don't have to put up with this." Olivia tried to encourage her.

"Yeah, I should've but now it's too late, I have to wait another cycle. And besides, I'm not old enough yet to get Medicare, still got six years before then. You know the university doesn't cover health care after you retire, that's outta your pocket. What I hear is that it's around fifteen hundred a month. That's why so many people don't retire." Nancy dabbed the inner corners of her eyes before the tears could spill over.

Olivia considered what was going on in Nancy's financial situation. Something had to be bad for her to keep wanting to be *there*. Ken wasn't working, he was sick all the time. Every time Olivia turned around Nancy was taking him to Mayo. The medical bills must be astronomical, and then there was the house. They'd just completed a major renovation, and she was looking to put in a gazebo.

"I don't know what I'm gonna do with Moma," Nancy added. "She's elderly, and her doctors are calling for her to have bypass surgery. I'm the only child so it all falls on me. Between her and Ken, I swear, I'm going crazy."

And to make it worse, Nancy had a spending addiction. Her closets were stuffed full, with clothes, shoes, purses, and costume jewelry, unopened sheets, towels, and decorative stuff she'd not used.

"Ken'd told me I need to "stop shopping" if I intend to retire. And I got no intention of doing that, Miss Olivia." Nancy gave Olivia the throat-snap and a wink. "He can kiss my derrière!"

"It seemed like fewer faculty were at the President's speech this morning; something like, what, seventy people resigned or retired last year?" Olivia moved on from Nancy's excuses for not retiring.

"True, and those few they replaced were with adjuncts." Nancy shook her head, closed her eyes. "But, we'll get through it!" She put on a plastered smile, and moved her legs up and down real fast while she sat, like she was marching.

"Nancy," Olivia couldn't delay any longer. "I moved my things to California, and I sold my house. I'm commuting to Roadims, and I'm here on Monday, Tuesday, and Wednesday — most weeks. Some weeks I won't be in at all, especially if I'm going to a conference or something. I know I have one in Pittsburg. And, oh, my son is leaving for Iraq right before Labor Day so I'm going up there to see him."

She looked at Olivia. "So, you're saying?"

"I'm saying I'm planning on making myself scarce. Blend into the woodwork. I'll support you as best I can over email and phone conferences, and serve on my committees, but my goal is to get positioned to leave. The best way to do that is through peer reviewed publications and conference presentations." Olivia let this speak for itself.

Nancy remembered that Patrick said Olivia wouldn't be able to leave because of the economy and her PhD, so she wasn't worried at all. "When is the sabbatical application due?" She kept going before Olivia could answer, "Do you know about your Fulbright yet?"

"No, I don't. I should know sometime in late fall about the Fulbright. As far as the sabbatical, I'll do like we've been doing where I'll write a recommendation letter you can mark it up, and then send it off." Olivia did lots of Nancy's work for her that way, and Nancy said she was glad 'cause she didn't know what she was supposed to write half the time.

"Good deal," Nancy looked at her phone, "Oh, that's Patrick calling, I better answer."

"See you later," Olivia got up and left. As she was walking out, Alma Watson was standing at Olivia's door, looking at her Office Hours card.

"Hey Alma, how are you? What're you doing down in this neck of the woods?" Alma was the Assistant VP of Assessment and Research, and her office was in the Physics building, just down the hall from the

Grant's Office. "Come on in." Olivia opened her door, motioned Alma to the chair next to her desk.

After a moment, Alma blurted, "Olivia, we have to hold that vote of no confidence. I was at church yesterday, and I heard some things that are just astounding about Arnie. Where does the faculty stand with it?" Alma looked like she was about to cry, like she was in agony from pain. She plucked her fingernails on her thumb and forefinger.

"I don't know where we are; Wes is the senate President now. You probably should talk to him." Olivia hoped the summer would have distanced her from all this, but apparently it hadn't.

"A friend of mine is on the Board, and she said they were trying to get rid of Arnie, but Darnell was the swing vote, even with John as the Chairman, they couldn't get the vote to shift in favor of getting rid of him. If the faculty do the no confidence vote, the three Board members feel that would be enough to take action."

"Well, I can have Wes give you a call?" Olivia was trying to wiggle out.

"Oh, no, absolutely not. I don't want anyone to know I was in here talking to you." Alma shrank back into her chair like she'd seen the devil himself. "Look what happened to Jim. I'm not putting my neck out there. I'm not tenured."

"That's not a guarantee, Alma," Olivia tried to reason with her.

"Yes, but it's a hell of a lot harder to get rid of faculty than staff." She pursed her lips.

Olivia couldn't tell who Alma was mad at, faculty or Arnie. She was in her late fifties, wore her hair short and blond, dressed professionally with pantsuits from Macy's. Whenever Olivia had been in a meeting with her, she found Alma to be defensive, always saying her office provided the data the university needed. But really they didn't. Olivia heard from Patrick and Kevin that she'd been promoted to Assistant VP because she was incompetent. One thing Olivia knew was there's nothing like being in a job you know you aren't qualified for.

"So what do you want me to do?"

"Call Wes and tell him to go forward with the vote, that he has the backing of the Board. But don't tell him I told you." She waited for Olivia's answer like a teenager pleading not to be grounded for this one little thing.

"Okay, I'll call him." Olivia looked at Alma. She was genuinely scared, and Olivia hadn't ever seen her that way. Most of the time she was overbearing and pushy, self assured that she had the right answers with her data.

"Thanks, Olivia." She got up, pulling a tissue from her suit jacket pocket, and dabbed at the corner of her eyes, as she walked out of Olivia's office.

Olivia called, and Wes said he would be right over.

———

At the August Faculty Senate meeting, the first of the 2009 2010 academic year, the faculty unanimously adopted a resolution forming a committee to gather evidence to support a vote of no confidence. An email went out to the campus asking people to forward documents and materials to the Executive Committee members by the end of August. They sent stuff by the truck loads: memos, emails, stories, articles, inappropriate poems Arnie'd written, and community testimonials.

The meeting in September called for the adoption of the secret ballot procedure to hold the vote, defining a successful vote of no confidence as that of the majority of faculty voting "Yay". All faculty, including administrators with faculty appointments, tenured faculty, tenure-track faculty, instructors, and adjuncts were eligible to vote. Human Resources would generate the list of academics who could vote.

At the October meeting, a list of twenty-five allegations supported by what was considered documentation of incompetence was adopted by the senate as evidence of the faculty's lack of confidence in Arnold Williams, and it was sent forward to the Board of Governors. They were made aware of the procedures the senate followed and established under the American Association of University Professors, and were advised that the vote would occur in early November 2009 if no action was taken by the Board to remove him.

On November 2, 2009, more than two-thirds of the faculty brought their IDs and cast a secret ballot affirming their lack of confidence in the President.

At the regularly scheduled Board of Governors meeting in that same month, the Board determined to take the results of the vote into consideration at their upcoming retreat in February 2010. No action was taken or had been taken, and the only closed session was held back in June. At that time, Arnie's contract was extended until June 2011.

Olivia stood looking at the "Departures" schedule. Her connecting Houston flight to San Diego was delayed. She was tired, hungry, and disillusioned. Turning around and spanning the terminal, she spotted the signs pointing to the Admiral's Club.

Inside, she settled down in a quiet corner. Maybe Kevin'll be around. It's only 6:39, not too late to call. She and Kevin had these unspoken boundaries, totally respectful of the evening hours for personal time. But he answered, and she was thankful.

"Dr. O-livia! What you up to girl?"

"I'm in the Houston airport, waiting for my flight to San Diego."

"That's right, it's Wednesday ain't it?"

"Yup, you got a minute?"

"Of course, hey, what's wrong with Patrick has he gone fucking crazy?"

"Yeah, everybody's saying he's drank the water. When I talk to him I tell him 'listen this is *me* you talking to don't gimme that VP crap' but he's gone off the deep end."

"He better watch himself else he gonna find himself shot. He cutting programs, firing people, no due diligence, no nothing just out the blue crap, like he took lessons from Arnie. I can't stand him. And what happened to his being all behind the faculty and shit?"

"Yeah, I know." Olivia sighed. "He's turned into a Dr. Jekyll, and he act like he never spewed the venom about Arnie. Whatd'ya think the Board's gonna do?"

"What they've already done—NOTHING. They ain't doing a fuckin' thing. If my grandmother didn't live down in Little Rock I would find me another job so quick. Speaking of that, how's Harmony?"

"She's fantastic, loving being away from here, doing great. You know she's from New York, right?" Olivia missed Harmony so much.

"Right, I do. Glad to hear she's fine. Good thing she got out this mess."

"I got recommended for a Fulbright, Kevin. And I got the grant for France. I'm leaving next month."

"Whoa, awesome. When will you hear about the Sabbatical? You know those fucks ain't gonna pay you." Kevin heard people saying Olivia got Arnie to give her a paid sabbatical in exchange for not holding the vote of no confidence last year. When he told Olivia about it, he was happy they were wrong.

"I don't care, I'll take the stupid unpaid sabbatical for 2010. I just need a breather, so I can get placed somewhere else. But I'll be in France for two months next semester, December and January. Thank God I got Patrick to sign off on that last year, and Dan too."

"I am so totally jealous." Kevin admired Olivia's creativity in thinking about ways out. "Speaking of jealous, I saw Luis and Michelle the other day. They've been offered a sweet deal down in Fayetteville."

"What, at the new multimillion dollar museum and art center?"

"Yeah, Michelle's taking the piano competition down there. All the big donors just followed her there. And Luis is on the board of the Leighton Community College District. They're paying him big dollars for his strategic thinking, getting credit for financial acumen instead of criticism for what he did with ACHEIP."

"That's great for both of them." Olivia felt a warm feeling in her insides. "I always liked Luis, and Michelle. Well, she was a piece of work!" She didn't want to bring up the way Michelle was always pushing people around.

"I hear that," Kevin laughed.

"Oh, shoot Kevin, they're calling my flight, I gotta go."

"No prob, have a good time in Cali, tell Jonathan I said hello."

"Thanks Kevin, talk to you soon."

After she got seated on the plane, she remembered the meeting she had earlier that day with Patrick and Nancy, which she would have to process with Kevin in their next phone call. But she still turned it over in her head as she sat looking out of the tiny window.

"Faculty needed to be on campus five days a week," he began. They were all sitting in his office, he was behind his desk, and she and Nancy sat opposite him. "Did you think you were going to work remotely for the entire spring semester?" His tone was adversarial, and he didn't wait for her to answer. "Soon HR would start taking your leave time to make up for your absences."

Olivia was confused. She was being accused and convicted of something without being allowed to explain or defend herself. This felt all too familiar.

Nancy added, "We need all the help we can get. I understand that you're trying to better yourself but your being gone to conferences and France is not helping the department." She looked over at Patrick, and then continued. "We're down several faculty, and students still need advised, student-run clubs need faculty leaders, the Program Review needs done, accreditation is coming and what with Claire gone, classes need covered. What will the other faculty think? You didn't keep your office hours over the summer and the faculty are angry about that." Nancy sounded like she had rehearsed what she was going to say. It pissed Olivia off.

Patrick chimed in with "And, what's this about a Fulbright? No Fulbright will be awarded to someone who has been to the selected university already. The chances of getting that are slim to none. The University isn't funding sabbaticals this year. Faculty aren't going to take too kindly to anyone accepting an unpaid sabbatical either, since that's a Faculty Welfare issue."

Olivia decided it would be best not to react. Instead she told them she never got her expense reimbursement that she was promised from a trip that took place eight months ago. Nancy said that wasn't her fault but it was Patrick who kept dragging his feet until the fiscal year closed.

Then, Olivia told Nancy and Patrick she had over six months of accumulated leave time that could be used if needed; however she was covering her responsibilities and wasn't absent from campus. "But if you feel the need to use my leave time, so be it. I'm not vested in the retirement program so it wouldn't go with me when I leave, and I wouldn't get a check for it either." She let that sink in for a minute, then she continued. "You tell the faculty that when they get some papers accepted to top-tiered conferences, when they get the honor of being a grant recipient, when they get off their asses and their own money and pay for the trips themselves, then I'll listen to what "the faculty" had to say. Until then, I don't want to hear it. Is there anything else?" She did not hide her anger, but she wished she could have expressed how it hurt her that they had pulled a stunt like this. It looked too much like Mallory and Dick all over again.

Nancy and Patrick said, nearly in unison, "That was all we had."

She got up and left.

Still looking out the window of the plane, she assured herself, "I only have one more month," Olivia said out loud. Her seat partner couldn't hear her as the plane was taking off.

"Honey, I've been invited to two campus interviews at two different universities," Olivia shouted and danced around their shared office on the bottom floor of their townhouse. "Can you believe it?" Olivia was ecstatic.

"Wow, that's fantastic," Jonathan was happy she was getting somewhere. She had been awfully depressed about all the rejection letters. And, frankly, he needed her to work so he could eventually go on and build his consulting practice. It was the only way he could see that they could accumulate wealth nowadays, since the world's economic engines came to a grinding halt. The prospects for investors and buyers in his company shriveled like an inflated balloon someone forgot to tie.

"Isn't it? I'm going up next week. One's in Malibu, the other is in Pomona. University of Tullcot and Claremont. Those are both great, because they're private schools, not reliant on the government cheese," she smiled, taking on a British accent.

"Well, now that's excellent, yes, yes." He followed her lead, put his index finger to his chin. "When will you tell that chap Patrick about it?" Jonathan could do the British accent so good, and he looked British too. Dark hair, fair skin, chiseled nose and chin.

"Oh, yeah, I do need to talk to him don't I." She dropped the role-play. "I dunno." She padded back to her desk.

"I'm sure he'll take the news quite well," Jonathan kept going with it. "Though he himself, with all the self assurance in the world, and the doctorate in business, has not gotten a single offer. I'd call that karmic justice if I believed in reincarnation." He quipped and they both laughed.

She kissed his face. "Thank you my Love. I hope you have a great day at the office."

"Yes, well someone's got to go to the salt mines to dig into the technology shafts. Cheerio." He picked up his briefcase, kissed Olivia and left. He did have a knack for that British thing.

Not having been to Roadims since the first week of December two months ago, Olivia found her sense of balance, and some semblance of normalcy returning to her life. Their one-month stay in Lyon, France was great. She would have stayed longer but their semesters didn't coincide exactly with hers, so she squeezed two months of teaching into one, over December and January around their holiday breaks. Nancy and Patrick knew she wasn't going to be there for the spring 2010 opening speeches, or the faculty meetings. Olivia had no intention of going to Roadims until March, and she was going exactly once, and only once. If they had a problem with it, then they could look at the documents they signed last year permitting her exceptions and talk to her lawyer if it came down to that. And, if they wanted to she didn't care if they tapped her leave balances.

As if she contacted Patrick intuitively, he called her the next day. Olivia played phone tag with him for a while, but eventually they connected. "Hey Patrick, how are you?"

"Fine, you?"

"Good, what's going on?"

"Are you in France right now?"

"No, I'm not."

"I didn't think so. I called over to the University there and talked to their President. They say you left in January."

Olivia was mortified. "What? Why did you do that? I gave you all the information about where I was going to be and how long."

"Faculty wanted to know why you weren't here. Hey, did you hear anymore about the Fulbright?"

"Patrick, it's February, I'm not going to know anything until later in the semester, I told you that too." Olivia was not hiding her anger and her disgust at his audacity.

He restated what he'd already told her before, "You probably aren't going to get it because Fulbright scholarships are reserved for people who haven't been to the host institution." Patrick was jealous of Olivia, who did she think she was, just running off, doing what she wanted to do? He believed she was lying to him, and making him look like a fool. "The sabbatical committee is going to hold its meeting next week. Are you going to be here for that? You haven't been keeping your office hours, and the faculty are complaining that you aren't pulling your weight."

"No, I can't make it next week because I have couple of interviews to go on."

"Well, you need to get here as soon as you can. Talk to Nancy and let her know what you plan to do about your office hours, and when we can expect you here."

"Patrick, you do know you talking to me, right? I don't care if you been appointed Interim VP, I am the one who listened to you insist on a vote of no confidence, and watched you say how the President was stupid, diss the strategic planning process, and listened to your soap-boxing on the republican agenda in higher ed. I'm the one who got you hooked up with Judith. Remember? So don't give me that crap about 'talk to Nancy.' I'll talk to you." Olivia was hot. How dare he?

"We can't have faculty out of control like you are Olivia. So when can we expect you?"

"Here's what you can expect Patrick: expect my letter of resignation. How 'bout that Patrick?"

He didn't know what to say. He sat up in his chair and held the phone. Most of the time he could intimidate faculty by implied threats, and acting like he forgot what he'd approved. What was it that Arnie said. 'I hate faculty?' He now had to act like he hated faculty too, especially ones like Olivia who thought they could just waltz on campus whenever they wanted to. Patrick would have sworn Olivia had gotten worse since Obama was elected.

"You'll have my letter first thing Monday morning. You can tell Nancy that yourself. And by the way, I have two job interviews, TWO, and they are both in schools of business. Have a nice weekend."

"Olivia?" She heard him calling before she pressed the End button.
"What."

"Are you going to teach summer school?" He knew that was at least $10,000 she wouldn't want to walk away from.

"You know what Patrick? No, I'm not teaching summer school either, I don't believe in online teaching in the first place, so if you want the classes I would normally teach to increase your retirement base, or Eric or whomever for whatever wants them, knock yourselves out." The money after taxes wasn't worth the headache to her anyways. All the whining about Blackboard not working right, or some body's grandmother dying, or they want to take the quiz later because they've got a wedding or whatever. It was just a pain in the ass, and there was no teaching, more like, she shook her head, she didn't even know the words to describe it. It wasn't what she went into academia to do.

"What do you want me to tell people about your sabbatical application?" He tried to hook her with that.

"I was just trying to help *you* out with that. So many faculty have left and all that from the mismanagement and disrespect. I mean, in France, people acted like I was a professional, not like here. Tell you what, you pull my application from consideration. I'll let you know when I'll be on campus, I'll make an appointment with your secretary. Bye." And before he could say anything else, she pressed the button and ended the call.

The unmitigated gall! It was hard for her to believe that she was talking to Patrick, the guy who'd sent his sons over to rake her leaves and cut up her trees, the guy who came to visit her in the hospital. The guy she'd pitched to the Board, the guy whose directives she'd always carried out, even with they didn't make sense. She started replaying in her mind the interactions with him over the last six years and she saw something she didn't like. It reminded her of Shane. All he wanted was to profit. And he, like Patrick, painted himself into a corner he couldn't get out of. Shane had been convicted on felony charges and lost every dime.

She sat down right then and drafted a memo of intent to resign, set up the email delivery for Monday morning February 8th. She would hand carry the formal letter to him when she went to Roadims next month.

*Roadims, Arkansas, March 2010*

Patrick looked like a man whose spirit was gone. His eyes were vacant. His skin was pale, his smile fake. Olivia felt instantly like she needed to tell him something, to be a mirror for him so he could see himself. Actually she felt sorry for him.

"Here, I brought this for you." She handed him a blue sweatshirt with 'La Jolla California' embroidered on it.

He held it up to his torso, and looked down. "It's nice, thanks. I'll put it on tonight." He folded it and put it in his inbox.

"Hey, give me a hug, this is me, you know." They hugged briefly.

Patrick hadn't had a faculty member give him anything or care about him since he saw her last. He missed it. "So you haven't seen my new digs here, huh? See my new ceramic bowls?" He pointed to a credenza with the clay artwork on it.

"Very nice. Is that some of Jane's work too?" Olivia looked over at the wall.

"Yes, it is." He sat down in his chair.

"How are the boys?"

"Fine, fine, making me have to keep working until they get out of college, reminiscing about you and Sebastian. How's he doing?"

"He's good, thanks. Army's treating him well, I think it fits him. I'm glad he found where he belongs, finally."

"Olivia, this place is killing me. I… you know Renee is going back to teaching? I told Arnie I would stay on until the end of June, but then

I'm going back to teaching too." He looked at the floor, crossed his legs, and rested his chin on his palm, elbow on the arm of the chair.

Olivia noticed he was grayer.

"Good for you. Did you get any job offers?" Olivia hoped he did.

"No, I didn't, I went on a couple of interviews here locally, but nothing materialized."

"Patrick, you need to retire. This place is depressing. Look at you! Look around! It's a sinking ship. It was going to be something but it can't now. It's going to take YEARS for it to be turned around if it ever is. You can't fix it, Patrick. Staying here is going to kill you."

He said nothing, only smiled a weak turning up of the corners of his mouth in a forced smile. "Jane doesn't want to leave now. She used to want to move to Paris, or near the city, but now she doesn't. Both boys are in college..." he trailed off.

"Whose gonna be VP AA if you leave then?"

Patrick shrugged his shoulders without moving his hand from his chin.

"So, how are you? Did you get the jobs?"

"Fine." Olivia stood up and handed him the letter, ignoring his question. "Patrick, I want you to remember the good things we did. You had a vision, you moved in that direction. You had a goal for the School of Business. We built the international program, we did the alumni network, the Global Leadership Institute. You can't let this pull you down." Olivia was talking to a dead person.

Patrick stared past her in silence. "Yeah, well that was back then, and this is now. I should have left when I had the chance." He picked up his ink pen, rolled himself up closer to the desk. He opened the envelope, took the letter out and read it, then let it fall onto the desk.

"Arnie is crazy." He looked at her in the eye.

"I know." Olivia held back her tears. She sat back down, hunched over in concern.

"The Board is crazier." He pushed himself back from the desk and put his feet up on it, leaned back and laced his fingers behind his head, looked up at the ceiling, closed his eyes.

Olivia sat there for a few minutes with him like she was visiting someone in the hospital. Letting him be with her, she sent positive energy towards him. Then she got up, "Patrick I need to go now, I have a meeting with some folks over on the sustainability committee. It was good to see you. Let me know if you need anything; you know, I hope, that… well, I will not be back to Roadims. My work here is finished."

"I'll give a copy of your letter to Jan in Human Resources. She'll contact you for the exit interview." He got up. How did she do this? She got two job offers he got none? Who was she? He waved at her.

Olivia went behind his desk and hugged him. He hugged her back, as best he could.

She left Patrick without looking back.

Later that day, she packed her office, gave away what she didn't ship back to San Diego. She met Nancy at Johnny Carino's and told her she wasn't teaching summer school, gave her a copy of the letter she gave to Patrick.

"We're sure gonna miss ya, what am I going to do without you?" Nancy nearly cried.

"You're the Dean, you got people who know the system who have been Dean's and VP AAs that'll be workin' for you. Just pick their brains. That's all you gotta do." Olivia didn't give a rat's ass what she was gonna do, really.

"True. How about you? What are you doing?" Nancy was intrigued about her being able to get job offers.

"I'm going to take the University of Tullcot job most likely. But I haven't fully decided yet. My personal email and stuff is on the letter, and you have my cell number. So stay in touch."

"Will do. Oh, hey, by the way, would you be willing to donate your unused leave hours to a 'pool' of hours for people who need them in case of emergency illness or family crisis?"

"Sure, I'm not going to use them, but I thought they had to be used to offset my missed office hours? Well, even if you did that there'd be like six hundred hours left!" Olivia laughed. In a world where there was nothing, people grasped for anything.

"Yeah, Patrick changed his tune on that. He also told me he was thinking he should spend more time with his kids, that he'd made a huge mistake in putting this place first. I told him this place'll run itself, and nobody gets any credit unless they give big money. You know they extended Arnie's contract again at the retreat, didn't do anything about the vote." Nancy laughed.

Olivia listened, nodding attentively.

Nancy just gossiped on about Renee, Arnie, her neighbor Darnell, and the rest of the characters at Western State. "I guess I'll make a good Dean." She smiled.

That night, Olivia got on the plane, and flew to the center of a new and better reality — for good.

*San Diego, California, May 2010*

"Honey, I got the offer letters! I think I should take the University of Tullcot position."

Jonathan listened and thought about it for a moment. "Whatever you want Love, it is kind of far." Oh God, why couldn't she get a job in San Diego?

"Right, the other choice is Pomona. It's closer but... I don't know, I think University of Tullcot is more my speed. And they offered more money and a smaller course load. Ultimately that gives me more time to write and research."

"Good point. So, it's up to you."

"Great, I'll send back the Tullcot offer letter!" Actually, she'd already sent it but she didn't tell him that.

"Okay." The lights started to dim as the concert got underway.

"I'm looking forward to hearing some Chopin," Jonathan whispered. "These are great seats, by the way."

"Yeah, I know, and me too," Olivia settled into the chair next to his, and held his hand. Life was grand. "This is the last concert in our season package, but I'll try for these seats again next season," she reminded him.

"Good, that gives us time for the cooking school," Jonathan smiled, turning his attention to the stage.

*July 2010*

They'd stopped at a scenic turnout on the way back from Monterey.

She closed her eyes and breathed in the salt air and turned around in circles drinking in the hillsides and the horizon. Olivia had totally relaxed probably for the first time in her life.

"This is so great Jonathan."

"Olivia, I have something I need to tell you," Jonathan stammered.

"Yes, what is it?"

"I lied to you about something."

"Oh?"

"I have adult late-onset schizophrenia that I treat with medication and therapy."

"What?"

"I have been meaning to tell you this but I just couldn't find the right time."

"What do you mean you 'couldn't find the right time'? In three years you couldn't find the right time?"

"I am sorry."

"Wow." Olivia shook her head and stopped smiling. She took off her hat and bent over and leaned on her knees. "Why didn't you tell me?"

"Would you have married me if I had?" He grabbed her hand and she pulled it away. Jonathan worried she would eventually leave him. But for now she was there, and she knew the truth. He smiled to himself knowing he had someone to take care of him.

"I don't know, maybe, but you should have let me decide instead of manipulating me." Olivia started walking to the car, "I don't believe anything you've said now." She started to cry.

Jonathan tried to hug her but she pushed away from him.

They drove the rest of the way in silence.

Days went by and Olivia tried to get over her feelings of betrayal. She couldn't seem to move past them.

Inside she felt hurt and disillusioned. Oh God, why can't I see? The implications were huge for her. She didn't want someone she had to take care of. This piece of news shook Olivia to her core, and caused a change in the way she felt about him, and how she felt about the marriage, about herself. All she could think was she had been stupid — again.

Within the next week, she filed for divorce.

By the first of August, she rented a cute little house to live in Malibu. Olivia figured she would recover sufficiently before her new position started in September.

Besides, her new Dean said he'd support her endeavors for writing and travel.

www.ingramcontent.com/pod-product-compliance
Lightning Source LLC
Chambersburg PA
CBHW031056020726
47495CB00007B/1908